BUCK ALICE AND THE ACTOR-ROBOT takes a wry and insightful look at human behavior after apocalypse. Mr. Koenig finds that people remain human—both mean-spirited and heroic, both aimless and persistent—in the gravest circumstances. It's a complex worldview, all articulated in a well-conceived science-fiction thriller.

—Leonard Nimoy

BUCK ALICE AND THE ACTOR-ROBOT
WALTER KOENIG

Manufactured in the United States of America

To ...
Joe Dimaggio, Max Zaslofsky,
Wally Hergeshimer and
Bill Swiaki—my childhood.

I wish to thank ...

My wife, Judy, whose unfailing support has made this book a reality;

George Clayton Johnson and Shimon Wincelberg for being its early champions;

Janice and David Cohen for their enthusiasm and for pointing me to ...

Gary Brodsky, my publisher;

and Leonard Nimoy who always comes through.

PROLOGUE

I wrote this story at a time when events seemed to be conspiring against me and I found myself teetering on the brink. However, when circumstances changed for the better and the crisis state did not, I began to understand that teetering was less a consequence of a single traumatic episode and more a constant in my nature. With the realization that I was permanently thus impaired, the inevitability of it all took hold and I began to relax. Since relaxation is the key to balance, I was able to make an accommodation with my instability.

Therefore, if the characters in this story appear to be a trifle out of kilter, it is because my brain has long been postured at an acrobatic angle with the medulla oblongata flailing precariously in very thin air and the cerebral cortex perilously close to scraping the cement. Or is it the other way around?

Walter Koenig
10/31/87

ONE

"IF only I were to keep my eyes open and not turn away. No one in his right mind could expect a blind man to save the world. I could stumble around for awhile and then, like frightened old men who drool down their nightshirts, cry out for momma." "Momma, momma," Joshua said, pinching the skin above his Adams apple and shaking it vigorously. "Momma, momma," he rattled again, testing the effect achieved when his other hand shut off the air from his nostrils. "After awhile I could lie down somewhere and then, weak from hunger, fall into a deep sleep from which I would pass into my untimely death. *THE UNTIMELY DEATH OF JOSHUA CHAPLIN.* Lawsuits would be filed over the rights to the title. The world's greatest authors would be reduced to squabbling boys. . . ." At that moment Joshua's eyelids lowered and the searing rays of the sun were replaced by purple dots, vermilion explosions, violet rods, and Milliginian silhouettes. At this point the idea of quitting had not yet strongly taken hold.

Joshua's body turned and, on their own, his feet began to move. He watched the activity below him with the happy innocence of a backwoods farmer suddenly astraddle a fiery pink carousel charger. "Lookee, lookee dag burn it, hogtied and feathered, that thar machine sure are a wonder. Whoopie," he yipped as his feet began to move faster. "Ride 'em cowboy," through clenched teeth, as the carousel spun faster and he met the challenge of his galloping doggies. High in the saddle, he rode a hundred yards before the music stopped and the bumpkins clambored off and he fell to his knees in exhaustion. "Plumb tuckered ain't you, stout fellers, gallant lads?" And, had it been there, stuffed deep in the side pocket of his jeans, just as sure as shootin' he would have plunged in his hand and brought forth the biggest lump of sugar his feet could eat. Joshua wiggled his toes. The four smaller ones had really very little to say. To be sure, there was a symmetry in the arc they formed that was rendered with subtlety and taste, like a quartet of doughty pillars steeped and graded for harmony of thought and action. Reassuring in its way but at a sacrifice, a sense of restraint; the subjugation of the individual for the common good: conformity. All in all, good architecture but not great art.

On the other hand, there was the big toe. THE BIG TOE. No humble petitioner, a craggy tower—intense, feverish, excessive. Not only above but beyond the crowd. Proud, insolent, a testimony to personal commitment. The nail—jagged, splintered, uncompromising; a pioneer. A tuft of hair-like fire in the desert—stark, defiant, liberated. The superstructure itself, a thousand planes and textures, the face of the people, and yet, free-forming, spontaneous, beauty through truth, the soul of the artist bared.

Joshua cursed his single-jointedness. His lips could reach no farther than the cap of his knee.

Joshua felt the earth moving from beneath the sun's eye. The sweat drying in his scalp turned his hair sticky and clumpish and the heat in his brain leveled out at luke warm. "Early afternoon," what a homey expression. Soft bellies easing over beltless slacks on tip-backed chairs on small town porches, overlooking cut green lawns from behind splashes of light and shadow. Joshua stood up. "Now let's take a long hard look, maybe there's something I missed. To my left I see . . . white, yep, it's white all right. Everything within ninety degrees to my left is pure white. Now to my right . . . white again, wait, is that . . . nope, white again. Thought I saw a fleck of cream there for a moment. Now behind me. . . ." But his heart had gone out of the game. " 'Tepid tissue equals joyless reality.' Get it framed Mrs. Cummings and hang it up behind my desk." Joshua started walking again and the white dust—which was all there was to mark the end of civilization and which altogether was all there was—smoked around his feet but left no impression that he had come or that he had been.

Before the invasion he had been a thirty-four-year-old JEWISH INSURANCE SALESMAN. It had been his custom, ad nauseum, to dismiss, with elaborate indifference, all cocktail party questions regarding "line of work" with a perfunctory "Jewish Insurance Salesman." Behind the studied nonchalance, however, was the mischievous little boy who announces to his harried household that the neighbor's great dane, trained since birth to open oven doors, had just slipped in through the kitchen window and stolen the family's holiday dinner.

Those who were not Jewish inevitably challenged the demand for "Jewish Insurance," exclaiming in the same breath that anti-Semitism had all but disappeared. Those who were Jewish, of course, raised their eyebrows knowingly, inhaled deeply through shuddering flames and nodded their heads sympathetically. To both reactions Joshua enjoyed an inward chuckle. The meaning of the gag, obscure to all but himself (which in turn gave him a feeling of superiority), was that being Jewish and selling insurance was a contradiction in terms. Insurance gamesters the world over were named Berkley, Thomas, and Fellows. They all had mean blue eyes tucked deep into pink faces, handshakes patterned after the Quakers and three "Manny" jokes in their repertoire. Joshua interpreted his survival in this world not as a compromise but as a victory for his "people," through infiltration in the "secret war." Telling himself that at least gave his rather dull existence a little more meaning. Besides, Joshua loved to daydream.

Joshua at thirty-four lived "comfortably but not in comfort." His life resembled the cardiograph of someone recently expired: a straight line continually repeating itself, traveling predictably from left to right, without interruption. His success at the office resembled the fabled tortoise *only* at the starting gun. The rest of his life, as if to preclude any mistake in his aptitude test, crawled along at a dead even pace.

Joshua "sort of" liked bachelorhood. The prospect of a family did from time to time warm the cockles of his heart, but the addended thought that a haranguing wife and bleating children might change warm cockles into self-immolation did much to extinguish the flame. So

Joshua "sort of" liked bachelorhood. Unfortunately, everything he experienced had the ring of "sort of": sort of good, sort of interesting, even sort of okay. The overall effect was to leave him sort of empty. Much of the problem could be laid to his lack of drive. Anything beyond the cleft of his chin was beyond his reach. He aspired only to goals discernible to the naked eye, leaving for others the ones requiring vision.

He did daydream a lot, though.

"We will serve you," said the six monsters. "For dinner?" flashed the answering thought. "No," said the six monsters who could read Joshua's mind. "As your slaves." They were, of course, hairy and hideously yellowish maroon. They had, as well, the mandatory number of fangs and claws, but what really made them monsters was the mellifluously rendered, soul-rending sincerity in their voices. It was like a tulip in a tar pit, he decided: how much uglier the tar pit for the beauty of the tulip. Joshua instinctively backed off. Quickly, however, he regained his composure and with one deft thrust brushed away both the fear and the compassion that surfaced in the tear that hung from his eyelash. "Now then," he said in a steady voice, "what's this all about?" The monsters waddled closer. "Together," they chorused, "we can defeat the Milliginians," and with a great display of strength they reduced to rubble the complex of skyscrapers immediately to the northeast. "No, no, that won't work," mused Joshua. "There aren't any skyscrapers anymore. Perhaps they could build skyscrapers from the dust, but then again that smacks of urban renewal." Joshua looked up. It was the dusk of another day. He thanked the monsters and filed them away for another time, when the consuming loneliness of his existence might start again to eat from his brain pan.

Joshua was on a journey. It started on Dyckman Street in the Inwood section of Manhattan, in the city of New York, and had carried him several hundred miles in the direction of the Everglades, in the state of Florida. "Misteh, misteh, my baby broder fell down the sewer," the child said, pointing to the opening in the gutter beneath the sidewalk. Without so much as a backward glance, Joshua ripped off a nearby manhole cover, pulled his tie from his collar and, otherwise fully clothed, climbed down twenty feet beneath the street into the dank underworld of alligators and prophylactics. He heard one burst of maniacal laughter before the light disappeared and the manhole cover was pushed back into place. Besides the squish of his own damp shoes, the only other sound he heard that day was the thud of something heavy, very heavy, shoved across the skylight of his subterranean bastille. Worse still, there wasn't a sign of the "baby broder."

Periodically, Joshua heaved upwards against the manhole cover from the top rung of the sewer ladder but, weighed down as it was, it never even vibrated. In a wink he lost all sense of time and space and with a hand to his nose was one last effort away from leaping off the brink of insanity right into the teeming labyrinth.

The manhole cover did not move, it shattered. It had the consistency of wood shavings. As his hands went through it, the lack of resistance caused him to lose his balance and, accompanied by the raining powder, fall backwards and down. He remained in the sewer two days more. His back was badly wrenched and the slightest movement was an agony, but now at least a shaft of daylight penetrated the abyss and his sanity teetered to a precarious balance. Alone and in pain Joshua Chaplin had no way of knowing that at that very moment he was one of only one one-thousandth of one percent of Earth's human population still alive and the only one of the species in the entire city of New York. If such a thing could be considered a stroke of good fortune, then his descent into the depths, and the subsequent injury to his back, was indeed a lucky break because the malevolent laughter, the last human sound to penetrate his asylum, was also the "fun city's" valedictory. No sooner had the gurgle died in the wretched child's throat than he and the rest of the city's eight million inhabitants turned to crumbly powder and died where they stood. The life span of the lethal radiation that accompanied the attack was four days, a period that was exactly five hours short of Joshua's first above-the-surface breath.

Joshua looked about him and decided he was frightened. "Where was everybody and where had all the white dust come from?" Where he stood it was ankle-high but he could see in the distance that he would soon have to trudge knee-deep in it. With an eye toward investigation, he freed his foot and sent a spray a football yard. Nothing happened: it gently settled back to earth. Joshua, his prospects as insubstantial as the surface he trod, reluctantly started walking. Had he known, he might have garnered some little comfort from his punter's toe. Inadvertently he had fulfilled the five-day-old promise of retribution on the architect of his predicament.

Joshua's fingers tingled as he remembered.

He had been wandering about for some days looking for something to eat and had come across a forest replete with trees and green leaves and furry little animals. It was a heavily wooded area somewhere in Connecticut and like the rest of the non-man-made world had been left unviolated. Oh sure, here and there was a desecrating heap of white, but basically the verdant landscape remained verdant and its furry inhabitants, had they been so charged, would have rejoined "Milliginian who?" in testimony relating to the invasion.

Joshua's fingers tingled as he remembered.

He had made the forest his home. He began by eating roots and berries. "A JEWISH INSURANCE SALESMAN does not eat roots," he told himself one day after throwing up, and with his hunter's cunning, took to pursuing little furry animals.

For a long time after that, he ate a lot of berries.

Then one day, he strangled a fourteen-year-old rabbit who, grateful to be put out of its misery, thanked him with a parting flap of one ear the tip of which struck him in the eye and caused a bothersome sty that lasted for weeks. Having tasted blood, however, there was now no stopping Joshua. Out of the wilderness he forged a bow and arrows and through sheer craft hacked out a spear. Then he waited. When hunger at last reappeared, all was in readiness. "Snap-buckle" went the tools of destruction as he shouldered them into place and, with body slung low, ear to the ground, nose to the wind he went, as all hunters have before him, in search of game.

For a long time after the rabbit-murder, Joshua ate a lot of berries. Joshua's fingers tingled as he remembered.

He had lived this way a long time, two months, maybe three. Then came the moose. Joshua discovered it defiling a small water hole with the indigestible refuse from its breakfast. Enraged beyond reason (he had used this very pool for his bath), he surprised the animal before it could extricate itself from the mud and beat it mercilessly about the antlers with the handle end of his spear. The animal in turn lowered its head for a charge but in so doing dipped it beneath the surface, panicked, inhaled three times, and drowned. Joshua dragged the beast from its watery grave and feasted royally. At a time when despair had succeeded depression and a reason to continue living grew more remote, the image of himself as "JOSHUA, KILLER OF MOOSE," became a valuable cudgel in his arsenal of maintenance weapons. It can be a good thing sometimes to be a city boy and not know Moose from Deer.

Joshua's fingers tingled as he remembered the exact moment he saw her or rather felt her.

He was sitting Indian-style before the fire thinking about enchanted berries that turn into medium-rare steaks directly after (1) the underside of the middle leaf is rubbed, and (2) thoughts that are pure are thought, when he received a wet, fishy slap across the back of his head. His heart missed cadence and was one dropped beat from a total halt when, through dimming vision, he perceived a little old lady with sprung Jack-in-the-Box eyes and a mouth frozen wide in a silent scream. Fortunately, she immediately fainted. During her unconsciousness Joshua recovered and in the process, discovered that the little old lady was, in reality, a teenager upon whom events had taken a severe toll.

Joshua's fingers tingled as he remembered how he had gathered her in his arms and had begged the rocks and the fire and the branches of the trees to not let her die. Joshua's fingers tingled as he remembered how her eyes had fluttered and how she had rested content in his arms and told him about the invasion and about the colony of humans in the Everglades and how and why she, Catheleen, had run from them. Joshua's fingers tingled as he remembered the long silences during which they looked into each other's eyes with love and gratitude for each other's presence. Joshua's fingers tingled as he recalled the absurdly concerted effort required to pry from his fingers the knuckle-bleached death-grip of her hand.

And so Joshua decided to go south.

TWO

ISOBEL was ten years old. She had a forehead and ears and eyes and a nose. She also had a figure that looked like a loaf of mud, removed from the mold of its Jack-and-Jill pail and turned upside down to dry brick-hard in the sun. She also had a pair of pancake-shaped (children's plate-sized) jowls that hung from her cheeks and eternally shaded the upper half of her stubby neck. Lining the inside of the jowls were secret pockets in which was stored all the terrible malignity of her nature. Isobel had only to puff up her cheeks and the ground, for miles around, would tremble with the quaking of knees.

By any rule of thumb, Isobel was no good. Nevertheless, she was also the singularly most revered object in the settlement called "New Hope" now that Catheleen had disappeared.

The main body of New Hope was formed from an organization called the Pathfinders, a group of sixty

husband and wife teams who believed in the frontier
spirit and were out finding paths in the Florida Everglades when news of the invasion came over their transistors and interrupted the ball scores. However, not
until the dying broadcaster announced that "until further
notice all American sports events are from this moment
suspended" did the Pathfinders abandon the hope that
the radio bulletins were the doctored joke of warped
intellectuals. Nevertheless, once recovered from the shock
of a world purged of non-Pathfinders, a prickly sensation traveled the skin of all the corps and left in its wake
an overwhelming feeling of pride. "If the rest of the
world had been where it belonged, out finding paths,"
they reasoned, "it wouldn't be in the spot it was now."
Awe succeeded pride and with it, a sense of mission to
reconstruct the world in an image closer to God's pio-
neering spirit. In no time at all, a plan was devised to
build a settlement, and since the invaders were still
hanging around Earth, to begin life anew in the jungle.

It had been the busy season in the swamp when the
attack on Earth occurred and the Pathfinders soon learned
they were not the Everglades' only vacationers. Before
long "Just Call Me Robbie—And His Mincing Ways"
minced into camp. He, in turn, was followed by Claude,
the Parisian tart peddler (the kind with cherries in them);
Buck Alice, the science fiction epistler; Eric and Catheleen, the young lovers and the mother of the child, as
well as the child herself, the dreaded Isobel.

It was exactly three o'clock in the afternoon in the
fifth month in the life of New Hope Settlement. Punc-
tual as the attack on Hiroshima, Isobel stuffed her hair
into her mouth and screamed loudly. She did this every
afternoon at three o'clock. It made her feel good. It also
scared the hell out of everybody in the camp, which

made her feel better. Predictable as land devastation after the flood, Isobel, in a torrent of tears, came splashing out of the swamp with eyewitness reports of Milliginian mayhem that, each time, further eroded the now thinning colony spirit.

The growing morale problem, a full month now in incubation, was not, curiously, environmental in origin. Food and water in the lush wilderness were both accessible and plentiful. The weather, although hot and humid, was certainly bearable, particularly if one didn't move around too much, and the tents, erected to house the community, proved ample protection against the seasonal rains. No, the waning of group ardor had more to do with the lyric than the pragmatic, concerned as it was with Catheleen's organs of reproduction and her reaction to the manner of their disposition.

Eric had been sixteen and Catheleen fourteen years to the day when, having lost all hope, they stumbled on New Hope. They were simply two water skiers with a poor sense of direction who couldn't remember where they had moored their craft. For a fortnight (and ten days since the invasion) they had crawled about in the woods fending against all manner of trap and snare with the additional inconvenience of Eric's hair lice and for the last seventy-two hours, Catheleen's first menses. At last they were spotted near an outpost of the camp and, with the aid of supporting hands, were warmly ushered into its midst and generously accepted into the fold. Eric and Catheleen celebrated their survival and her new womanhood by making love for the first time. Afterwards Eric rolled over on his back exposing, in the process, the soul of his left foot to a sharp sting and almost immediately thereafter died of snake bite. Catheleen made several stabs at writing an ironic poem commemorating the whole ordeal but, in the end, settled for becoming pregnant.

Several months later, she reluctantly made the announcement. To her surprise, not only were congratulatory handshakes passed all around but a festival, heralding the blessed event, was immediately conceived. (In time, the nature of New Hope festivals, under the direction of Hank Hank, the retired army major, took a decidedly different turn but at this early date, scarcely four months into the young life of the settlement, orgies had not yet come into their own.) In its own way, the current festival was terribly excessive, so extravagant, in fact, that old Pathfinder spirituals like "Ole Lonesome Trail" and "Tumblin' Tumbleweeds," formerly in safe keeping like precious mementos in a hope chest, were unpacked and chanted non-stop from dusk to dawn.

The reasons were twofold: (1) during the four months since the invasion, not one woman in New Hope Settlement had become pregnant, and (2) in the absence of periodic evidence to the contrary, no woman appeared capable of fertility. As was their want, the sixty-odd ladies in the camp exchanged notes and before long an hypothesis, slow in germinating, took root and blossomed into a fully subscribed-to fact. Just prior to Catheleen's belated announcement, Titheria, the female biology student, described the situation to the entire community. Any woman who had been even minimally exposed to the Milliginian attack must, inevitably, have suffered some consequence from the accompanying all-pervading radiation. In the case of those hidden away in the Everglades, the effect, although not mortal, was devastating to female ovaries, the high metabolic function of which, after puberty, made them acutely sensitive to disrepair by any potentially lethal agent. Since the only women who were not minimally exposed were those who were maximally exposed and had ceased to care about quantitative measurements, the unavoidable conclusion drawn in great despair by all concerned was that even without detection by the Milliginians, human life in the swamp would span only the length of their own lifetimes.

Harbored in each man is the belief that in all succeeding generations, the essence of himself is passed, in effect kept alive, and so somewhere deep in his subconscious he basks in the illusion of his immortality. With the sure knowledge, as presented by Titheria, that with his death dies all of the human race, he does, in his despondency, unwittingly hasten the inevitable.

No wonder, then, that Catheleen's surprising pregnancy was a cause for jubilation. It did not, however, obviate the logic of the "radiation" premise. On the contrary, the child's pending maternity lent it support because she did not achieve pubescence until more than a week after the Milliginian invasion. Therefore, her gonadal activity at attack time was below the sensitivity threshold and by the luck of the draw she was not susceptible to the radiation and its ninety-six-hour life span.

Immediately after strains of "don't fence me in," on its one hundred and twentieth repetition, faded in the night air, on the last day of the festival, Catheleen was enshrined as the resident baby farm. At one of the rarely-called town meetings, it was unanimously decreed that, from a volunteer handful of men, Catheleen would each fifteenth month be fertilized and produce an offspring as long as she might live and was capable. It was hoped that by changing the male partners, her children, who would in turn cohabit, might produce new generations with a minimum number of mutant characteristics. It was the informed opinion of Titheria and her husband, Gardner the gardener (who once successfully crossbred six different strains of weed), that with good care, proper nutrition and plenty of sun and water, the figure might climb as high as twenty-five.

An oppressive gloom followed Catheleen's disappearance. It led directly to the aforementioned state of demoralization.

Thus was established the setting into which each day, punctually at three, lumbered malevolent Isobel with her tales of torture and decapitation. Established also was the reason the settlers of New Hope were restrained from fulfilling the promise of infanticide central to her theme of outer space atrocities. After all, Catheleen had flown the coop and Isobel was the only chick left on the farm.

Piqued at the shabby attendance for her latest dramatic unfolding, Isobel unfolded all the creases in her cheeks (something she was never before able to accomplish) and gave birth to a whole new dimension in cacophony. "EEEAHAHAHAHOHOHOOOOWAWAU-GUGGGGGGYIYIYIYIIIII," said the future mother of the human race.

THREE

CASEY Milligin, the lovable rascal, walked with a hitch in his gait, leaned on environmentally dimpled elbows, snorted through a red nose and talked to elves. The limp was caused by O'Lafferty's inordinately high footrail. The puckering was due to his habitually damp counter top, and the broken veins and the inner dialogue were the sad result of O'Lafferty's violently short temper.

It all happened years before, when Casey, then a bright young son of the Dublin sod, decided, one late night after work, to visit the "one for the roader" across from the Planetarium. He had just discovered a new heavenly body in the moors of the galaxy and full of triumph announced as much to the proprietor, one Murphy O'Lafferty. "Why haven't I seen it in the paper then," sneered Murphy with only the prospect of a cold dinner and an even colder Catholic wife (she believed the evacuation of bodily waste to be disgusting mortal sin) in his future. "I only found it tonight but you will read about it tomorrow," said Casey in a fine tenor voice. And so it went back and forth becoming more and more heated. "Next you'll be saying it's the home of the leprechauns," cracked O'Lafferty. "Who's to say no?" challenged Milligin, throwing reason to the bog, his dander now totally erect. Shorter and shorter burned the fuse until, at last in the wee small hours, a Rosary fell from Casey's pocket and O'Lafferty, seeing black, let fly with the King James version of the Sunday Punch. Poor Casey Milligin never was the same. They kept him on at the Planetarium but now, instead of plotting stars, he plodded about sweeping stairs. His future was gone and also his memory. He continued to frequent Murphy O'Lafferty's but never again was Milligin's planet discussed.

How different things might have been for the world had Casey's astronomical charts for that fateful night been found the next day and not so many years later.

"Saints preserve us," gasped Mrs. Cluny, the washerwoman, sneaking a swig from a cobweb-covered bottle of ten-year-old "Shamrock Whiskey" and tasting naught but rolled parchment.

The scientists, in belated recognition, called the distant twinkle "Milligin." Milligin, far out himself, did with a twinkle dance naked a jig in front of O'Lafferty's.

Immediately a sophisticated laser system was directed at the new planet and five months before the invasion the data came back that "Milligin" had an extremely dense population of human-type organisms quite a few of whom were preparing to make a long trip. "In one year's time," proclaimed Earth's leading Astronomers, "we will be able to make voice contact with the Milliginians and let them know we are harmless." The Milliginians already knew that.

*   *   *

Imhor generally was blue. Today he was greenish-blue because he didn't feel too good. He had again failed to bag his monthly quota of humans. "There are no humans in West Germany," he had pleaded but they sent him anyway. He returned with a decrepit runaway Tzarist Princess whose best feature was thirty-three inches of colon at the tail end. "Your work is deteriorating, Imhor. You're letting us Cobalt Blues down," he was told by way of welcome from his month's journey. Not one word of sympathy for his condition. To make matters still worse, several paces from his overheated compartment and a much needed rest, he crossed paths with one of the boorish Aquamarines. As they moved around each other, the latter, eyeing Imhor's greenish pallor, snickeringly accused him of trying to "pass." Imhor blushed furiously and, to compound his misery, turned bright turquoise. Of course, Imhor wouldn't lower himself to gutter-baiting, so he collected his poise and continued forward to his quarters.

(It was not as if Imhor was prejudiced. "I am the first to say I believe in equality," he used to tell the "bright lights" and "button downs" at work. "I have one strict rule that I insist my sky-blue brood follow," he said, punching several of his key operators. "When we are extended an invitation to an Aquamarine function, we go, are polite and eat whatever they serve . . . no matter what it is.) "Cloddish Greeny," Imhor shouted back down the hall and then quickly shut the door to his room behind him.

It was a good thing for his digestion and his family's sense of values that Imhor never married and was hardly ever invited anywhere.

The planet Milligin was the size of Earth and had

developed along an exact parallel course. The only difference was a seventy-five-year head start. Being that much older, there were proportionately more complex problems as well as proportionately greater technological advances. Of the problems, the greatest was the insufferable congestion. With the aid of federal funds, competition was initiated to discover a habitable planet on which some of Milligin's population could be relocated. The search extended through many solar systems and was close to bankrupting the treasury when information about a tiny speck of a planet at a distant point in their own galaxy was fed through a computer. So it came to pass that Earth was deemed the "final solution" in the quest for Milliginian elbow room.

Most encouraging of all was the computer's determination that people living on Earth had the same physiology and attendant life-support systems as the folks back on Milligin. That fact, as far as it went, was totally correct: Earthlings living on Earth and Milliginians living on Milligin did respond with the exact same body chemistry to their respective environments. The very small leap in logic that followed, which in turn led to the invasion of Earth, appeared faultless only while airborne.

And so, five months from the day that Casey Milligin, at one and two-eights time, celebrated his belated triumph, the benefactors of his name descended upon the Earth in two hundred ships and never even said "thank you."

"Thank you for nothing," Imhor muttered to himself, remembering the honor that went with appointment to the fleet of earthbound ships. He had riveted his mind to the pre-invasion days in an effort to block out the pain that had invaded his stuffy quarters and threatened his post-invasion body. Back on Milligin, Imhor had been a

Meteorologist. In the advanced time of that planet, his work was concerned with coordinating a vast network of mechanical brains dedicated to analyzing and prescribing for all possible atmospheric disturbances. The information he did not publicly reveal about his world of computors was that beyond the knowledge they could impart, he had imparted to them fully realized personalities. The "bright lights" and "button downs" with whom he associated were really just lights and buttons, as well as charts and graphs. For Imhor, however, they were more. They were the close friends with whom he discussed the day's pressing problems.

Rarely did he overlook anyone. "Temper, temper, mister," he would caution, a red light flashing madly to indicate a non-machine error in computation. "Feeling a bit low, old sport" was a mild rebuke to a sagging graph. "Buttons Class AII through Class BIV, I only want you to hear this," and he would promptly shut off all other circuits. Very often he would bring to work current, controversial, philosophical questions and conduct trials, acting as attorney for both the prosecution and the defense. "I ask you gentlemen of the court," addressing the odd-numbered charts to his left, "can we, in good conscience, permit the destruction of this great society's foundation, molded as it has been, by the sands of time, at the hands of a few maladjusted malcontents?" And in rebuttal, "My esteemed jurors, if a handful of idealistic thinkers can so threaten our system, then surely this molded foundation has turned moldy and is no more dear than the admission price to a museum." It is here, too, that Imhor discussed the problems of coexistence between Cobalts and Aquamarines, and here as well he evaluated the coming invasion of Earth, speculated on the nature of the crews to be recruited, and deliberated on the moral questions to be answered.

On an evening like any other, Imhor closed down his machines, locked away his notes and started out of his workroom. This time, however, he stopped and turned on the threshold. The ball bearings in two of the smaller computers clunked together involuntarily and several lights started to glow in surprise. Imhor stood there with fists clenched and tears running down his cheeks. "If only I could make them listen, I could help them solve so many of the problems of the world. Tell me, dear friends, tell me, I beg of you," he addressed the entire room of nuts and bolts. "What should I do? How do I make my presence felt?" Not one condensor spoke up. Imhor dropped his arms, raised his shoulders, lowered his head and stepped from a small pool of light into the shadows of the alley.

The next day notice of his conscription for the inter-planetary armada came down. Imhor, in a state of apoplexy, proceeded to assail every accessible avenue in the futile effort to get his name stricken from the list.

Imhor only briefly considered registering a complaint. It would be better to live with the clogged air vent, he decided, than to risk a check into his case history. He would dearly love to take a walk outside but this was foolhardy, as well as ultimately suicidal. Earth was off limits except on raids and to be caught sneaking a stroll would definitely lead to a case history check and a physical exam. Imhor looked at himself in the mirror: the button nose; the almost transparent lids; the watery eyes; the thin lips; the fragile chin. "It's a weak face," he told himself, "one which never truly told the story of the man within. And now it's too late. The man inside is as weak as the face and God knows neither can stand another operation. I just won't have it," he told himself bravely.

But then his bowels began to hurt and he could tell from the signs that this was going to be the worst attack yet. He had been stricken three times since returning to the ship and sensed a pattern building. "They're coming faster and harder," he thought and immediately told himself that he would not give in to the pain. The way to do that was not to think about . . . "it." He must wipe his mind clean of the "It" or, like the gift-bearing Ancients who humiliatingly cast themselves before their terrible icons and begged for salvation, he would run with his offering and throw himself in shame at the seat of "its" omnipotence. "I won't let a 'thing'—an 'it' —take over my life, tell *me* what to do. The 'its' and the 'things' in the world have been the only things I *could* control. I have always dictated to them, pumped the levers, pushed the buttons, pulled the knobs. I never did their bidding, they did mine. 'It' will not make me leave this room; 'It' will not give me away; 'It' will not land me back on the operating table. Permission denied. I WILL NOT BE SEDUCED. Coils and transistors, I'll think about rainbows of coils, all different in color, disappearing into mysterious crooks and crannies and transistors. I'll think about transistors designed for a thousand different functions in a thousand different designs. Oh yes, oh yes. . . . OH NO!" He bit on his tongue to conceal the sudden pain that ate at his rectum. "Click-click little lights. Hum-hum little buttons. No no, the other way around . . . oooOOHHH!"

The Spiked Milliginian Broadboar tunneled through to his brain and lay scratching itself behind his eyeballs. "Click-click little buttons. Hum-hum. . . ." His eyes closed as the agony throbbed on. "I mustn't think about 'it' . . . hum-hum little click-clicks, I mustn't. . . ." But already from some pink gauze-covered burrow the "It" began to emerge and grow. Then the pain redoubled and Imhor abandoned all thoughts of coils and buttons. He stiffened out like a board and the muscles in his buttocks tightened to a high-pitched hum. "IT HURTS, IT HURTS," he cried out at last, and the "It," sensing the cue, suddenly appeared all swollen and bloated in front of his face. There, the alabaster base and there, the oval-shaped mouth, gurgling fetchingly, beckoning. Last time when he had given in, he had dashed from his room, illegibly scrawled his name, and amidst the raising of eyebrows, was permitted entrance to the "chapel." This time, this fourth time since his return and they would know just how sick he was. "Damn this liver, damn, damn, damn. Oh God, another operation. More needles, more knives. Blood and more blood. A little more of my life sponged away each time along with the slop. I can't go through with it again!" Panic gagged his mind and the apparition momentarily receded. One deep breath and the pain again, this time in battalion force, and also the vision now bright and clear, ten feet tall, maniacally flushing itself over and over again in his ear.

Imhor was in the corridor waddling toward the Medical Bureau Station. His left hand, flappingly extended, was making involuntary scratches in the air. I-M-H-O-R he had written a dozen times before the quill was thrust into his sweaty palm and his signature surfaced on the check-in pad. "Let them raise their eyebrows, see if I care. Let them put me on the operating table, anything, just-open-that-door!" Another torturous second and the latch was released. For one brief moment before his eyes welled, before he sank down, he saw "It": the oval seat mounting the white alabaster base, enveloping the gurgling bowl of water, paying homage to the imperious lid, archly at attention, awaiting his supplication.

Outside, the bureau chief was duly noting Imhor's uncontrollable Gastro-hepatic disorder.

FOUR

"'MOBAWAMBA, Mo-ba-wam-ba, da lordy ob da jumbo, thas who!'' With that, the black man let fly from a favorite perch and soared through the air a dozen feet. Nothing in the world was as exhilarating as an early morning swing, Mo told himself as he spun back into space from another of his elaborate network of vines. He chose a tree in the near distance as "touchdown" because, he decided, it had a particularly incorruptible look that assured integrity of character. "Okay tree, address yoself to dis here den," said the jungle lord, gunning his engines in reverse and taxiing to a halt on its most scrupulous limb, "ifn ah ain't da lordy ob da jumbo, don who den?" The challenge, as it did every morning, went unmet. Behind half-closed lids, Mo nodded approvingly. "You better believe it, baby." With that he loosed a sigh of impressive dimensions and dropped lightly to the ground.

Alas, once earthbound and in the company of his

subjects, reality intruded and the well-rounded sigh deflated into vacuity.

Mo was the leader of a group of ex-pug "runners" for the Syndicate who (before Milliginians) had worked faithfully at their jobs right up until they stole the "organization's" bet-money on the big fight and high-tailed it to a small island in the Gulf of Mexico. Arnoldumbo, Samatoba, John, Raymon, Damon and Mobawamba made up the gang. However, when Raymon said he wouldn't go without Damon because he only trusted him with the insulin shots, and Damon said he wouldn't go without their sister, Louella, and Damon owned the sailboat, and John said, "Then I ain't going without Pearl," and Samatoba asked would it be all right then if he brought along Celestealulu, and Maytagagawa got wind of the extra cargo and bit Arnoldumbo in the leg and wouldn't let go until her own passage was secured, the gang grew in size from six to ten.

No one, however, took the precaution of stocking in additional food and water for the trip there and, as a result, supplies were depleted a full day before the island roost was reached. In an effort to improvise a meal from the briny deep, fishing tackle was thrown over the side. Unfortunately, the boat was so small and so overcrowded that not only was the miraculously hooked Marlin too big to bring aboard, but in trying to tame the creature, the other end of the tackle, lying loose on the floor boards, got entangled in the feet of the crew. The effort to release their seaworthy legs from the imprisoning wire led to the reduced mobility of their ensnarled arms and shoulders. Maytagagawa, of the sharp incisors, tried to bite through the wire but succeeded only in getting it caught around her neck. The sixty-pound Marlin, having revived itself, torpedoed off about that time in a mad dash for freedom. "Zing"

went the hooked line, drawing taut as a bow. "Slump"
went Maytagagawa, going limp as a fish. The only hope
for her life was to decrease stress on the tackle by
throwing her overboard. At precisely the moment she hit
the water the fish freed itself of the hook and everybody
let out a big cheer. The elation was premature, however,
because now Maytagagawa was in danger of strangling
from the line pulled taut at the other end, wrapped as it
was around the ship's crew. Naturally, everybody leaned
over the water as far as they could to slacken the
line. . . .

The capsized boat, although a total loss, was something to cling to and eventually everybody reached the
island.

Several previous excursions to the hideaway by Mo
and Damon had built up a secret storehouse of food and
clothing which, as it turned out, was about a quarter of
what they really needed. Not only was the size of the
gang almost doubled but the period of their exile, extended to seven weeks by the construction of a new
boat, was almost twice the original length.

No wonder then, when at last they took leave of the
island, they were a sickly group, all bones and skin
rashes. Which was not to say they weren't a lot better
off than most everybody else.

At a mid-ocean conclave it was agreed by all that
despite the way they looked and felt, the enforced delay
was a blessing in one sense. Immediately following the
theft, the "Big Boys" had undoubtedly turned the heat
on full blast. Yet despite their most strenuous efforts,
the gang had succeeded in eluding capture. It was safe
to assume, they agreed, that after so protracted an in-
terim, there was no question but that the Syndicate had
tempered its efforts and things had cooled down.

The enforced delay was not only a blessing, it was a

blessing in disguise; it also gave the entire planet a chance to cool down. The Milliginian attack came just five days after the gang was originally slated to return to civilization.

They did not know this, however, and so when they landed in Miami Beach and discovered that among all the other things obliterated, the Miami racetrack was gone, Arnoldumbo, reneging on his part in the agreement, concluded in terror that the havoc wrecked on the mainland was the work of the vengeful Syndicate sworn to turn every stone in pursuit of the guilty.

For several days after, they had no other clues to go on. They wandered aimlessly because as far as they could see there was nothing to aim at. The white powder was there, was in all directions, and to make matters worse, it squeaked when they walked on it.

Eventually they stumbled into what had been the city of Palm Beach. (If anything, the powder was whiter there.) No one had said anything for a long time but now John grunted and the others, looking up, saw it too. In front of the backdrop, inside the sidedrop, and behind the frontdrop of the dusty white landscape, smack in the middle of all the surrounding nothingness, sat two old ladies in rocking chairs beside a sunken fallout shelter, knitting sweaters for absent kittens.

"What happened to everything; what happened to everybody?" asked Mo, the first to reach them. Without dropping a stitch, the one with the tooth said, "Now who all heyar do you all think you are addressin', boy?" The white contingent in the gang stepped forward and between them—Arnoldumbo, Maytagagawa, Raymon, Damon and Louella—they extracted from the cobwebbed biddies at least part of the story. The hoary grannies had been canning peaches in the shelter when they heard a disturbance topside. "Screamin' an carryin' on an all," but lasting only a few brief seconds. The pectin wasn't in the jars yet and figuring what they didn't know wouldn't harm them, they sniffed away any curiosity, and in the process, preserved not only the summer harvest but their hirsute octogenarian noses as well. "Well now," said the one with the hole in her forehead, "when we did come up, two weeks later, here were these nice people all dyed Easter Morning Blue with these strange machines they kept waving in front of us."

"What is the meanin' of this here, boy, I said," bitingly said the one who still had the wherewithal.

" 'How old are you, mother?' the John Gilbert-looking one asked me," said the drafty-headed crone through peach-stained gums.

"An then ah said to him, 'mahnd your P's and Q's, *foreigner*,' " triumphantly interrupted the carnivore of the duo. "Then they started in about what to do with us, and one, pointing to his crystal set or whatever, said something about it not making much sense to take us back, seeing that we was . . . sort of elderly and that we had nothing they could use."

"But where did they come from," Mo persisted, jumping forward. "What did they do to everything, what do they want?" "Harumph," said the proud owner of the Doctor Lyons can, eyeing the color of his skin, "*you* should know *that* better than *I*."

"But, but . . ." sputtered the group surging forward. Too late, too late, the old ladies "pearled two" simultaneously and put down their needles. It was time for a fitting. The anxious gang closed formation and huddled nearer still. It didn't seem to matter. "Here kitty-kitty-kitty," chanted the imperturbable hags, looking directly through Mobawamba, Celestealulu and Samatoba and establishing a fix on Georgia, the Carolinas and the three states to the northwest.

Even so, they had learned enough to give specific direction and velocity to their hitherto aimless wanderings. The gang, with the stolen money satchels firmly in tow, didn't stop running until they reached the Everglade jungle.

It was in the swamp that Morris Leverne Tate became Mobawamba and Sam, Celeste, Arnold, Maytag and Louella were rechristened. "We'd rather not," begged off Raymon and Damon, the homosexual twin brothers, explaining that additional syllables wouldn't go with their self-conceived images. John refused on other grounds. "I ain't no jungle bunny and neither is Pearl," he said, spitting defiantly and kicking a tree for good measure.

The idea was Mo's and he came upon it as a symbolic means to indicate the metamorphosis in their lives. "This is where it's going to happen, brothers, and we sure as hell better start making the best of it. We got to live like Africans and live off the land, maybe for a long time and maybe for good." Sam looked over his shoulder and saw a statue of himself in feathers and a loincloth and said, "Oh yeah, oh yeah." It went without saying that Celeste would then also approve the name change. Arnold looked over his shoulder and saw Maytag who was elbowing him in the kidney and bobbing her head rapidly. "Okay, okay, but does it have to be Arnol*dumbo*," he said sheepishly, referring to John's impugnment of his "mental works." "Course not, call yourself what you want," replied Mo. All eyes turned on the truncated macrocephalic and the heat from their looks ballooned the size of his head another six inches in diameter. He put his hands to his temples to hide the telltale swelling and covered up the coverup by pretending to scratch for a new name from behind his ear. "I know," he brightened at last, "I'll call myself Arnoldumbo like in the elephant who could fly. That was pretty terrific you know.'' For Arnoldumbo, a change in connotation was as good as a change in name. "Glicki-glicki," said Maytag who rarely said anything else. "Fine, then from now on I'm Louellalulu," said the sister of the twins, looking deeply into Mobawamba's eyes.

And so it came to pass that the "gang," like civilization, turned to whispy dust and the "tribe," like the jungle underbrush, sprang sturdily to life and flourished.

Everybody agreed that Mo should be the leader of the tribe because he knew the most about Africa and because he had always been the leader anyway. It also helped that he was best liked.

"Even on the island when things was bad, Morris always smiled and kept everybody's spirits up," said Celestealulu.

"He's just one of them naturally light-headed people," said Pearl.

"Yeah, but he's got brains too," said Arnoldumbo, admiringly.

"He's strong," said Samatoba, "like me."

"A tough mother," said John, grudgingly.

"Mostly he's kind and good," said Louellalulu.

"And cute," said Raymon and Damon.

"He's the one that's going to save us all right. We're lucky to have him," they whispered in tandem, as if afraid something in the forest would hear them.

Mo was off by himself. He propped himself up against a tree and laughed a big toothy hyena laugh and then another. He listened to it ring through the jungle and then tried again, this time changing the tone and pitch. "Merry Christmas to all and to all a good night." And then, "Sheeeet man, this am what ah call Sunday noon in da mibble of da week! My, oh my, this ole body done feel soooo gooooooood an fine an. . . ." He looked around restlessly. "Maybe I should do some swinging, but then that's what I do to fill the mornings . . . when they're sleeping." And then, "Damn them for sleeping late, the lazy bastards!" The headache began. "No, no, I'm sorry, bless them, bless them and their innocent little asses. I'm glad they're happy, cause . . . ah is happy too, ah is sooo haaaapy." And he rolled his eyes and snapped his fingers for emphasis, but by now it was too late. The cavalry was galloping across his skull. But still, "I am da lordy ob da jumbo an everything is as sweety as sweety potatoey pie." The words kept tumbling out, one after the other, as if by regurgitating a specific quota he would relieve the pressure on his brain. And then finally in a shout, "I mean what's the matter with me man, why does my head hurt?"

The problem which he did not understand was that he was off by himself and being off by himself he had to work very hard to keep from thinking about another time in another place when he wasn't everything to everybody, just one thing to one man, his murderer. He wasn't succeeding. "If only the honk was here," he barely dared to think.

FIVE

"HOW many times can you point to the right field
bullpen with the count three and two, two out, the bases
loaded, and the other team leading three to nothing in
the ninth? What's the point of hitting home runs, giving
new hope to the blind; assassinating dictators, and being
top hand on the carousel circuit anyway? It's all just
stupid fantasy, childish day dreaming."

In the time before the Milliginians, Joshua best liked
to consider his imaginary exploits on Fridays. Friday
was the day he deposited a portion of his weekly salary
at the bank and the accumulating entries in his passbook
seemed to make everything a bit more possible. On the
way home he was either the only comedian ever to
conduct a telethon for Paranoid-Schizophrenics and with
his brilliant wit, "uncanny as it may seem ladies and
gentlemen," keep an audience of thirty-five million rolling in the aisles for forty-one consecutive hours; or the

man to whom the world's ten most beautiful nympho-
maniacs swore everlasting subservience as a result of
having saved their lives, "miraculous as it may seem
ladies and gentlemen," by carrying the entire bevy out
through a burning building all at the same time without
singeing so much as a false eyelash. Or, among his
favorites, the only American on the great Argentinean
soccer team who personally won the World Cup for his
adopted country by scoring the last-second goal, "astounding
as it may seem ladies and gentlemen," by kicking it on
the fly the entire length of the field from in front of his
own goalposts . . . off his right knee . . . just above the
point where his leg had been blown off . . . in the "BIG
ONE" . . . during his heroic charge . . . against insur-
mountable odds . . . in defense of liberty and justice.
On those occasions when he misjudged story length and
arrived home before all the climactic moments had been
served, he would circle the block a couple of times
before parking and dutifully detail the remaining hero-
ics. On Fridays Joshua always stepped into the winner's
circle when he stepped out of his car.

Something had gone wrong. Today, all day, nothing
good happened when he tried to pretend. His stories
would not come to life and, worse yet, they suddenly
seemed ridiculous. It was more than sad. It was terrifying because there was nothing to put in their place,
nothing to fill the void. The box of goodies was gone
and all that remained was the discarded cellophane wrap-
per. "There's nothing inside me," he said. "I'm empty.
I might just as well lie down and die." Joshua laid
down, crossed his hands over his chest, and waited for
the Milliginians.

In the old life he had worshiped before the reality of
his savings account. It was not a very imposing god and

could only bestow blessings on Fridays. The altar at which he knelt in his new life conferred canonization on an around-the-clock basis and every day had become Friday. There was one stipulation: the flight of fancy had to be tethered to an element of reality. In the past, it had been money in the bank. In the present it was his faith that he would reach the Everglades. As long as he had that one bond, his imagination needn't recognize any boundaries. But days had turned into weeks and alone by himself, traveling for all he knew in circles, a sense of futility began to grow and the tie began to fray. Today, the day he finally gave up on reaching his destination, it at last broke. When he stopped believing in his goal, he stopped believing in himself completely, and the self of his imagination with no anchoring line was caught by the perverse winds of self-ridicule, sent spinning and finally crashed at his feet. ''Stupid fantasy, childish day dreaming,'' he had said.

The man who then laid himself on the ground was Joshua in name only. Gone was the meat of the man, stringy though it may have been: the small ambition, the faint character, the insurance salesman and the Killer of Moose. And gone also was the soul of the man, the part that only surfaced in his dreams. What lay there, spread-eagled, in anticipation of man-eating space monsters, was only the unappetizing scooped-out cellophane shell of the man through whom the white dust swirled and blew as through a hollow.

But the monsters did not come and at last Joshua found a reason to get up and continue.

He had remembered something. Something that wasn't a fantasy; something that really happened. He couldn't remember the circumstances nor the details but he knew for a fact that somewhere, sometime in his past he had saved a man's life. ''How could I have forgotten that?

How could I have forgotten the most important thing that ever happened to me? I saved a man's life; snatched him from the jaws of death as it were; caught him at the edge of eternity. . . .'' Joshua stopped. It was beginning to sound all too familiar. The thing he didn't want to do was muddy the experience by coloring it with the same brush he used on his imaginary murals. "Actually, all I did was save a man's life, that's all . . . a simple thing really . . . nothing to get all that excited about . . . a small event, insignificant in the light of man's greater accomplishments . . . a testimony to man's humanity to man perhaps but still. . . . NO, DAMN IT, THERE I GO AGAIN! Look, it wasn't all that much. Anybody would have done the same, okay? Okay!''

It was enough, however, to fill the cavity and put Joshua back on his feet. He had found a new reality.

"Hell, if that girl could find me, what with her miscarriage and all, someone who had saved someone's life sure as hell should be able to find a tractor and make it to the Everglades.'' Catheleen, it seems, didn't come the whole way on foot. Somewhere in the Mississippi backwoods she had come upon an abandoned tractor and ridden it until she had seen the spaceships in the distance. Before she died she told Joshua where it was hidden. "Among some trees in the Mountains,'' which was better at least than "somewhere in the North American continent,'' he rationalized. "If that little girl could come all that distance without knowing where she was going or who she would meet,'' he told himself again, "I sure as hell ought to be able to find that tractor, get to the Everglades, and live again among human beings.'' Tanked up on new faith, Joshua cranked himself up off the sacrificial ground. "I mean you can be just so humble, but if you've saved a man's life, you've saved a man's life, and there's no other way to slice the pie.''

Joshua then shifted into high and sped away from his surrender. "I mean if that teen-age girl could come all that way. . . ."

The only thing missing from the overhaul he had done on himself was the where and the when and the how and the who of that legendary Homeric triumph in his past.

SIX

RETIRED Army Major Hank Hank had finally gotten across his idea; back in New Hope Settlement, the third orgy of the month was currently in full swing. At the appointed hour everybody (who had one) had grabbed his mate, dashed into his tent, and in the manner of his belief, according to the dictates of his conscience, did "it." Unlike other such festivals in man's history, New Hope conducted its orgies with strict adherence to the principles of the private enterprise system.

The catch phrase for all behavior in New Hope was "Everything is Private." Every family, consisting always of two or one, worked on its own strictly for itself in any activity related to survival. It was part of the original Pathfinder philosophy that in order to make it in the wilderness, each family had to be as "pioneer tough" as America's first settlers. It was the consensus that those frontiersmen, with neighbors few and far between, learned quickly that if they were going to prevail against nature, they would have to do it by themselves, without help. Since the entire colony was carved from a rare 300-square-foot piece of flat, dry land, these latter-day settlers were forced to erect quarters that were no more than a few yards apart. Nevertheless and against almost impossible odds, this policy of isolation was courageously maintained. Each family forced itself, with steadfast New Hope resolve, to conduct all life-sustaining functions while operating in a vacuum. For example, Buck Alice, the science fiction writer, got caught in an animal trap of his own invention and hung upside down for nine hours (until the rope broke) in full view of the entire camp because he had come to the settlement alone and had no family to cut him down. Even more to the point were the circumstances surrounding the death of the wife of Buck's closest neighbor. One hungry day she was dragged off and thoroughly chewed by a big bear. The neighbor ran to Buck and begged the use of some heavy stones to divert the animal. Buck, who was building a rock garden and had by then learned his lesson, responded as if born to the Pathfinder cloth and said, "tough shit."

This is not to say that the people of different families did not speak or pass the time of day. The exchange of pleasantries was perfectly acceptable just as long as nothing important was said.

The concept of the orgy was introduced by Hank Hank in the fifth month in the colony's life. "The definition of orgy," he explained, "involves *the* most personal kind of behavior in the atmosphere of the commune and that little old atmosphere, my friends, is the very complete antithesis of what we believe in. What better way to secure the beachhead for our way of life," he reasoned, as the echoes of cassons marching along rumbled through his head, "than to win a victory over the enemy by undermining it at the very root of its ugly heart. We'll take their foul decadent rites," and again he was knee deep in the mud, reviewing the troops at Fort Dix, "and turn it into something decent and reverent. We'll have orgies all right," he said flicking the dust from his imaginary general's bar, "but we'll have them by the democratic process in the spirit of capitalism and private enterprise."

The humanitarian tie-in to which Hank Hank alluded was the settlement's preoccupation with procreation. "For the love of babies," the old militarist cried out each time an orgy was to begin, and the troops marshaling behind ceremoniously chanted in return, "I only wish I had a life to give to my country." After each such "engagement" the old warhorse would pop from his tent with an expanded chest and in full dress uniform. He would then parade the camp grounds, shaking hands, slapping backs and uttering words of encouragement like "well done" and "atta boy."

In passing, it should be noted that early in the game Hank Hank extracted at bayonet point a New Testament vow from his wife never to reveal either the history of the high picket fence or the result of his inability to clear it . . . or for that matter, the surveillance maneuvers he conducted through open tent flaps after everybody was safely bedded down and festivaling it up.

In defense of these separate but connected carousels, it can be stated that many wives noted a new vigor and enthusiasm from otherwise "too tired to" husbands. (The exercise of male imagination, triggered by the knowledge that the neighbor's more attractive spouse was getting "it" at the very same moment, no doubt played an expanding role in the rejuvenation.)

All in all, it didn't take much to get everyone into the teepee.

The orgy currently in the works was sparked by screaming Isobel who punctuated her announcement by kicking out the underpinnings of the three nearest tents. She danced insanely about the settlement, waving her blouse in time to a mad little ditty about budding bosoms. "Yes, yes, she is bigger, definitely bigger, and now her womanhood can't be far behind." In anticipation of her impending puberty, warm kisses were generously bestowed on Isobel's forehead and other places. Then the villagers, responding as one to Hank's cry of "Babies or Bust," deflated the child's triumph by dashing pell-mell for their tents. There stood Isobel in the center of the small settlement, abandoned and alone with only bitter tears and her now slightly smaller 32A-sized breasts for company.

No wonder she was a rotten kid.

SEVEN

IMHOR had long ago adopted the practice of nestling his hands in the hollows under his arms when his body was in repose. The limbs, thus foreshortened, caused the elbows to angle rakishly and called to mind the attitude of some winged creature poised for flight. What Imhor was doing, in reality, was incubating the tips of his fingers. He liked to imagine that the warm area at the abutment point for his arms and body acted as a greenhouse and in some undefined way provided the conditions for perpetuating the health of his extremities. It was a theory he had come by in his formative years and despite the lack of confirming evidence, was one to which he resolutely clung.

Because Imhor was much too aware of his fingers, this posture never reduced itself into simple habit. (Even as a child his mother had said, ''Imhor, you are much too aware of your fingers.'') Consequently, despite the countless number of such ministrations, each time he tucked his hands under his armpits it was with the conscious design of maintaining their salubrity. Although Imhor's fingers were nice, they weren't that nice. It's just that when you have a weak chin and transparent eyelids, long, smooth and shiny fingers add up as ten important digits on the plus side. No wonder then his chagrin at their desertion in his hour of need.

He was on his stomach desperately clawing the hard ground in an effort to keep the planet from rolling from under him. At last he spied a partly embedded stone. As he grappled for a hold however, his fingers turned to milk toast and with a soft spungy squish, bent this way and that. "Rotten, they've turned rotten," he told himself, lamenting again the deceitful nature of everything. With no way now to anchor himself to the smooth earth, he began to lose ground and rapidly slide backward. "I'm going to drop off into space," he cried aloud, viewing the precipitous fall through the transparent lids of his tightly shut eyes. "What have I done to deserve this?" No sooner had he spoken than the planet came to an abrupt halt. Imhor struggled to his feet and began pulling himself inch by inch through the soft, gummy tar surface. Up, up he climbed toward the top of the world and the lone tree positioned there. He would be able to hold on to his dear life by wrapping himself around the trunk, he told himself, if he could just reach the tree before the planet started moving again.

Suddenly there was a loud grinding sound like gears on a ferryboat meshing into activity and the Earth responded with a violent shrug that threw Imhor from his feet. Like a man listening for the report of the rifles at his own execution by firing squad, Imhor, with hope gone, waited for the planet to resume its movement. False start, nothing happened. At last he pushed himself from the glass-like surface and again began the ascent.

Once again came the sound of cogs and sprockets and
with it the rumble beneath him. But this time, he kept
his feet and, dripping mucky stuff, climbed closer and
then still closer to the tree at the top of the world. Again
the Earth shook, this time for a full twelve seconds, but
now he could see the coarseness of the grain and the
eddies in the bark where the knotholes were.

He knew he should conserve his strength and breath
for the last ten yards but he could not contain himself.
"I love you, I love you," he shouted to the tree, not
unlike a young girl racing across a bridge toward an
abandoned beau hanging from a guardrail. "Thank goodness," he said at last, wrapping himself around the
bark. "Thank goodness you're still here!" He had no
sooner gasped his third triumphant breath than the planet
began spinning in earnest and almost incidentally shook
Imhor loose from the tree and sent him sailing off into
space.

The sensation of slowly tumbling through a galactic
limbo was a pleasant one. Despite the vastness of space,
he experienced a feeling of snugness as if he were all
the time curled inside a velvet-lined, form-molding plas-
tic bag. Involuntarily his knees reached up toward his
ears as his chin pressed down against his chest. "This is
good, this is good," he thought. "Coooo" is what he
actually said. "Happy, happy, happy," he thought. *"Oh
My God!"* he shouted as he suddenly remembered why
he had tried so desperately to find a handhold on Milligin.
It wasn't space that was so terrifying but the prospect of
where he would ultimately land. The climax to all his
sweaty dreams was the real nightmare, EARTH, and as
he emerged from the anaesthetic his worst unconscious
fears were once again realized.

Imhor's new liver was the third organ transplant he
had undergone since he first stepped out onto Earth's

surface that dreaded day six months before. That dreaded day succeeded by a week the actual moment the two hundred Milliginian spaceships entered the Earth's atmosphere. Their battle plan had been simple: annihilate the whole of the human species and destroy all of its structures and products. Turn Earth virgin-white and then, with 21st century Milliginian know-how, rapidly cultivate and develop the planet into a model society. (Although unspoken, the plan was in no little way motivated by the desire to exorcise feelings of genocidal guilt. Milliginians were strong believers in the old axiom "out of sight, out of mind," and with the slate truly and totally wiped clean, as it were, the occupation of "Milligin II" could proceed with a steady hand and a light heart.)

The attack was aimed at the world's most strategically sensitive areas and the fight was over before any nation could fire even one volley in defense. From that point on, it was merely a matter of Swoop Craft patrols on seek-and-destroy missions.

It took the Milliginians six days and six nights to complete the job. They rested on the seventh.

A never-ceasing marvel of Nature is that every living thing has its own built-in defense system. Planets, apparently, are no exception. Within a very short time, Earth started to reject the invaders. Milliginian organs began spoiling in wholesale lots. Tissue malfunction caused the death of one hundred and twenty Milliginians within the first ninety days. Angry murmurings careened through the corridors. Scientists who had vociferously supported the "invincibility" theory of their Earth-stationed species were openly bumped and jostled outside staterooms. Aquamarines culled little satisfaction from the knowledge that infirm Cobalt Blues were turning greenish because afflicted Aquamarines were, in turn, turning orangish. "What to do, what to do," all cried, as one, wringing the brown spots on their hands. In no time at all the one hundred and seventieth alien succumbed. Immediately thereafter, one hundred and ninety-nine warships packed up and returned to the parent planet. The crew of the two-hundredth ship, including a disproportionately heavy contingent of bacteriologists, meteorologists, chemists and microbiologists, was left behind with the admonition that they either solve the mystery or die at their posts trying.

In no time at all, eighty-six of the remaining ship's complement of seven hundred and fifty expired. Under these circumstances, it became a growing possibility that three and a quarter billion humans had died in vain. Finally, someone came up with the idea of stimulating research by developing a formal competition between Cobalts and Aquas. It was conjectured that competition would also have the therapeutic side effect of lessening the tension generated by the prevailing situation. In no time at all, the Blue-Greens were divvying up a dozen extra bowls of bouillon and the Sky-Blues were flipping for the five additional servings of sauce. An entire range of techniques in bludgeoning and strangulation was showcased through the deaths of the seventeen crew members. To make matters worse, no one felt less tense. The competition was ultimately abandoned.

Then Glogmor, the healthy philosopher, stood up and stated that he held the answer to their sickness. Before he could continue, however, he was rudely seized and tossed into a crypt. (Milliginian scientists as a rule hate philosophers, particularly when they exhibit absolutely no signs of failing health.) As fate would have it, shortly after his interment, the chief scientist developed a dispeptic ulcer and in a state of panic, had Glogmor exhumed and brought forth to expound. Everybody took a big gulp of air in preparation for holding their breath in the presence of the soft-spoken Glogmor. The death rattles that accompanied the group inhalation caused the halls to reverberate and the chandeliers to sway. Glogmor smiled, not because he was mean but because he was a PHILOSOPHER. Then he spoke: "Only natives of Earth can survive on Earth. We are not natives of Earth; therefore we cannot survive on Earth."

Glogmor was, of course, immediately reimprisoned but, alas, the damage was done. A curtain of despair encircled the ship and several ailing crew members, including the chief scientist, passed away prematurely. "After all," said many other scientists into their shirt fronts, "Glogmor is the healthiest of us all; therefore he must know something!"

The philosopher's syllogism, if not more accurate, was at least better constructed. Nevertheless, Glogmor was shortly murdered in his sleep. It was the assassin's idea that reducing the philosopher to a poorer state of health would reduce as well the weightiness of his words and rekindle hope in the dejected crew for an ultimate solution to their increasing mortality.

Imhor had been picked for the fleet because he was a meteorologist and a computers systems designer. His responsibility was to have been the engineering of a computer system to analyze and forecast disturbances in Earth's atmosphere. However, because of the emergency, there had been a change in priorities as well as directives. He had been relegated instead to Swoop Craft operator in charge of bringing back alive the few pitiful humans the Aliens had missed killing the first time around. "You'll be more useful tracking humans" was all the explanation he ever received.

His bitterness mounted with every patrol and reached crisis proportions when he was called for a tour of duty only six days after his most recent operation. He climbed into the craft knowing full well that a measure of his emotional as well as physical strength had been left on the operating table never to return. He felt a twinge in his still-healing abdomen as he triggered his secondary jets on the ship and barreled off across the barren terrain. "Viscera, where are you?" he thought, thinking back to the liver which originally came with his body. He had a vision of it lying at the bottom of a pile of snails and autumn leaves waiting to be hauled away to the local incinerating plant. "Not fair, not fair. It was a part of me. It was me. Soon there will be less and less of me. Who will I be then?"

He looked down at his body as if seeing it for the first time and shuddered discernibly. Then from the corner of his eye he noticed that his hands had started to inch their way up his trunk. The movement looked natural enough, but then why this creeping feeling of apprehension? They drummed along his ribcage in what he began to suspect was an exaggerated display of innocence. He looked away for only the briefest of moments and already they were crawling across his chest. The long, smooth, shiny. . . wait! These weren't his! They were less long, less smooth, definitely less shiny. SOMEBODY HAD SWITCHED FINGERS ON HIM DURING THE OPERATION. He watched in horrified fascination as they climbed toward his neck. "They're going to choke me, I know it now, they're going to choke me. 'Death by his own hands,' they'll say, but it's not so. They're not my hands . . . just like that new liver. . . ."

It wasn't until he had wiped away the cascading tears with the heels of his palms that he realized it was his mind of which he had momentarily lost control and not his hands. "If only I was doing the work for which I was chosen I could concentrate better," Imhor told himself, a bit shaken by the ordeal. "But no, they have me doing this. It's so beneath me," he said, looking below him for signs for fugitive Earthlings. "It's just not fair." Finding comfort in self-pity had become Imhor's principal diversion. The odious nature of his assigned Earth work gave him much on-the-job opportunity to wade and wallow; as in the present situation, he was more and more frequently in danger of going in over his head. "A garbage collector, scavenging for bits and pieces of human debris," Imhor sighed. The lyric quality of the phrase was comforting. He repeated it to himself. "Scavenging for bits and pieces of human debris." He reveled in its toniness. It gave him substance and identity beyond his present station.

He began to feel better. He activated the trap nets to stand by, reversed direction on the Swoop Craft, and powered down toward the human couple vainly seeking refuge on the flat plain. The cries of the ensnarled humans barely sifted through. "Garbage collector indeed. I'll show them, I'll show them all."

EIGHT

THE self you see is totally myself. As a rose is a rose, I am who I am.

"In other words . . ."

"No other words, no words at all. I am defined by being."

"And that is all?"

"In my case it is everything."

"We are more than just what we appear."

"I am not."

"We're made up of many things, a plurality . . ."

"Not I."

"Heterogeneous products of a complex world."

"I am the product of a simple world."

"And that is . . . ?"

"Nature, instinct."

"But civilization . . ."

"I am uncorrupted by civilization. I am the honesty

50

of a snake's rattle, the integrity of a cat's bristled back, the truth of a wolf's bared teeth. I am a fighter.''

Before the tribe had been the gang, they had earned their way running bets for the Syndicate. Before they had been bookie runners, they had performed in the fight game. From an economic standard, a low point in their lives was during the time they fought in the ring. From a spiritual perspective, the years spent fighting were the ones in which they achieved the dizziest heights, notwithstanding the fact that most of the time was spent flat on their backs.

''Remember the time I almost beat. . . ,'' ''Remember how they said I wouldn't last four rounds with. . . .'' ''The Champ, he still remembers the time I. . . ,'' they said. ''That's the time I knew who I was,'' they thought. Because of that golden time their lives had not been a waste. As long as they could remember that, they could at least coexist with the years that remained.

As for the years that went before . . .
''Are you a good doctor, daddy?''
''Yes.''
''What does a doctor do?''
''He heals the sick.''
''I want to be like you, daddy.''
''Thank you, son.''

''Daddy, who am I?''
''A fine boy.''
''But who am I?''
''Yourself.''

''They won't let me be myself.''
''Dance between the raindrops.''

*   *   *

"I'm soaked, pop."

"Sit awhile in the sun."

"The Pacific Ocean sits in the sun every morning."

"Doctors do everything backwards."

"I'm sorry."

"They shouldn't heal the sick."

"Not so loud, Morris."

"Curing a dying nigger is an illusion, father—a false sense of security. You should work to keep our wounds open because we are deceased and we should never forget that."

"We're not niggers, Morris."

"Yes you are, Charlie."

"Where are you going, Morris?"

"I'm going to make wounds."

"Why?"

"It's not right we should die alone."

And in the trenches . . .

"I had this terrible experience in my childhood, Morris."

"Somebody dip your hair in the inkwell, honk?"

"No, it really was terrible."

"You're lucky."

"Why?"

"I didn't have one."

"A terrible experience?"

"No, a childhood."

"Well anyway, these bastards were chasing me."

"Were they Negroes, honk?"

"No, Irish."

"They have freckles?"

"Yeah, I guess so, around the bridge of the nose."

"See, I was right, they were niggers."

"What do you mean?"

"All those chocolate spots on their faces."

"It wasn't funny to me. I ran away."

"You're lucky."

"How's that?"

"I couldn't, honk."

"Can't you call me by my name?"

"I just did."

"Do you hate everybody?"

"I think so."

It was almost like a vaudeville act the way their helmets pitched forward as they simultaneously whirled, fell back on their haunches and discharged their rifles. The yellow soldier toppled into the hole and fell across them without making a sound. There was one bullet hole in his head and a lot of his blood on their hands. "His face doesn't look like a mask at all," Morris thought.

In another moment the battle was on again and they were returning the fire from the distant shadows. Never during that whole night did Morris forget the reason the foxhole had shrunk in depth; each time he stood up to fire, he felt beneath him the give and displacement of human flesh.

Morris spent the weeks following the battle for "Junk Hill" in a hospital ward. The honk came by several times but Morris refused to see him. The honk wrote notes but Morris refused to read them.

"We know you have Morris' good at heart," the doctor told the honk, "but right now he reacts very badly to anything that reminds him of the war. He's still

in a state of shock." "It's not that I expect any gratitude," the honk told the Doc, "it's . . . just . . . that
. . . I'd . . . like to say . . . hello."

The honk finally got the idea and stopped coming by.
"I would have seen him the next time," Morris wept,
"but the bastard quit pretending and gave up." Morris
interpreted the honk's easy defeat as further proof of his
own unworthiness.

"I killed a man," he had said that first day when he
awoke in the hospital. "I shot him right through the
head. He was standing as close to me as the tip of my
rifle and I murdered him. I put a bullet in his face. I
stopped his heart. I stopped him from breathing. He was
going to live till ninety and his children loved him and
worried about him and were proud of him and I ended
all that, I destroyed all that. I KILLED HIM. I SHOT
HIM THROUGH THE HEAD, RIGHT THROUGH THE
CENTER OF HIS HEAD." As many ways and as often
as he said it he could not verbalize the enormity of the
horror he felt. Worst of all, there was no salvation in
confession; each admission of his guilt just added to his
burden.

"I'm a Black Man," he told himself another time. "I
have been oppressed and suppressed all my life and I'm
full of hate and frustration and bitterness. I have the
right to taste blood. I have the right to kill. It is the right
given me by a world that has made me black first and a
human being second. I HAVE THE RIGHT TO KILL."
The muscles in Morris' face buckled from the strain of
his contortions. At any moment the skin would rip from
his skull and like a punctured balloon, dance insanely in
the air. He went stiff and fell back on his bed, helpless.
If no one came soon he would drown in his own tears.
"GOD, I KILLED A MAN."

The world had not succeeded.

The only person who could have relieved Morris' agony was the honk. He had been there in the hole with him. He knew it was self-defense. He would have told him that he had to kill, that it was war and the soldier was the enemy, that nobody, not even the soldier's family, could hold it against him. The honk would have reassured him that he wasn't a murderer. The honk was never permitted an audience, however, because deep down, Morris was not yet ready for exoneration. During the weeks in the hospital he had developed a built-in safety catch against inner peace. On those occasions when his attention was diverted from his "cross" and he was in the middle of a small smile, the pin automatically slipped into place and shut off his mind to all but the vision of himself climbing over a heap of scraps in a junkyard.

It was always the same. He wasn't blind and yet there was nothing he could distinguish by sight. He saw himself scratch about for something and then he saw himself run his fingers across the cloth folding compartment from inside an attaché case. He dipped his fingers inside and felt the sloppy lips of wet suckly things all squirmy and alive. He withdrew his hands and swept them in an arc but could not find the housing for the compartment. It had started as a recurring dream during the first week in the hospital. After the seventh repetition, he knew the details as well as he knew his multiplication tables. It became part of his conscious reality and he had no need to ever dream it again. As soon as Morris saw himself on that junk pile he would stop smiling. He didn't know why.

Eventually Morris recovered from his battle injuries. The psychological wounds that would not heal, however, precipitated his early release from the service and he was never again asked to shoulder a gun. The Army doctor was replaced by a civilian psychiatrist with a goatee and a watch fob.

"The junk pile is Junk Hill and the content of the pocket inside the attaché case is the inner conflict between your ghetto-conditioned need to hit back and your super ego that says such things are wrong. In the middle, being pulled this way and that, is the actual act, the killing of the soldier." Without pausing, the doctor withdrew a pad and began notating from memory the introductory passage from a Richard Strauss tone poem. His other hand was vigorously engaged in rubbing his beard with short rapid strokes.

"The case within which the compartment rests is you, the self-conceived you." The right hand was now busily engaged in changing the clef sign from treble to bass. The soft clinky sound of a key chain in friction came from within the fist of the doctor's other hand. "The reason you can't see the briefcase with your eyes is because your super ego is winning the battle and in so doing, has thrown your self-conceived image into disorientation." "Dum-de-dum-dum-dum" sang the analyst under his breath for three bars while he simultaneously tumbled an obelisk statuette between his palms.

"As a result, you are condemning yourself" (sotto voce), "rejecting yourself" (forte), "DENYING YOUR VERY EXISTENCE" (fortissimo). The good doctor's grip slipped as he reached the crescendo and the obelisk splattered all over the carpet. "There is a reason you see yourself as an attaché case"—the consultant rubbed away the far-off look in his eyes with his near hand while his far hand, near the end of its travels, was designing the character for a "full rest" stop—"but to find it might take fully the rest of our lives." "On the basis of all the notes I have been making," said the doctor turning to Morris with all the involvement of a wind-blown weather vane cock, "there is one thing I can definitely tell you." The virile psychiatrist reached again for his stiff pointed van dyke. "You are not a murderer."

It didn't help.

He left the doctor's office and went searching for the honk. It was his last chance. He would never find peace anywhere, he decided, unless the honk told him he was innocent. After a week of not knowing where to look, his search became a gradual retreat from the world. If he could not find equanimity in one way, he would find it in another.

He drifted through his old neighborhood from street corner to street corner. He came to know all the lamp-posts by name. They never bothered to learn his. To them he remained as disdainfully anonymous as the other faceless drunks. Progressively he ceased to see, ceased to hear and ceased to feel. It wasn't heaven but for a long time it was better than dealing with sloppy-lipped, suckly things.

The weeks grew into months and he withdrew still further, but now with each step backwards, he drew a step closer to changing direction and beginning the long return journey. He both reached the end of the road and took his first cautious look over his shoulder on the night he was beaten and robbed by two small boys. With no place to go, he lay mutely in the alley. Towards morning his hands reached out against his will to soothe his aching parts. He discovered in his pain an awareness of himself more acute than ever he had known during his long retreat. As he touched himself, he felt corroborating evidence of a dawning suspicion: he was not only a living thing but had form and substance as well.

On another afternoon he saw a million dust particles lazily floating in a shaft of light and in recognition of the August day he unbuttoned his worn Mackinaw and let it fall where he leaned. The supporting lamppost lit up and took notice. The word spread quickly that he had begun as well to shed the layers of emotional insulation and along his route the light standards beamed their approval. The day came at last when he tipped himself up straight, said good-bye to wooden poles, and went looking for human companionship.

He began by hanging around with hung-out hangers-ons. After a while, he wanted more. He went to New York and met Raymon and Damon and was invited home for dinner. Louella made an unexpected appearance and whatever ideas the brothers had for dessert were forever abandoned. Morris read in Louella's eyes her suddenly awakened feelings. His own attention turned from the crème-de-menthe-flavored hamburger to the knowledge that he had completed his evolvement and returned to life.

The homosexual brothers decided to take Morris under their wings. They introduced him to boxing and he took to working out with them at the gym. Raymon and Damon had classic bodies and looked like made-to-order gladiators. They had shoddy records as fighters, however, and the reason became painfully apparent once they ventured between the ropes: they lived in mortal fear of being hurt.

"Why did you decide to be fighters?" Morris asked discreetly. "Because," they said, shifting all the weight to the left hips as they bent the right knees, "we promised mother."

If the reason for their ring failures had not been so obvious, Morris might not have hit on the idea of becoming a boxer himself. He knew that unlike the twins, he was not afraid of getting hurt. The guilt that had hounded him into oblivion was there to welcome him back, and he saw in the fight game not only a way to earn money but a chance to do penance. In the succeeding months he became known as a middleweight who could take punishment.

Boxing helped in another way. In the ring he was a different man. He had no history. There was no yesterday and no tomorrow. His life was only one second at a time, one clean second of animal reaction, of instinct. No tortured mind tearing scabs with dirty nails. No exposed, festering wounds bubbling disease. In the ring he was free—freer even than he had been during his mind-dulling descent to lampposts and back alleys. In gratitude he began to win.

In counterpoint to Morris' immediate success, the twins found it increasingly more difficult to get fights. Their manager (he had chosen his profession after recognizing in himself the prototype for the sleazy, creepy, crawly character in a "B" film called "Gut Punch"), armed with twin boxes of tissue napkins, called them into his plasterboard office one day after six months of unemployment.

"Hiya kids," he said, sweeping to the floor with his elbow the uneaten corner of a carp sandwich. "I've got great news. By the way, you both look very beautiful today, like Greek statues. You've really got to say something for homosexuality if it can turn out real-men-looking guys like you." The sleazy, creepy, crawly manager then grabbed himself by the crotch, flapped his tongue between his teeth, and winked his warted eye as if to say, "If only I were twenty years younger." Raymon and Damon responded with a pretty gesture of their long fingers that inhibited the return engagement of their noon meal past their lips.

"Anyway, the reason I called you in was to tell you. . . ." The manager, looking for just the right words to express his lugubrious news, hesitated a moment. At last his eyes brightened. "You're all washed up as fighters." The boys gasped and in the process almost swallowed their knuckles. "However," he continued as he passed out the boxes of tissue, "I love you like a father and so I booked you into St. Nick's Arena as a tag team for wrestling matches."

"Boo hoo, boo hoo," the twins bleated like lost lambs as Raymon reached for a vile of insulin.

"My children, my children, I have not decided on this maneuver idly," said the manager, twiddling his thumbs; "believe me, my sweethearts, it's for the best."

"Never," cried Raymon, injecting himself. "Never," cried Damon, throwing his wadded napkin at the cigar.

"Starve then, you lousy faggots," the manager rejoined in an entirely different tone of voice. The boys leaped from their chairs, contemptuously ground the uneaten square of garbage fish beneath their heel, and snatched the manager from behind his desk.

"See, see," he choked as his lungs collapsed from lack of air, "a perfect headlock! Born naturals. . . ," as his eyes rolled out of their sockets and he collapsed in a faint.

The twins reconsidered.

Several nights later they held a "Raymon and Damon Name Game" party. The purpose of the celebration was to introduce the new tag team and enlist the guests' support in inventing a name for the act. The winning entry, "The Siamese Soufflé," had to take second place, in terms of historic significance, to another event that occurred that night: Louella and Morris found each other.

She had been attracted to him that first time at her brothers' dinner and afterwards began to quietly follow his career. Although they rarely spoke he became aware

of her in the background and ritualistically came to look
for her in the crowds before his fights. She was always
there. He would tap his gloves and she would play back
a secret smile that said, without a word, 'the time would
come when they would fall into each others arms.'

They embraced for the first time that evening at her
place.

"Are you happy?"

"Sure."

"Are you sure?"

"Yes."

"I'm glad."

"Good."

"I feel so close to you, how do you feel?"

"The same."

"Really?"

"Yes."

"That's wonderful."

"Yes."

"Tell me about yourself."

"No."

In the months that followed, Louella discovered that
she was gathered close to him with one strong hand
while held at arm's length by the other. He was black and
she was white and although it didn't keep them from
going to bed, it did, for a different reason, keep him
from baring his soul. With the return of his guilt came
back Morris' need for exculpation. The only person who
could provide redemption was the honk. ("Hi, Mo."
"Hey, remember that time . . . ?" "Oh, that, shit man,
that wasn't your fault." "Are you sure?" "Sure I'm
sure, that was war." "But are you sure?" "I was there,
wasn't I?") Now Louella had given him another reason
for finding the honk. He had looked into her eyes and
seen that there was something in him worth caring

about, something about him worth loving. He hung this concept out before him like a carrot on a stick and used it to strengthen his will to hold on until he could find peace. He would return her love when the honk gave him absolution.

White people had forced upon him the need to kill and yet, by accident of birth, two white people had become the most important human beings in his life. It was inevitable then that they would become inextricably tied together in Morris' mind. He found that he could not accept the ideas of one without it influencing the way he felt about the other. He knew that if he bared his soul to Louella, she would tell him what he wanted to hear; yet Louella had not been in the trench, had not felt the soldier's blood, had not seen the soldier's dead eyes staring up at him from beneath his feet, and therefore could not bear witness to his guilt or innocence. If the testimony of the one white person he needed was to be thrown out, then what of her twin, the other white he desperately needed; could he ever trust in him? Morris decided not to take the chance and kept his silence.

Louella was in love with Morris, but each time her feelings raced ahead of her reason they ended treading the insubstantial air that filled the breach Morris created to keep her from coming too close. More than anything she wanted him to share himself with her.

"Tell me what's bothering you."

"Nothing's bothering me."

"You're distant."

"I'm right here."

"I want to help."

"I don't need any help."

"What do you need?"

"You."

"Do you want to make love? . . . I want to make love."

"So do I."

It was always the same. She pressed her hands against his spine and traced the cord down to the small of his back. She tantalized herself by withholding her hands from his buttocks until the urge to touch him was over-powering. At last she cupped his cheeks and felt the muscles tense under her hands. It was always the moment she looked forward to, the moment all the doubt and equivocation she felt in their relationship vanished and he came alive, wholly alive, only for her. She rolled her chest from side to side so that he would feel her breasts rubbing against him. She bent her knee so that her thigh caressed his genitals and then she scraped her toenail against his calf as she straightened her leg. She made him aware of every plane of her body in a panto-mime that was meant to communicate far more than to arouse. "When I touch him like this, his thoughts are here. When his body touches me there, there is where he is. At this moment I know exactly where his thinking is, what his feelings are. How could I have been so stupid! His mind is as clear to me as my own because we are one mind, one person. We are in love." The celebration of this knowledge was always the moment he could wait no longer and entered her. "My darling, we love each other, we love each other," she repeated again and again until finally it was over and they fell apart and the chasm between them again yawned wide.

"If I didn't have Sam to look at, I'd just as soon pull that ole raggity quilt over my head an' go to my maker," said his mother. "I sometimes think that Captain Marvel, Jr., is gonna drop outta the air an' take me away from the screamin' an' the bugs an' you know what? He always has the face of Sammy Kelly,'' said Celeste, a shy fifth grader with glasses.

Sammy Kelly had dark intense eyes set off by heavy black brows and thick black eyelashes. His V-shaped head was formed from a series of subtly tapering concentric rings that were in turn extravagant, boisterous, vigorous, energetic, and hearty. Celeste had been only partly wrong; there *was* something familiarly heroic about Sammy's face. It's just that its identification lay more in the direction of the Submariner than the Marvel family. It was not his magnificent face, however, that brought grace into all their lives and evoked in them the feeling of his predestination—it was his magnificent body.

''I tell you man, it's a stinking world and us niggers is the stinkingest—all except for little Sam; he is so beautiful that tomorrow I'm gonna shove this jug up some ofay's ass and go searching for my religion,'' said one of his ''uncles'' who slept with his mother out of respect for his father who had been gone a long time and was as good a man as ever had walked on Dwight Street.

''It's gonna be summertime again and all the kids will be running around this hot city without half their clothes.''

''Yeah . . . what do you think he's going to be?''

''I think he's gonna be anything he wants, he isn't just any ol' black boy,'' said the old men who sat on the stoop and watched the cracks in the pavement grow.

At the tender age of eight, Sam had begun to develop the kind of physique that is found only on old, cheaply illustrated, duotone wall charts which hang from blackboard frames in improvised offices of carpetbagger chiropractors. Like those body chart diagrams, Sam's physique was perfectly symmetrical and perfectly proportioned. Where the muscles should be flat, his were as smooth as slate. Where they should have bulk, his were emphasized in heavy outline. The big difference was that Sam made people feel good, gave them hope, while those charts were always hung next to full-length mirrors to evoke despair and guilt. Sam made people feel that beauty could crystallize from filth and poverty and ignorance and pain, and as a result, made their lives a little less meaningless. Those charts, which don't call you "sir" or "Mrs." or bless you with a smile, served only to remind of one's descent from glory.

Sammy sprinted through his childhood happy and secure. He was ten, he was eleven, he was twelve, and then he was thirteen. The love and admiration and respect that were his right were still there, but now there was an added thing: a restlessness, a shifting of the weight, a drumming of the fingers—a growing perceptible impatience.

"Come on baby, do your thing, rise above the sea of drowning black faces and pull us with you. You're thirteen now and it's no longer enough to be pretty and happy. Soon you'll be fourteen and then twenty and you'll have missed it. You'll fall back and spend the rest of your days talking about how great it was to have been a kid on Dwight Street."

"What are you gonna do, Sammy? What are you gonna be?"

"No sense fooling around now, Sam."

"Lots of people depending on you."

"We're all so proud of you, Sammy."

"What you gonna be, Sam?"

"Tell us, tell us, TELL US!"

"C'mon, goddamn it, what the fuck you gonna be."

"I'm going to be . . . I'm going to be . . . a . . . Chiropractor! I'm going to be the living example for all those tacked-up wall charts. I'm going to heal people and make them healthy and beautiful like me. Yes sir, I'm going to be a Doctor.''

''A Doctor.'' The word spread through the dirty tenaments like the gush from an open hydrant. It swept away old condoms and broken wine bottles and the stuffing from torn, discarded sofas. The black jungle let out a sigh. It had put its money on Sammy and now the board had flashed back ''no contest.'' He would be the great black savior knight after all. They would chuckle with possessive glee into their broken gums and wink to each other when his name was mentioned. Sam belonged to them. They had created him and nurtured him and his success would be theirs.

At sixteen Sam went to his first Chiropractic Seminar and learned that the charts had nothing to do with life. He learned that the charts were only icons before which cancer-wracked patients were made to prostrate themselves. ''Spinal manipulation to oppose Trapezoidal, Caucasoidal and Suicoidal atrophication,'' the high priest teachers chanted, and the novitiates screamed back, ''Ahmen.''

In the seclusion of his hotel room Sam took off his clothes and looked at his reflection in the mirror. He began to wonder whether his own body had perpetrated a fraud and, like the charts, held out a promise it couldn't deliver; that despite what he had been led to believe on Dwight Street, the world was not there for the beautiful and innocent.

He returned to the streets without his diploma. They said that they understood, that of course he was right, but they never forgave him their dreams. Politely they asked, ''What now?'' and he said, ''I'm going to be a fighter,'' and they said, ''That's nice.'' He continued,

"Because people are dishonest and want to take advantage and make you have to fight for what you want," and they said, "That's nice," and then they closed their eyes and folded their arms and hummed old spirituals. The people on Dwight Street knew all about fighting and also knew that for black people the fight was lost before it began. They had hoped that Sam with all his beauty would not have to struggle and now he had come and told them that this was the only way to make it. Sam was not yet seventeen and already they began to speak of him as in the past.

"Remember Sammy?"

"Yeah, what a wonder that boy was."

"He was going to do great things."

"What ever happened to him?"

"What ever happened to us?"

And they were right. Six months later he put on his first pair of boxing gloves and by the time he was twenty-three he had forgotten that he ever wanted to be a Chiropractor. There were a few good years in between when he fought to win, when he still struggled to benefit from his disillusionment and to fulfill the promise of his youth. They passed before he succeeded. In his middle twenties he was an ex-pug. He had traded his chance to be someone for a different kind of identity—an old identity—the identity of defeat: non-identity.

Sam never stopped being Captain Marvel, Jr., for Celeste. It wasn't that she figured his luck would change and her comic book dreams would come true. It was simply that she never woke up. It didn't matter that he would never be champ or even a contender, that his face was broken and his body grown thick. For her the facts of life were only mist on a window glass; if you tried hard enough, if you really concentrated, you could see through the fog to the rolling hills and bubbling brooks beyond.

As children and through their adolescence, Celeste had remained a respectful distance to the rear. She had been thrilled and humbled to step where he had stepped and would have gladly dogged his footsteps the rest of her life. But then one day, when he no longer could get fights and his mind had begun to peel, she unexpectedly overtook him and found him walking in circles. He did not understand that she had no other life but his.

"Why do you hang around?"

"I love you."

"Why?"

"You're my man."

He turned bitter when he found that he could not stand without her.

"You've got to fight to make your way."

"Yes."

"You've got to do it by yourself."

"I know."

"What?"

"I said, I know."

"Right."

Worst of all, her unblinking devotion seemed to give the lie to his early promise. If she saw no difference in him now, then maybe he had never changed. Maybe it wasn't bad luck and cruel fortune. Maybe he was never meant to be anything but what he was now. Sam could not bring himself to make her go, and never being told she simply stayed and drained his hope and his will with her love. She heaped it on him, covered him with it, and he, finding comfort in her arms, began to die in earnest.

John was the third black member of the tribe.

"Aren't you going to draw a picture?"

"Uh-uh."

"Children always like to draw pictures."

"Who do you love most?"

"I don't love nobody."

"Everybody loves somebody."

"Hey man, you comin' to the protest meetin'?"

"Nope."

"We all gonna be there."

As John grew up he learned what he was not. He was not a "children" or an "everybody" or a "we." He didn't belong, not anywhere, to anyone. He was dropped into the steamy Harlem ghetto one day when nobody was looking and by the time they turned around he had faded away unseen, unheard and unfelt. While black brothers all around were struggling to find out who they were, John was struggling to find out why he was. He didn't know a reason for his existence.

He left the orphanage when he was nine and spent the ensuing years drifting between foster homes. He bade farewell to his last detention camp when he was fifteen. He developed a narcotics habit and took to the streets to pimp and steal. He went straight when his body, in a fit of petulance, rejected even "dope" as a purpose for his life and he discovered his addiction wasn't genuine. With no pressing economic need he then sat himself under awnings and begged for his cans of tuna fish and hog jowels.

He lived in the cellar of an apartment house where Fleetwood Flyer sleds and pee-stained carriages and old dresser mirrors were stored.

"You don't belong here," they whispered to him late at night.

"I am Stevie's."

"And I am the Johnsons'," the shadowy sentries boasted.

"I've been with the tenants in 2C all my life."

"And I belong to . . ."

"Eat my ass," John muttered under his breath.

There was a game John played. It began with the superintendent who lived just above him. "This movie stinks," he could hear him yell through the floor boards. The superintendent always kicked off his television precisely at midnight when he didn't like the eleven o'clock movie. (Inevitably, it took him an hour to make up his mind.) Each evening John passively waited for the critique from above. If it didn't come, he curled up and to the sounds of blasting six-guns and galloping hoofbeats, lulled himself to sleep. On those nights when the midnight silence made the whispering in his room even louder, he climbed into his clothes and slipped out into the street through the basement window.

"You don't belong here," whispered the rocking horse from 4G in a parting shot.

He boarded the subway train at 116th Street and rode the local down to 34th. He then switched to the uptown train and took it back into Harlem. He spent the time on the rides walking slowly from car to car. Whenever he found the kind of people he was looking for, the forgotten and the woebegotten, he took a seat across the aisle and spent long minutes in observation. When his list of flotsam reached fifteen, he stopped looking and became impatient for the train to arrive at his station. At last he crawled back through the window of his room and into the corner where he slept.

He did not sleep. He listened for the sounds of his detractors. He heard nothing, not a peep, not even from the chromed two-wheeler that had all its spikes. John let out a sigh and settled into the heart of his game. "Everybody has a reason to be alive," he began to himself.

"And I will prove it." One at a time he called to mind the dregs he had met on the subway. The whites among them he dispatched immediately. They were alive because they were white; it was a divine right. The Puerto Ricans and the Blacks were the challenge. Sometimes the game went on for hours: "Let me see now . . . yeah, *that* guy *really* looked bad," and he chuckled to himself. "I mean baby, he had *nothing*. I mean the beetle bugs are still flat on their backs with their feet waving in the air trying to figure out how he climbed out of the grave. I mean. . . ."

Further and further into a corner he backed himself until suddenly he remembered a clean fingernail or a dirty fingernail or a broken fingernail that was the clue to the purpose of that man's life. Eventually he found reasons for them all. Even the guys who didn't sleep in the subways but laid in the alleys and peed on their shoes and were never not drunk. They had to stay alive so that the guys who laid in the alleys and were never not drunk but who didn't pee on their shoes could feel that they were a rung higher, and they had to stay alive because their bodies scared away the alley cats who kept awake the drunks who were not always drunk and needed their sleep, and they had to stay alive. . . . "With all those reasons," he said to himself as at last he began to drift into sleep, "there's gotta be one for me, too."

From time to time he would try to find the reason. He would pick fights, smash windows, run in front of trucks, and then wait for the police to come and arrest him. It was a ritual. He would grapple with them, scream curses at them during the whole trip in the police wagon, and then laugh in their faces during the booking at the station.

"You hate me, don't you?" he challenged them.

"Don't deny it, you're scared shitless of me, aren't you? I know, I know," as they dragged him away. "I disgust you, that's it, isn't it? One of these days you're going to answer me." Then to himself as they threw him into the tank and he dissolved into the shadows, "and then I won't have to play 'the game' anymore."

The day finally came when they told him he would be put away forever unless he straightened up. He promised he would be good, so they took him by the hand and with a note pinned to his mittens deposited him at the door of the same creepy-crawly manager.

"This man is a born killer," the note read. "Make him a fighter and divert his hostile instincts into socially acceptable behavior . . . and the state will pay you fifty bucks a month for care and maintenance."

John was big: six feet two and two hundred and forty pounds. He had a Roman column for a neck and a steel bullet for a head. The manager's feet began to stink from the sweat of his excitement.

"Now I know man, now I know! I'm a goddamn mother-sucking professional fighter. That's where it's at!" exclaimed John triumphantly as he awoke all battered and bruised from the merciless second-round beating of his first boxing match. "I always was a sucker for a bargain," spat the creepy-crawly manager.

Pearl, of the enormous ass and enormous thighs and enormous breasts, was John's woman. She had manufactured herself from the mold of her race's stereotype and was pleased as grits about it. She looked like Aunt Jemima and laughed like Beulah. She carried a bottle of rum in her purse and drank it out of a paper bag. She called everybody "honey" and "darlin' " and loved tap dancing and harmonica playing. She didn't know from "black" or "white" and just wanted to be the best gold-toothed colored lady there was. She genuinely didn't care if white folk liked her because she didn't recognize that her image of herself was the creature of their mind. She didn't care, in fact, if anybody liked her because she was already crazy about herself. Unlike John who couldn't find himself in the world, Pearl's world, only as vast as her girth, was as plain as fat to see. While John got his head battered in the search for his meaning, Pearl stirred batter in the search for smoother pancakes.

"Lan' sakes, lan' sakes, just look at all you've gone an' done to yourself, John Burns," as her thumb and index finger twitched convulsively in anticipation of an ear-tweaking reprimand.

"I dwant tum ga-ga pweeze." Arnold talked baby-talk until he was four. It was the last time he was cute.

By all rights Arnold should have been a dwarf. His massive skull with its thick forehead and sunken features teetered on a skinny neck that was loosely supported by barely angling shoulders. From the shoulders abbreviated arms abruptly hung like knotted kites caught tight on droopy tree limbs. His trunk was disproportionately long and caused his waist to stop at about the point of his knees. With no place to expand, the lower extremities, crammed into the remaining area between himself and the ground, predictably buckled into an exaggerated bow. The overall effect was to make him appear even smaller than his actual four feet eleven inches.

When Arnold was six and had no friends and was still in kindergarten, he developed a rash on his neck. For a period of a week he came to school with his hands manacled together to prevent him from digging holes in the erupting area. The teacher explained this to his classmates who responded by curling one side of their upper lips and crinkling their noses in a show of disgust that even exceeded the one they usually reserved for Arnold's appearance. "The real reason I'm tied up like this," Arnold told the least timorous of the children on the third day when the rash had cleared considerably, "is because I'm so strong and they're afraid of what I might do." The explanation was an immediate success with his classmates who, on the one hand, were ready to believe in any adult conspiracy while maintaining, on the other, that nobody as funny-looking as Arnold could be without some redeeming virtue.

On Thursday and Friday, Arnold was dragged around the schoolyard by his proud classmates and presented to the first and second graders with a flair reminiscent of a barker's at a carnival side show. "Here he is, here he is, the strongest and ugliest boy in the whole world. He's so dumb he's been in kindergarten for two years and he's so strong they have to keep him tied up." Arnold was the center of attention and he loved every minute of it. He never forgot that week. It was the highlight of his childhood.

"Hiya Johnny, I've got a new hat Sally, remember Friday Louie," Arnold rehearsed to himself as he raced to school the following Monday fully recovered from his skin rash. All weekend long he had anticipated greeting his newly acquired friends of the week before and now he could see them standing in line in the schoolyard. "Hiya Johnny, I gotta new hat Sally, remember Friday Louie?" he rattled off, running at everybody at once and failing to hear the teacher directing him to silence and to his place in line. "I gotta new hat Johnny, I mean Sally," he repeated all out of breath, suddenly confused by the lack of response from his classmates.

"Remember Friday, remember Friday," he implored and in turn began shaking Sally and Johnny and Louie.

"Arnold, you are making noise and everyone is supposed to be quiet so get in line and shut up." But still Arnold did not hear the teacher. If he did, what she said had no meaning because it was not what he was prepared for.

"You're my friend, you're my friend," he began chanting to each person in the line and still they wouldn't talk to him or look at him. "Thursday, remember Thursday?" he yelled at everybody. But maybe it wasn't Thursday, maybe it was Wednesday when they had had such a good time or Tuesday or. . . . And then Arnold began to cry and someone began to giggle. It was the boy with the blond hair or the girl with the braids whose names he couldn't remember. Arnold charged the girl with the braids and threw a punch that missed. She shoved him back and he fell to the ground and the giggles of the one erupted into an avalanche of laughter. Johnny and Sally and Louie were laughing the loudest. The teacher was yelling, "everyone back in line" and "eyes straight ahead," but Arnold only heard the girl with the braids asking him if he had lost all his strength when they untied him. The rest of the kids picked up the taunt. At last Arnold got up and crawled to the back of the line and was never heard from again.

That Monday marked the low point of Arnold's childhood.

When Arnold was twelve and still in the fourth grade he happened to look in the mirror one day and was struck by an insight that left him comatose and bedridden for a week. He suddenly realized that although it had been years since the bonds had been removed, his hands were still tied because the world holds out few opportunities for monumentally ugly and stupid people. It was during the week of his convalescence that he invented the "ugly and stupid kingdom of Arnold." In this realm the very drawbacks that had set him apart from the crowd now placed him in the center of it. "We will follow you anywhere," they chanted to him from their knees, "Oh greatest ugly and stupid one." "They can laugh at me now," said Arnold to himself as he combed his hair without the benefit of the draped-over mirror in his room. "But someday I'm going to be king."

And someday he was.

When he was fifteen and still in the sixth grade he left school and went in search of a way of life in which he could hide. He had seen pictures of broken-faced fighters and had heard stories about how they hit the sides of their heads with the heels of their hands to quiet the bells in their batfries, and he decided he could find companionship with such people. He also concluded that boxing was a profession in which being stupid and ugly, if not actual marks of distinction, was at least only the result and not the cause of failure.

Said the creepy-crawly manager on first meeting Arnold, "You must have had some really rough scraps." "Yeah," said Arnold proudly, catching in the manager's inflection the echo of the heady times he had known back in the good old bound-and-tied kindergarten days.

"Where you been fighting?" asked the manager. "Tank towns," came the well-rehearsed reply. Arnold didn't know what tank towns were but he had been coached to give that answer. The manager remained quiet for a moment and Arnold was thrown into confusion. He had not anticipated the need for any further explanation but the manager's silence seemed to demand it. "You know,"

Arnold continued weakly, "where they make all those tanks." The manager didn't stop laughing until long after Arnold had signed the contract and left the plasterboard office.

The sleazy, creepy-crawly manager, as befitting his title, had a little business going on the side. Although Arnold signed on as a featherweight, he did most of his fighting against broken-down heavyweights as comic relief to the dirty movies shown at stag parties. After everyone had gotten a good erection watching the pornographic pictures, Arnold and some lumbering punch-drunk giant would climb into the improvised ring, on the way to falling back through the ropes, in the course of throwing many wild punches, and uproariously helping the guests to work off their turgidity. Despite the circumstances, Arnold, with a strong fix on his one emotionally satisfying experience, was able to turn the inevitable fistic failure into a personal triumph; while in the ring he was for a few minutes, as he had been in kindergarten, the center of attention.

Only one pair of hands was ever permitted to scrape him off the ringside chairs and return him to combat. They belonged to his handler, charge and companion, Maytag. Anyone else who tried to help Arnold caught the wrath of her salivary glands all over his waning sexual ardor. (In some damp and musty dead end of Maytag's mind throbbed the belief that a zapped zipper rendered a man helpless.)

Maytagagawa came by her name in three stages. The last three syllables were of course affixed by Mobawamba. Her christened name comprised the first syllable and that was doubled in length when her obsessive need to wash things was discovered. As a child of nine or ten she had been known to run up to shirt-stained strangers and tug fitfully at their clothing. The fact that she never learned to speak and only made sounds like "gliki-gliki" and "tumpara," and a noise that sounded like a fish out of water flapping convulsively across the curled pages of an old *National Geographic*, put the fear into more than one ill-kempt male that she attacked with rape in mind.

As she grew older she learned to restrain her impulses in public. Partially through habit and partially because her short square figure did resemble a washing machine as much as it did anything else, she did not outgrow the nickname. She was deposited on Arnold's doorstep for a weekend when she was twelve and he was twenty-three. Her parents, Arnold's distant relatives, geographically underscored their blood ties by going far away and never being heard from again. Arnold looked after her first as a kind of pet, then as a ward and companion and later, when he got drunk enough, as a lover. Maytag's other distinctive characteristic was her total loyalty and maniacal possession of Arnold. Arnold was forever apologizing to people whose flies she spit upon when they inadvertently came too close.

After only three years Morris had become the fifth ranking middleweight and was perhaps only two fights away from a shot at the title. He was twenty-nine years old and at the peak of his abilities. All across the nation, God-fearing, mother-loving sportswriters were tabbing him a future champ. "Super terrific," they proclaimed, and "peachy keen," and all the other expressions of innocent joy that are befitting the last stronghold of America's romantic adolescence. "A credit to his race," they wrote at the climax of their ecstasy, and then fell back spent, went to church and prayed for his strong right jab.

Morris again won decisively and suddenly he was the leading contender for the middleweight crown. Back went the sportswriters for new expletives but in the process of trotting out "stout-hearted," "forthright," "some kind of a fighter," "humble" and "patriotic," they stumbled over a sizeable mound of unAmerican activities. "Say it ain't so, Mo," they cried, bemoaning more their own disillusionment than Morris' fall from grace. Torn between "loyalty" and "truth," with thumb and index finger they wrenched loyalty from their hearts and in the process increased circulation two hundred percent. All over the land that day typesetters were receiving wet and blurry copy that told of Morris Leverne Tate's wrongdoing. "Masochistic Homosexual Miscegenationist," whispered the headlines between the headlines. From all over the country letters poured in. It appeared to be a tossup as to which of his heinous violations against nature—his guilt-ridden compulsion, his innocent friendship with Raymon and Damon, or his relationship with their sister—would receive the most courageously condemning support.

The Boxing Commission, faced with having to choose between the antic outrage of the community and defense of its title contender, found an easy answer in a current Congressional probe of the rackets. The Commission immediately leaped into its own investigation and in no time uncovered a fragile link between the creepy-crawly manager and an underworld underling. Bravely the Commission put the blood leaches to its own wounds and successfully drew out the poisonous Morris, the sleazy manager and, to insure against the spread of infection, the rest of the manager's stable of fighters. "BECAUSE OF BAD ASSOCIATIONS ALL LICENSES ARE REVOKED," the lead articles gravely announced in three-inch type while war raged in Southeast Asia.

The Syndicate, of course, couldn't have cared less about the people involved, but in an arrogant gesture aimed at agitating the Congressional Committee and the Boxing Commission, it offered to find work for the entire displaced contingent. Thus it happened that Morris, Raymon, Damon, Sam, John and Arnold, as well as a half-dozen other fighters, became flunkies and book runners.

After five months on the job:

"This is no where," said John.

"Mother is upset," said the twins.

"How can I ever be king here?" said Arnold.

"You've got to fight," said Sam.

"Let's steal all their money and split," said Morris.

And they did.

NINE

MILLIGINIAN Swoop Craft had been spotted to the north of New Hope Settlement.

"Retreat," cried Buck Alice.

"Advance," roared Major Hank.

Everyone was so busy arguing the question that no one noticed that five days had passed and the invaders had not returned.

"Voice modulation," at last, said Just Call Me Robbie, offering a compromise position.

Catheleen and Eric had been under the surveillance of a private eye for several weeks prior to their Everglade adventure and J.C.M. Robbie was the very sleuth hired for the job. Catheleen's overprotective father had been convinced that Eric (not an American name) was an evil influence and hired the homosexual detective in the belief that it takes a degenerate to know one. Robbie and his camera diligently followed the couple into the swamp and, like them, had also become lost. He arrived at the settlement two days before the suspects in a comparable state of exhaustion. He explained his presence by producing his camera and relating a story of nature study and bird watching. For days he wept over the "best photographs ever taken of the Macaw in ritualistic sleep" that would sit forever undeveloped in his camera. Ever the private detective under cover, Robbie kept at his story long after Eric had died, Catheleen had fled, and the news that the world no longer needed private detectives had come over the transistors.

If he had been even more successful in his ruse, things might have turned out a lot different in New Hope.

". . . and so if we practice voice modulation, the chances are very good we will not be discovered at all since it is obvious that the aliens, having missed us the last time, don't see too well," explained Robbie with a rather curious logic. "Voice modulation is sissy stuff," complained Hank Hank, whose blood, to keep pumping, required a good atrocity now and then. "Not if it is practiced through a course in 'Supressing Cries of Agony'," countered Robbie, always one skip ahead. "I should think Major Hank would make a wonderful law enforcer for 'voice modulation' and I could be the teacher," continued Robbie, crinkling his nose. "It is easy enough to talk quietly in normal conversation but people in New Hope are forever shrieking over a stubbed toe or a . . . 'pricked' finger," he added, shuddering deliciously.

Robbie's credentials for teaching were the three years of Judo training he had undertaken for his detective work and possession of a Judo belt that in degree of excellence was of a shade somewhere between pink and chartreuse. No one questioned his qualifications but the point was raised that a classroom situation with all its give and take and rubbing of elbows was a dangerous intrusion of privacy and a serious threat to the settlement philosophy of isolation. Buck Alice, the science fiction writer, who had not even been a member of the original Pathfinder group but who had begun to stand out as a fierce defender of the faith, said (after counting to himself the words of the sentence), "Today classrooms, tomorrow communes." "What's a little class," said an ex-Jewish mother with a moustache who had been passing for a Pathfinder for years. "Such a class would help fertilize our way of life," said Gardner, the gardener. "Grumble," said Buck, always the writer, under his breath.

In the end, it was decided that Robbie should be given the go ahead to start his classes.

"Suppression of Cries of Agony" was founded on the principle of sublimation of the pain reflex into socially productive behavior. Any time a hurt was experienced, the recipient, through conditioning, would automatically grab a shovel and quietly irrigate a cesspool. Reconditioning of the pain reflex began with Robbie whacking the student about with a stick while the victim choked back a mouth full of dirt. Prevailed upon by a fear of suffocating, the abject trainee learned to keep his tongue still, his mouth shut and suffer in silence. Since nobody (with the exception of Isobel) raised their voice for the longest time after the training sessions, and since there was always a need for good cesspools, the classes were deemed a great triumph. The fact that more than one hole was baptized with the blood of its severely lacerated and expiring engineer did little to detract from the overall success of the conditioning. The fact that there was an immodest increase in the number of painful injuries suffered from painful falls into pits previously dug in sublimated reaction to painful injuries was acknowledged as a necessary pitfall on the road toward progress.

All in all, Robbie, through his role as teacher, became the singularly most influential person in New Hope. People began to say that voice modulation had kept New Hope together yet apart, whereas an attack on or a retreat from the Milliginians would have caused the settlement to fall totally together or, at best, only partly apart. A pat on the fanny in passing by Robbie (or in the case of females a sororitorial slap on the shoulders) came to be regarded as an honor, second only to receipt of the Pathfinder Eagle Badge for Good Citizenship, and that hadn't been given in a long time.

On the other hand, Buck Alice, who abhorred dirt and cesspools and had decided that one day he would become leader of New Hope, came to regard Robbie with an abhorrence that was second only to dirt and cesspools. "I'll fix him," said Buck quietly, after counting the number of words in the ominous threat.

Lack of volume did not dictate a corresponding state of emotional equanimity. On any restless and troublesome afternoon the air was pierced repeatedly with the sounds of frustration and anger carried on the breath of strangled whispers:

(In a whisper) "You're standing on my land, get off."

(In a whisper) "What did you say?"

(In a whisper) "What?"

(In a whisper) "Huh?"

(In a whisper) "Heh?"

(In a whisper) "Oh!"

And so on.

The source of the conflict on a day when the air was

particularly electric with charges and counter-charges was the disposition of the case of Claude Aefitte. At the heart of the debate was not the fact that Claude was crazy but the reasons for his insanity. (Just as it was with Robbie and his homosexuality, the actor-robot with his buzzing and clicking and Buck Alice with his speech difficulties, it was of little concern to the private enterprise community that Claude went around all day in imaginary clown makeup, holding an imaginary umbrella and climbing imaginary stairs.)

Claude Aefitte had peddled his bakery cart around Paris for twenty years, selling tarts on street corners and dreaming of becoming the incomparable Marcel Marceau. No child was ever permitted to purchase his pastries without first enduring his pantomime act. "The little ones love me," he told the ticket-wielding gendarme, who was forever fining him for creating a silent disturbance. "They could sit for hours and watch me perform, I bring so much joy," he cried, while in fact more than one moppet, in the desire for a speedy purchase, dressed up in dark glasses and white cane and haltingly tapped his way toward the sound of the little bell on the peddler's pushcart.

Claude Aefitte had come to America with his life savings for the first and last fling of his life and was passively drifting through the Southeast when the invaders came. Hours before the attack, he had boarded a single engine tour plane which subsequently stalled out a hundred feet above some alligators and fell into the Everglades. Like the legendary hero "The Heap," who emerged from the wreckage of his ship as part roots and leaves and only part World War One German fighter pilot, Claude, as the single survivor of his air crash, popped out from behind a broken wing part vegetable as well as part human. He had no clear memory of his previous life nor any idea about how to survive in this one. Nevertheless, he did know who he was. He was that gifted clay upon which all human foible is impressed. A flick of the foot, a shrug of the shoulder, and that clay molded itself into a record of human frailty that brought forth peals and gales of laughter and tears.

It was a good thing for Claude that he crashed so near to the settlement camp.

Claude spent all of his time in the settlement polishing his craft. The routine to which he gave the most loving care, his self-proclaimed pièce-de-résistance, was "the imaginary staircase." Everyone agreed that it was the high point of his act but, all things being relative, the majority interpretation leaned less toward "Man, the downtrodden, endlessly climbing nowhere" and more toward "Man, the careless, having left the pissoir too soon." Fortunately for Claude, his hearing had been damaged along with his brain and he went along without contradiction, blithely believing in his genius.

The town meeting, at which the charges and counter-charges were flying thick and fast, would never have been called at all had Claude stuck to his pantomime act and not felt the urge to create a little Marceau of his own. The Gallic call to duty was strong, however, and since, as he semi-reasoned, a gift such as his could only be inherited, the time had come for him to wear the mantel of fatherhood. Claude had learned through gestures that are part of a universal sign language that volunteers were being recruited for future studding with Isobel. He signed up immediately and threw the colony into some of the loudest whispering it had ever known. The crux of the discussion was whether the plane crash was responsible for his present state of mind or whether

Claude had always been crazy and carried defective genes.

The leader of those opposed to a mating of Claude and Isobel was Titheria, the brutish lady who, earlier on, had diagramed the effect of Milliginian radiation on female reproduction. Titheria was a seven-year Anthropology student who had finally achieved some notoriety from an otherwise indifferent University by presenting a Master's paper that traced her lineage all the way back to the Aurigacian Age and a Cro-Magnon family of blue-collar workers. Her classmates and professors had remained skeptical throughout the length of her dissertation but responded as one in, first, stunned silence and, second, an explosion of applause when she concluded her thesis by removing the drapes from a hitherto concealed three-times enlarged, life-sized nude photograph of herself. (The only sounds of dissent came from the purists who believed that the war club in the photograph was an excessive gesture and served no purpose other than to gild the lily.) Recognition poured in from all quarters and covered a wide range of expression, from countless gifts of raw meat to the affectionate nickname of "Prim" for Primitive.

On the other side of the argument was the Actor-Robot and a group of religious fanatics.

The Actor-Robot had been an actor who had played a robot for twelve years on a television series and who, somewhere along the line, had gotten his identities confused and had come to believe that he was a robot with an almost human talent for acting. The Actor-Robot felt there existed a professional kinship between himself and the pantomiming Claude and became his most voiciferous defender. The Actor-Robot monotoned as a succession of internal wheels and gears came to life: "(click whirl) Claude is a good man and an artist. (clank) The world needs (drone) more artists (thump) and more (whirl-clunk) good men. The Screen Actors Guild (chug-sputter) and Actors Equity (sputter-cough) don't do enough (sputter-sputter) for actors like Claude (click).''

It was an impassioned plea but no more effective than that of the religious fanatics who believed that Claude was divinely possessed. They were forever rushing up to him with statuettes and medallions of the Crucifixion and beseeching him to make the Savior's wounds bleed. Despite the fact that he would respond by pantomiming a horse in foal or the ashes of two lovers tossed on the wind, they held firm to their belief in his saintliness. Eventually the decision was made to avoid the possibility of a New Hope Settlement someday overrun by a horde of defective mimists. The deciding votes against Claude were cast by Robbie who had personal reasons and by Buck who had political reasons. For professional reasons the Actor-Robot duly noted the latter's voting position in his memory banks.

In celebration of the judgment, another private enterprise orgy was held. During the course of his surveillance maneuvers, however, Hank Hank noticed a lack of enthusiasm among participants in several of the tents. The cause was a vague, undefined uneasiness that had settled in the minds of some of the less easily distracted inhabitants of the community. Claude's behavior was irrational to be sure, and it was true he was a foreigner, but was the first perhaps only related to the crash and was the second sufficient grounds alone for a defective genealogy? Could so specious an argument, thought more than one reluctant lover, be a forerunner for other decisions that might eventually involve some of them on the short end? This train of thought, had it been ridden a cross tie further, might well have changed the vote. Unfortunately, to ride those tracks further required an exchange of ideas and everything of importance in New Hope was private. It was ironic, then, that in the course of preserving the colony's most cherished ideals, the entire philosophical structure of New Hope Settlement would eventually collapse.

TEN

"OHMS," cried the nauseous new chief scientist. "Ohms?" quizzed the surprised gallery of subordinates. Pontificated the wincing leader, "We have completed our re-evaluation of all life-involving variables and have concluded that the original prognosis of Milliginian and human interadaptability was totally accurate. People on one planet can live on the other without the slightest fear of physiological impairment . . . provided they don't have to travel to get there." "Provided they don't have to travel to get there?" repeated the dumbfounded audience of underlings.

Excitedly ejaculated the perspiring head expert, "We have discovered that our internal fields of electrical resistance undergo a profound change when exposed to the conditions of space for protracted periods of time. The result of this exposure is a manifold multiplication of Ohm units. Consequently, when our bodies impact with even low amperage electrical current, such as found in Earth's atmosphere, the result is a high-voltage internal generation of energy." "Praise to the wise new chief scientist for finding the cause," rejoiced the assembled idolators.

Continued the acknowledged master, trembling violently, "In short, our heightened sensitivity to the flow of atmospheric electricity . . . produces a proton-electron change . . . that short-circuits our organs and slowly electrocutes us." "Let's go home!" implored the panicked party of potential mutineers.

"In order to be able . . . to live on Earth . . . we need only . . . locate a way to reduce our ohm units and . . . locate . . . a way . . . to find me . . . a . . . new pancreas," concluded the not-so-new chief scientist, grabbing his stomach and passing out.

Imhor was among the crew in attendance at the beginning of the ship-wide conference. However, the scientist had only uttered the first words of his explanation when Imhor, his mind racing ahead, completed the diagnosis and angrily stomped from the room.

The ohm theory was the very one the computer meteorologist had settled upon three weeks before. The influence of atmospheric conditions on Milliginian health was a natural course of investigation for the weather-minded Imhor, and after extensive mental checking and cross-checking, he had concluded that the electrical resistance principle was indeed a possible answer. The beautiful part of the theory, he realized, was that one need only hook up an electrometer to test its validity. Days had gone by and all aboard the ship had grown progressively weaker but, curiously, Imhor had not come forward with his ideas. He alibied his recalcitrance with old Milliginian homilies like "Never postulate without proof" and "To thine own self alone hypothesize" when, in reality, all he had to do to distinguish fact from theory was to requisition the necessary measuring device from the science storeroom. He didn't do it.

"I'll wait for them to call me," he told himself on another occasion. "After all, who am I, a lowly Swoop Craft fly boy, to brazenly volunteer that I know more then they." When he had deemed that excuse hollow, he dug into another. "I'll wait until the last possible moment when everybody has given up and is preparing for his death and then I will step forward and explain very quietly so that everyone will have to strain to hear what it is that's been killing us. . . ."

Imhor slammed the conference door behind him and moved limpingly toward his quarters. Ordinarily he avoided corridors on Level Eight with an almost religious zeal but today his mind was elsewhere. "I knew the answer weeks ago, weeks ago, but did they call me in, did they ask my advice, did they remember even to tell me to wear my meteorologist's status sash? No! I was the only scientist there without his sash! That would never have happened back home." There was nothing ahead of Imhor but a far wall some sixty feet down the hall, but he suddenly pulled up short and reflexively jerked back his head to avoid a ghostly contact. Before his eyes stood an impressed visual memory of a great steel door with an enormous slide bolt. It was then that Imhor realized he was still on Level Eight. In what seemed to take a hundred and eighty steps, he slowly turned one hundred and eighty degrees. Twelve feet down from the direction he had come, he saw the original model for his after-image. It was then that Imhor realized the real reason he had failed to report his findings.

"What am I doing?" he asked himself only once, as

his hand slid back the heavy bolt and tugged at the slippery door handle. Imhor stepped through a narrow opening and entered a storage room that was quite different from the kind that housed electronic instruments.

Above him, sculptured from the open beam ceiling, hung a phalanx of mastheads crafted in the form of visionary men, sheltering women, valiant gods and beatific children. Carved from the crossbeams were their linking arms and the inscription, "As we shall seek the highest, so shall we endure." Tapestries of the same motif sheathed the walls and were repeated in the plush rug, now worn and stained beneath his feet. Imhor stepped deeper into the room and caught the stench of pervasive chemicals. He advanced further and saw his image reflected back at him on three sides. Gone were the pews and the lecturn and the great Milliginian organ. In their place, filled to brimming, stood rows upon rows of mirror-shiny seamless glass vats. Trance-like, Imhor moved closer. To each step, he added a word: "I-did-not-reveal-the-ohm-theory-because-I-want-all-my-people-to-die."

When he became aware that his breath against the vat walls had fogged his vision, he stopped. Like a child before a bakery window, he pressed his nose against the glass and peered vacantly at the human sweet meats within. "As we seek the lowest, so shall we endure." The words came by themselves and were meant to include, himself among them, every Milliginian on Earth. He sighed fatalistically once through his nose and laughed bitterly twice in his throat. Then he slowly backed out of the converted chapel and limpingly returned to his quarters. "When I get home," he told himself, all the while trying to estimate the number of Milliginians he would have to murder to get there, "I shall wear my sash all the time."

ELEVEN

"BOY, did I blow my childhood. What a waste. The fact of the matter is I didn't even have a childhood. There is nothing about it worth remembering, like the time when I struck out and, on my follow through, the kid behind me got hit with my bat, the elastic in my pants broke, and his mother called me a dirty Jap for weeks. Nothing. Or the time the ugly girl said she liked me and I invited her to the 34th Street Armory for the Boy Scout Jamboree. She told her girlfriends that my nose dripped the entire time and that was why she wouldn't kiss me good night when, in fact, I hadn't even asked her. That's the kind of things not worth remembering that I remember.

"The rest of the time I had no friends. Did you ever know a tall gawky kid with a big ass and flat feet who *was* popular? Saturday afternoons I went to the movies alone and tortured myself by imagining that the place was full of couples feeling each other up in the dark.

Saturday nights I hid behind my collections of trading cards, stamps and bottle tops. The rest of the week was one long trip through the Museum of Cement or something. Bored. Totally bored; empty. I never did anything, just sat around.

"Never got any encouragement either. Where the hell were the people who were supposed to say, 'sharp kid' and 'good-looking lad' and 'bright boy' and 'natural athlete' or, better than nothing, 'sensitive child'? Father was okay but he was never around and he died before I was thirteen, and mother . . . well, mothers are mothers. You can't believe anything they say because they've got this hairpin trigger system built inside their left breast, which goes off and drowns everything within five square blocks in a love gusher whenever your name is mentioned, regardless of the content."

"Mamma, I washed my hands." "Oh my wonderful darling sweetheart." (As the fingers spread, the eyes go wide and the lips turn inside out in anticipation of a gorgeous kiss.)

"Momma, my nose has stopped dripping." "All by itself? Oh my wonderful sweetheart darling." (As the hands clasp in prayer, the eyes shut tight and the lips turn inside out.)

"Mamma, I moved my bowels. . . ." "Oh my darling sweetheart. . . ."

"In my pants." ". . . wonderful darling." (etc.)

"Then there were the bad times, or at least . . ." Joshua shifted slightly. His shirt had pulled up under his armpits and he took a moment to pull it down over his exposed stomach. He then slumped back into the tractor seat and propped his legs up over the steering wheel as before. ". . . one bad time. I guess I was twelve years old, a Harvester, certainly no more than twelve years, six months, and I was invited to this dance. Actually it

was a dance class with a lot of rich little kids and my
old man was paying for it. But to the non-kids in my
non-neighborhood I let on that it was this great party.
After about forty-five minutes in my bathroom, however, I was about ready to forget about going and just
pull out the old collections. It was my hair. I had
already washed it four different times and applied four
different kinds of hair dressing, including Vaseline, and
still couldn't keep it up in front and down in back. In
desperation, I finally pulled out a thick lanolin compound of my mom's that was so pure and smelled so
bad you could almost hear the sheep bleating for their
lost secretions.

'' 'What's wrong with your sweetheart shoulders and
your wonderful neck and your darling head?' asked my
mother when I at last emerged from the bathroom all
tilted to one side in a position guaranteed by the manu-
facturer to keep my hair in place. Carefully I slipped
into my raglan sleeve overcoat with the ballooning shoulders (I always felt more vital in my raglan sleeve overcoat). Still tipped off center, I climbed down the two
flights of stairs to the street. 'Don't touch anything
rusty,' my mother called adoringly after me.

"Then it happened. I had no sooner come abreast of
the 'super's' entrance to the apartment house when,
out from that dark mouth, spewed two hundred and fifty
thousand 'Bagel Beaters.' I suppose there were only
six human forms blocking my path, but behind them
stood hatchet men, specters from Auschwitz, the War-
saw Ghetto, the Spanish Inquisition and Pharaoh's Egypt.
Wrapped tightly around the wrists of the mortal assailants were harmless enough looking strings attached to
harmless enough looking water bagels. From each of the
bagels, however, protruded one edge of a two-edged
razor blade. Curiously, for the first few moments, I

heard nothing but my mother's parting admonition, and in the glint of the moon I furtively checked the enemies' weapons. After all, to bleed to death was one thing, but to get lockjaw. . . .

" 'Hi,' I said, pleading for my life.

" 'Don't worry,' said the littlest of the half-dozen Irish kids, standing on my toes to look taller, 'we like youse.'

" 'Thank you,' I said, noticing in the process that he was half my size, had a marble for a nose, and freckles that in the dark looked like a blood spray from the severed artery of his last victim.

" 'Sure,' he continued, 'we're not going to cut youse' (Irish kids in my neighborhood never said 'you'). 'We're just going to beat youse up, Floyd.' Floyd. My God, they thought I was someone named Floyd, case of mistaken identity. What a relief.

" 'Wait a second, men,' I began. . . .

" 'Yeah,' said Lefty, who had only one arm and was bitter about it, 'we only use the bagels on Jews.'

" 'Yeah,' said Blackie, whose nickname was inspired by the predilections of his soul, 'we're just going to use youse to keep in shape.'

"The littlest guy then leaped off my feet and took a punch at my face. Fortunately my head was still tilted to one side and the blow only grazed my ear. He hadn't counted on missing me and a moment of general disorganization followed. Divining a once in a lifetime opportunity, I immediately went into my crazy act. The beautiful thing about feigning a fit while experiencing high fear is that once you get it rolling, it sort of takes care of itself. I began by barking and biting the air and pounding my hands against my sides. Before I knew what was happening, my body had completed a series of pliés and arabesques worthy of the mad heroine in *The*

Red Shoes. My disorientation reached fever pitch when my hands, like hunger-crazed blue jays attacking a sparrow's nest, dive-bombed into my pompadour and rooted insanely about in the lanolin-gorged hairs.

"Out to sea went the wave and in its place emerged the lost city of Atlantis. A skyline of steeples and towers, highrises and spires stood protruding from my sticky scalp. Their free design lent the finishing touch to my appearance of unsuccessful electroshock therapy. My one offensive gesture during the episode was to clap the cheeks of my marble-nosed tormentor with my gooey hands. It is difficult to determine whether the ensuing screams of horror originated with my small assailant or his revolted breathren who were quick to spy my hair ointment oozing on his skin. I was by this time in fine voice myself and together we—the Bagel Beaters and myself—became the first of the year's cacophonous carolers.

"I knew that this interlude would not go on forever and that eventually the gang would regain its composure. At a prudent moment, I turned on my heel and after several false starts (during which my legs pumped up and down but would not carry me forward) I tore loose of my hysteria and bolted back into my building. I didn't own a key to my apartment and, besides, I didn't want the Bagel Beaters to know where I lived, so I passed up the chance to wait outside my door for the eternity it would take my mother to open it. Instead, I headed for the roof. I had already reached the third-floor landing when I heard my pursuers opening the foyer door below and starting up the stairs. I burst onto the roof and immediately got caught up in Mr. Donnelly's green bathrobe hung out to dry and apparently forgotten overnight. I fell down on the tarpaper, my foot firmly entrenched in the sleeve of the robe, and my thoughts bitterly reflected on the truism that the Irish always stick together. A dribble of warm air trickled over my face and I realized the roof door had been opened and I was no longer alone.

" 'Good try, Floyd,' admiringly panted the hard-breathing Blackie, 'but now we're gonna beat youse up.' "

Joshua broke off for a second and for the twentieth time turned the ignition key in the tractor. As before, he heard the machine roar to life and vibrate heavily. As before, he pushed and pulled all the panel buttons and levers and, as before, he still had not found the secret of making it move forward. Joshua shut off the machine and returned to his former position.

Of all the events in his life, the sequence that succeeded the appearance of the gang on the roof was the most instrumental in forming the pattern of mediocrity that characterized the following years. "A broken metal clothes-line pole stood propped against a large round incinerator fan and, in a flash, I realized that such an instrument could be wielded in a manner not unlike, say, the jawbone of an ass."

Joshua didn't stop telling his story, he just stopped telling it out loud. It didn't seem to make much difference to the tractor anyway.

"They made a circle and started crowding me in toward the middle," thought Joshua. "The metal pole was still within reach but I didn't reach for it. If I hit them with that they'd *really* be angry. I looked down and there was the littlest assassin flailing away at my raglan sleeve stomach with his fists. I didn't feel a thing. Despite his bold front he turned out to be as weak as he was small. That didn't stop me, however." Joshua took a deep breath in anticipation of the painful part of the story. "In five steps I had reached the ceramic roof ledging and in one more rather long one I had leaped the seven-foot span between my apartment house and the next one over. A tremendous feeling of elation at having eluded my tormentors swept over me.''

"I kept the feeling alive by recounting the details of the chase later at the dance class. Those rich little kids were fascinated by my description of a roof (swank Park Avenue apartments don't have roofs) and the story of my exploits with the gang (rich little kids only read about gangs in their older sisters' thesis papers). Anyway, I was a great success and all the girls, and even some of the boys whose fathers were always away on fur-buying expeditions, wanted to dance with me. I was the toast of the town, the hero of the day, the brightest light on Broadway. Then I went home and crawled into bed.''

Joshua took another deep breath. "In the dark my thoughts began to clear. I was like the bespectacled English explorer with the walrus moustache, the short pants and the pith helmet who, having made a wrong turn, has found himself in the wilds of the Arctic Circle. There, in front of him, in this subterranean cave, is this ancient block wall of ice and inside of it, frozen stiff, is this shadowy figure. Against his better judgment he begins to hack away at it. The work is torturous, as much because of his pervading apprehension as for the compulsive physical exertion. 'Let it alone!' cry the ghosts of Stanley, Livingstone and Byrd but, relentlessly, he hacks on. The friction from the pick has greatly heated the ice; now it is a race between his chipping off the old block and the ice melting on its own. Suddenly, there is this slushy sound and the shadowy figure stands revealed. The explorer is perspiring freely and it takes several seconds to wipe the sweat from his eyes. When at last he looks up, it is too late.

Revitalized by his warm breath, the figure comes to life and bites off his head. As his eyes roll closed, he notes that he is passing down the throat of the arch monster, the 'Wolfman'."

"That's the way it is for me in the dark as I revoltingly realize that my heroic feat on the roof was really one of incredible cowardice. It dawns on me, there in the dark, that in order to avoid a fight and a few scratches, I chose to risk death by leaping across a chasm six stories above the ground. The most sickening thing, of course, was that I acted on reflex. There was nothing heroic about it. I acted solely in the manner dictated by my character. I acted solely from the governing element in my genes: FEAR. Well, Harvester old boy, when I realized that, I came to grips with my very own wolfman. At twelve years of age, or at most twelve years, six months, I learned that I was a permanent and irrefutable coward. In the jaws of that knowledge, I proceeded to live the rest of my life."

Joshua cleared his throat and resumed the audible portion of his soliloquy. "Now that I've told you my secrets, Harvester old boy, secrets which, incidentally, I have never divulged before, how about you living up to your end of the bargain and telling me yours? How the hell do I make you go!" Joshua again turned the ignition key, pumped peddles and shifted gears with no better luck than before. "It's just not possible that I could be sitting here with this dumb piece of steel and not be able to make it run. It is not possible that I could have come all this distance by myself and then finally fail because I never drove a Volkswagen or some other fascist machine that didn't have an automatic transmission. I mean, if I'm going to die, and I know I can't go any farther on foot, then it should be because I fell into a snakepit while trying to elude a menacing gopher, or because my heart stopped when I at last saw the monstrous Milliginians up close, or because of some other comparable situation in keeping with my basic cowardice.''

Joshua paused. He didn't feel nearly so droll as he tried to sound. "Frankly," as tears began to form, "I don't appreciate the irony. . . ." He got halfway through the sentence and began to weep in earnest. "What have I done to deserve this? It isn't fair, it just isn't fair." He fell to his knees and began praying to a god he never worshiped. "God, I'm not a prick, I've never hurt anyone. Why is this being done to me?" Joshua cried for a full twenty minutes and then, emotionally spent, he rolled over on his back and rested his hands across his stomach. "Okay," he said, "then this is it. This is the end. I'm going to simply lie here until I die. I've said it before but this time I really mean it. It's one thing fighting yourself to stay alive and quite another when it's something you have no control over. It was meant to be this way all the time. I know that now."

There was no pain but Joshua understood that his life forces were beginning to ebb. "I feel so woozy and so very, very weak." He tried to move his arms and legs but they no longer responded to his command. He could literally feel his heart slowing down. "Then this is death. It's not so bad. How foolish to have run from it for so long. Good-bye world, empty though you may be. . . ." Joshua breathed deeply one last time. Then, as he saw his eyes close and felt his heart stop, he exhaled the rest of the epitaph: ". . . I wish I could have served you better."

"Up yours, International Harvester," said Joshua when he awoke from his sleep and found that he had not died after all. "The truth of the matter is, I didn't tell you everything about myself. I'm not quite so stupid as you think. I figured you for a four-flusher all the time. If you won't start up for me, I won't tell you about . . . the great thing that has kept me going. I bet you'd like to know the reason, the real reason I didn't die before, huh? Huh? Huh?!'' After a moment of building anger, Joshua jumped up on the tractor and again went through the ritual of trying to get it to move. This time, however, he gouged and kicked at it too, which apparently is sometimes the only language certain things understand because miraculously the machine came to life and started forward. ''Remember the Alamo!'' came the war cry from his lips and for an instant he was riding in an amphibious boat that had just hit the beach and was charging pell-mell toward the enemy.

Joshua was unaware that all his thoughts, since wakening, bore a marked similarity to an image of himself in a war scene. It was no different now. ''I'm a hero,'' he said, whispering in the machine's ear. ''I once saved a man's life; that's the great thing that once happened to me. Now if I could only remember the circumstances.'' Joshua furrowed his brow very, very deeply. ''Oh well, right now I've got a trip to make. Swampland here I come.''

''Slurp,'' came the captious comment from the shallow contents of the gasoline tank. The taciturn tractor, although an acknowledgedly poor conversationalist, had succeeded in scoring the last word.

TWELVE

THE tribe had turned savage and was on the run again. "This ain't no place for me, I ain't no Mau-Mau," John told Pearl.

"Everything's too easy," said Samatoba to Celestealulu, "so how we ever going to get anywhere? You can reach out and cut yourself a dinner and the weather's good so how can we stay alive? You've got to fight to make your way, but there's nothing here to fight. Am I right, Celeste?"

"Someday I'm going to be king but I don't think the animals like me," said Arnoldumbo to Maytagagawa.

"What would mother say?" sobbed the twins to each other.

"It doesn't help that there aren't any more widowed wives and orphaned children and judges and juries left in the world," thought Mobawamba, "because the honk is dead too."

"The flowers around here make me sneeze," said the twins or Arnoldumbo or one of the others.

"The birds around here keep me awake at night," said Samatoba or John or one of the others.

"Let's go find another place then," said the understanding Celestealulu or one of the others.

And so, after a couple of months, they picked themselves up and moved on, and a couple of months after that they did it again.

Each time they traveled deeper into the swamp, they traveled further from their memory of civilized behavior. "We've got to wash our hands before every meal, and we've got to do our 'business' away from the camp and then dig a hole and cover it up. We've got to take turns fixing the meals, and we've got to keep the living quarters policed. . . ."

"Why we got to?"

"Because if we don't, after a while we're going to be just like some of the animals around here."

"So what," they replied as they turned their backs and walked away. Mobawamba didn't know what to say. How could he tell them about the pain in his head. How could he make them understand that with the honk gone they had become his last chance for some kind of peace. How could he explain that he had been on trial all these years and that the latest evidence on his guilt or innocence was the tribe's ability to survive. "I must keep them alive, I must keep them alive. I cannot endure the responsibility of their deaths too." And yet he was failing.

After six months, cleanliness stood next to deathliness in the order of things. Breast of alligator had become a menu staple and communication was limited to the grunts that accompanied an infrequent carnal appetite. The tribe had fled into the jungle to escape the Milliginians and also discovered in the process an escape from the oppressive conditions of the past. All too soon they found that they were no happier in the jungle than they had been in the city and it weighed heavily on their minds. They knew that in the Everglades there was no one better than they, no one to put them down, to deny them. Each one was his own man here, able, with few restrictions, to live his own life with the freedom to think and feel and be as he wished. "This is Paradise," the swamp called to them. "If you can't find happiness in Paradise, you can't find happiness," is the way it translated in their minds. Each in his own way slowly came to understand that they were still outcasts and as they did, they slowly began to stop covering up their "business."

"What's the use," they said, not understanding that you cannot treat the tree at the limb or cure a lifetime of affliction with a vacation.

"Look what's happening to us, look what's happening to us," beseeched Mobawamba from his own private torment.

"Mother is dead anyway," rebutted the twins.

"Arnoldumbo is alive to make everybody feel less stupid, and Louella is alive because she is white and that makes Mobawamba feel like a big man, and Samatoba is alive . . . ," said John to himself as the veins whispered in the night, "You don't belong." The tribe was not running from civilization—that was only a casualty of the chase—they were running from themselves.

Then the hurricane came and changed everything again.

"I sleep better under the stars." They long ago agreed to lie outdoors when the old shelters wore out and they couldn't find the motivation to build new ones. Thus they were bedded on the open ground when John broke a week's silence and said apprehensively, "Breezy, ain't it?'' The reply, if indeed it was ever spoken, was stolen by a robber wind that erupted from nowhere. In seconds it emptied waterholes and stripped branches and threatened to steal their breath as well. Before they could reach their feet the storm was upon them and sucked them up and creased and crumpled and tossed them about like note paper in the hands of a toddler. Shifting images, like slides set upside down and backwards in a projector, kept registering before their eyes as they floated into trees, hung from their knees, or slammed into ditches and saw the world from between their legs.

At last someone switched off the lamp and pulled the plug and one by one they lost consciousness. No one got killed.

"Holy shit," said one.

"Yeah," agreed the others after the hurricane had abated and they began to recover.

"What do you think?" said one.

"What do *you* think?" said another.

"What do you think I think?" said the first.

"Me too," said the second.

"I'll tell you what I think," said a third.

"Sssssccccchhhh," whispered nine.

"*Balls*," said the tenth. "I'll tell you who caused that storm," continued Mobawamba in a fury, "You did. That's right, you did."

The tribe members, each with the knowledge of his own innocence, started to inch away from their guilty brothers and sisters.

"Hey Raymon," began Mobawamba.

"Yeah!" interrupted the snarling tribe, pointing to the homosexual twin.

Continued the leader, "What was it you told me about your auto insurance?"

"Some of our most important statesmen are gay . . .

queer . . . were . . . were queer," the diabetic Raymon retorted, not to the question, but to the unspoken accusation in their eyes that "gale" is a derivative of "gay" and that homosexuals are responsible for storms.

"How could you?" cried Damon in a deep voice designed to disassociate himself from his sibling.

"What I mean is," returned Mobawamba, "didn't you tell me that the day after your insurance ran out you had an accident?"

"It doesn't apply, it doesn't apply," sniveled the frantic Raymon, reaching for a vile of insulin and sure now that a sacrifice to the wind god was in the works.

"It does so apply," insisted Mobawamba.

"Yeah," snarled the interrupting tribe, panting hard at the pleading pansy.

"When you let down, man, when you stop caring, that's when stuff like this happens. No better than animals, that's what we've become. Just take a walk through the jungle and count the number of dumb animals dead from the storm, and when you get that all totaled up just add another ten for us 'cause if we're not dead this time, we will be the next time." Then the tribal chief spun on his heel and, in his own way, stormed off. Louellalulu ran after him.

"It's not your fault," she said when she reached his side. "I never said it was," he spit back at her. "I've done as much as I can . . . What else can I do? . . . If they want to fall apart and just die out here, well, it isn't my fault. To hell with them. Let them. I'm not responsible and as of now I quit being leader. . . . I'm not going to take the blame."

"Nobody's blaming you," said Louellalulu, trying to understand. "Oh yes they are, oh yes they are." There was a hitch in his voice and for a moment he had to gulp for air. She looked into his face and saw the anguish and begged with her eyes that he open up to her this once.

"Please" is all she said. He avoided her gaze and started to shake his head, but the smallest movement intensified the pain in his skull.

"I killed your husband," he said at last.

"I had no husband," she replied steadily.

"And your father and your. . . ." The tragedy in his voice was so plain to hear. She put her hands to his trembling lips. "I'm sorry," she said with tears of her own. "My poor darling, I'm sorry. I'll never ask you again." And she didn't. The moment passed when he might have lessened his burden by asking her to share it with him.

Louella returned to the tribe and told them that they no longer had a leader.

"How will we get along?" asked Pearl.

"You don't listen to him anyway," came back the answer.

"But what if there is another storm?" Samatoba wanted to know.

"Or an earthquake?" included Arnoldumbo.

"What if," rejoined Louellalulu.

A long silence followed during which the tribe stared at the campfire and evaluated the consequences implied by Mo's abdication. For many months they had been living a lingering death. Maybe now it was time to bring it to a conclusion. Maybe now was the time to once and for all 'throw in the towel'. Like a keyboard musician with his tuning fork, each plucked away at his mind and listened for a match in pitch between the thought of total surrender and the sense of conviction to carry it out. The unfed flame grew brighter as night fell and extinguished what was left of the day. The silence grew louder. When the words came at last they were dull and flat. In the darkness they seemed as likely to come from the creature-shaped silhouettes of rocks and trees as from the rock-still humans still frozen around the campfire.

"Remember my fight with Hodges? I hit him with a right cross." And then nothing for a long time.

"I could always move fast," and in a whisper, "jab, jab, feint, one-two, one-two. . . ."

After another eternity: "I was good." And then after only a millennium: "I was good too."

Slowly, very, very slowly, the tribe crawled off its back, then climbed to its knees, then pulled itself up straight, and then dusted off its gloves.

"Remember the time I almost beat. . . ."

"Remember how they said I wouldn't last four rounds with. . . ."

"The champ, he still remembers the time I. . . ."

The next morning they began the construction of a housing development. The ground was graded for a shallow incline and the shelters erected at the high end so that drenching rains would run off and not undermine the foundations. Pelts were retrieved from casualties of the storm. When they grew scarce, the survivors were hunted and brought down. The skins were cut and stretched and used as insulation against the weather, both as clothing and for the sturdy mud- and wood-reinforced walls of the huts. Brush and trees in the surrounding area were cleared of overhanging growth, and breakers to fend against future storms were erected at the camp's perimeter.

People talked and laughed and policed the area and did their business away from the living quarters. Mobawamba assisted physically but rarely spoke and never offered counsel. He maintained a distance at first because he didn't believe they would follow through with their plans. He kept it up even after the work was in high gear because he realized that a large part of the impetus to succeed was their desire to return to his good graces. He understood that it was to the advantage of all that he not give in too easily.

Everyone benefited from the infectious sense of accomplishment. It was like coming back after being knocked down at the bell and winning in fifteen by a decision.

"Fuck you," said John to the whispering vines.

"Anything's possible," said Arnoldumbo, surveying his shiny new palace.

"Bring on another hurricane," challenged Samatoba, rubbing his hands together.

"Mother always wanted a thatched roof," said the twins.

"We're alive," said Mobawamba.

THIRTEEN

IT was three o'clock and banshee time. Isobel galumped into view as usual but this time she didn't wail. She stood trembling center stage. While her diaphragm went through a series of sudden involuntary contractions which closed her glottis at the moment of inhaling, she breathed out her bulletin in a strangled wheeze.

"Someone's (hiccup-hiccup) Claude's (hiccup)."

"Babies or Bust," shouted Hank Hank, missing the meaning of her message.

"Someone's (hiccup) off Claude's (hiccup)."

"We know Claude's off, honey, but don't you worry, the vote went against him," said several people, thinking about next Wednesday or the Chicago World's Fair of 1936.

"Someone's (hiccup) off Claude's thing," she said, stamping her foot so hard that her cheeks, set to flapping violently by the vibration, actually touched beneath her chin.

"As long as you have your health," slipped the moustached ex-Jewish mother, fearing for the child's fallopian tubes.

Isobel was frustrated but determined. "NNNNNAAA-AAAAHHHHHH," she said, requesting both silence and attention. She settled quickly into a squat position with her feet angling toward the Earth's opposite axis and, to the accompanying sway of the nearest tents, proceeded, toad-like, to huff and puff until she was all swollen and bloated. With at last a sufficient air reserve, she managed to fill in the missing word. "*Cut,*" croaked the doom harbinger shrilly, at last living up to her reputation. They found Claude's naked mutilated body fifty yards from the perimeter of the settlement, half submerged in a mudhole.

"Everything's private, we should mind our own business," cooed Titheria and the other strict constitutionalists, attempting to quiet the thick, fast-flying questions. "It is obvious that somebody was just trying to insure against the cross-pollination of Isobel by Claude," added Gardner, with the final word on the subject.

"Claude was in the middle of creating a new secret pantomime and now it is lost to the world," said the lost world's only Actor-Robot. "His murder must be avenged," he finished with all circuits flashing.

"Suppression of Cries of Agony is the real killer," said Buck, bifocally eyeing on one side the poly-worded speech from which he read, with an eye on the other side to discrediting Just Call Me Robbie. "If Claude had cried out when he was attacked he might still be alive."

"But, but Claude was mute, he would never have cried out in the first place," protested the fluttering Robbie. "Then why waste the taxpayer's (6ch-b9-ww-1) time with a course in (j09-4y) Suppressing Cries of Agony (888) in the second place," countered Buck, punctuating the brilliance of his spontaneous comeback by tearing his note card in half. "Babies or Bust," bellowed Hank, still misreading the cue.

Several days passed and the controversy began to subside. It started to look as if parochialism would prevail and the Titheria-led contingent would rule after all. Then a second, even more startling event occurred. On the morning of the fifth day, the colony was turned inside out when the conservative element reversed its field and suddenly lent its voice to the cry for justice. The reason was deeply pitted with the gravest of implications despite the fact that on the surface it was only six feet shallow. Sometime during the preceding night, someone had exhumed Claude from his mud pack and given him a more conventional interment. In the absence of existing family, and in the presence of settlement policy, it was understood that Claude's body was to have remained where it was until time and nature saw fit to dispose of it. Yet there was this neatly made mound with its tiny cross of twigs.

"Sedition!" cried the constitutionalists, with all flags flying. "After all," they harangued, "it was one thing to transgress against God's commandment and murder the foolish 'Frog', and quite another to defile the philosophy of isolation and private enterprise and bury him."

For the first time, fear gripped the community. Anyone, it was reasoned, who would purposely undermine the law of the land could not be trusted to kill only once.

In the wake of this revelation, the physical appearance of New Hope changed drastically. Overnight trees were leveled, new ground cleared, and the borders of the settlement pushed deeper into the jungle as greater distance from suspicious-looking neighbors was sought by suspicious neighbors. Moats filled with water were dug and sharply hewn stakes were placed around dwellings. Plank bridges connecting tents with dry land were pulled in at night and transformed into standby weapons of defense. During the day no one ventured forth without a heavy rock and a large stick. Even then, with trust at a premium, each gave the rest the widest of berths. The most disciplined traditionalists reveled in this new high of vacuum existence while others, fearing for their personal safety, began arguing for cooperative action. "Just this once, just his once," they pleaded to the stronger quarter of resolutely deaf ears.

"Let's have a town meeting and get this thing cleared up," said two of the arch conservatives after two weeks, and the night when they awoke in a sweat and discovered their tents being burned around them in protest.

Debate was not nearly as fierce as it might have been in other times and a decision was reached very quickly. For the first time, jurisdiction of settlement affairs was to be taken from the hands of the individual and placed in a central governing committee. However, a safety valve against creeping totalitarianism was written into the plan by expressly limiting the influence of the involved agency to the functions of investigation, detection and apprehension of Claude's killer. Furthermore, the lifespan of the committee was defined by the successful completion of its duties. Specific disposition of the killer's fate was deferred until after his identity became known. (Sacred article seven in the Pathfinder Charter diagrams the philosophy of reward and punishment based on individual merit as opposed to blanket law.) Any residual doubts concerning the virtue of such an organization faded with the addendum that the committee would be voluntary in nature and its members anonymous to each other as well as to the rest of the colony. The holy writ of self-determination (article eight) was insured by the "volunteer" element, and the dual ideal of maximal individuality and minimal cooperation was served by the anonymity factor.

To make the plan work, one person to whom all the committee members would independently report, and through whom their results would be made known, would be chosen. Nominations for the post centered around Buck Alice, who had already proven himself a devout constitutionalist; Just Call Me Robbie, who had saved the settlement once before; and the Actor-Robot, who had expressed the strongest desire for revenge on the killer. In this particular circumstance, the majority concern, leaning as it did toward the pragmatic, found its greatest reassurance in the Actor-Robot's overwhelming hate.

A box with a slot for volunteers to deposit their names was placed at one end of the compound. After twenty-four hours the Actor-Robot retrieved the receptacle and in the seclusion of his tent emptied the contents onto his bed. He did so with growing astonishment.

Buck Alice was a portly 39-year-old man with webby fingers, rounded shoulders and the beginning of a hump. He projected the image of a plump, medium-sized turtle who, caught by surprise and garroted around the neck, vainly seeks to make his head disappear. In Buck's case, however, being a fully realized paranoiac, the noose was around his mind and his tucked-away head ducked away from mostly imaginary assailants. Understandably then, Buck was tense. He liked it that way. As long as the muscles in his neck were knotted and quivering, he couldn't be caught off guard. To hear him tell it, never, since the serpent first buttonholed Adam in an alley and offered him "dirty" apples, had life been so actively committed to catching one man off-guard.

Tension, of course, does have its drawbacks and in

Buck's case the most notable example was his inability to string together more than five consecutive, intelligible words. On the other hand, he had no trouble speaking if he could first see the words written out. Apparently he needed the reassurance that the words, because they were down on paper, did exist and would not catch in his throat and come out all dangling modifiers with commas and semicolons misplaced. To this end he carried a large briefcase containing a dozen pencils, a vast collection of catalogued index cards and reams of note paper. "What kind of a day do you think it will be, Buck?" Press-snap-pop the briefcase would open and the answer, cleverly cross-filed under "strata data" and "Arthritis," would, after an apparently casual glance, spring glibly from his tongue. On those occasions when the answer was not to be found among his cards, he would simply pull out his note paper and scribble a reply. With the simplicity of Jesus announcing "I am the Christ," he would dismiss all challenges to this practice with the pronouncement: "I am a writer." It generally worked.

Pressured into lengthy discourse and rendered valiseless, either through emotion or by circumstance (as when the dictates of nature prohibited the assignment of his fingers to unrelated activities), the walls of his larynx, like the rubber band in a model airplane, convoluted into a twisted rope and strangled his breath. Apoplectic at such times, but wishing to appear in control, Buck would take the offensive. In great heat, he would list through his nose a compendium of his thoughts using only letters and numbers. The code, an insoluble cryptogram to all but himself, had the effect of disarming the interloper and, more often than not, encouraging the beat of a hasty retreat. "Xz5h-k931-lm-7iiiii . . . ," he was likely to go on endlessly.

"Buck Alice" was a nom-de-plume. The science fiction writer's real handle was Stanizlas Pulsutski. He changed his name, and in the process paid homage to his two greatest fantasy heroes, Buck Rogers and Alice from Wonderland, when he grew tired of the old joke that science fiction in the hands of a Pole was more autobiography than invention.

One day when he was nine and still Stanizlas and wondering why his longshoreman father liked to sneak up behind him and pinch him on the head, he was suddenly struck by the resemblance between Killer Kane and Marshal Stalin. Unlike his father, who as a boy caught a 120-pound crate of liver paste tossed by his dying grandfather, Stanizlas knew, even then, he was not qualified to carry on the dockworker tradition. "The pen is mightier than the grappling hook," young Stanizlas observed. "I shall become a science fiction writer and devote myself to fighting present-day evil through futuristic fiction. Through thinly disguised parables, like certain others before me, I shall denounce Russian commies and other commies . . . like Polish longshoremen," he said to himself as his barefooted father snuck up behind him and pinched him on the head. Thus Buck came by his given name. As for his surname: The obvious similarity between the family's weekly celebration commemorating the Polish liberation from the Turks and the Mad Hatter's tea party in Lewis Carroll's story served to strengthen Stanizlas' already strong identification with the little girl who fell down a hole and landed in an alien world.

"My new name is Alice," gleefully said the twenty-year-old writer to his dying father as he carefully dodged the 120-pound sack of Crane eggs and, in the process, hastened the poor man's demise.

Buck had been called down to the Everglades, some

seventy-two hours before the invasion, for rewriting on a science fiction television series being shot there. In no time at all he had identified a half dozen Com-Symps in the crew. He was well on his way to flushing out the Com-Symp-Symps when, on the third night, the disgruntled brigade snuck off in their motorboats leaving Buck behind with nothing to rake but swamp muck. Needless to say, the plan to return for him the next day never reached maturity.

Buck Alice had never experienced very much sexual passion. As a consequence, the thought of bedding down with Isobel was even more repugnant to him than it was to the other volunteers. Nevertheless, it was Buck Alice who proposed that the frog-girl's perspective mates be drawn in alphabetical order. The thought of being first with "droopy jowls" appealed only to Buck and the colony readily agreed. Then Claude Aefitte volunteered and Buck was forced to vote with Robbie in order to get the first whack at Isobel.

The reason for Buck's machinations lay in his craving for power. He knew that respect and prestige would come with siring the settlement's first born and he meant to garner the honors. "No neck" Buck genuinely believed that only through his enlightened leadership, based in part on his thorough knowledge of certain fantasy literature, could the "Dog" and the "Horse" prevail over the "Pig" and the "Hog," or to put it another way, he wanted to make New Hope safe from Big Brother by becoming Big Daddy.

Buck considered Robbie to be his main rival, and when Claude was murdered he seized the opportunity to discredit the teacher by casting aspersions on his classes. When this ploy failed, he took his plan a step further. He buried the tart peddler with a shovel borrowed from the tutor's tent; before tossing it into a nearby thicket, he took the added precaution of scratching Robbie's moniker on the handle. Everyone naturally assumed that the person who buried Claude was also his killer. Therefore it was only a matter of protocol when the Actor-Robot individually polled the anonymous committee after the shovel was found. Robbie, of course, was found guilty of both violations.

"But, but would I have left such telltale evidence where anyone could have found it?" protested the private eye in his own defense. "HKN-95W-7-B8B8," exploded the self-righteous Buck, forgetting in his excitement the carefully prepared rebuttal he had written. "The fact of the matter is," read Buck, as his larynx unwound, "that is exactly the kind of maneuver one would use to throw trackers off the scent. In my story 'The Secret Subversives of Sigma Six', published by the American Opinion Library just nine years ago this month, the very same ruse was used by a group of pink androids who left their anvil and scythe marks on their victims to divert the authorities into thinking that they were being framed. They didn't get away with it either!"

Faced with the uncontestable evidence of the written word, everyone turned to Buck and said, "What should we do with him?" Buck smiled to himself. Everything had fallen neatly into place. Robbie would be disposed of and the future head of New Hope would be free of a bloodstained past. "Let the committee decide," he offered, knowing full well that it would have no choice but to order an execution. "A good idea," they agreed, wishing to avoid responsibility for the popular Robbie's punishment. "I will poll the committee and return with their decision tomorrow," said the Actor-Robot pensively.

"Someday soon when I am head of New Hope," said Buck Alice that night, after he said his prayers and pulled the covers up tight, "I will make the Actor-Robot reveal the people who were on the anonymous committee and severely rebuke them for condemning Robbie to his death. Yes sir," he said, as he snuggled close to his pillow, "it certainly was smart of me to stay off the anonymous committee."

"Now's the time," said the Actor-Robot that night, as Three-in-One oil dripped from the crack in his munched-upon lip and stained his blankets. "Now's the time for me to get Buck Alice. Yes, sir," he said, as his lids clanked shut, "Buck Alice must pay."

"If only I could change the past," said Claude's murderer, tossing and turning the whole night long. "If only Claude hadn't started that secret new pantomime. If only tomorrow didn't have to come. Yes sir," said Claude's murderer, "if only."

"The assassination of Claude Aefitte was merely the will of the individual people in individual action," droned the Actor-Robot the next morning. "The burial of the body, which was ostensibly an act of sedition, was in reality a strict interpretation of the law. With Claude buried and out of sight he was also out of mind which in turn made it easier for everyone to mind his own business—as set down in article one of the constitution and in verse three, chapter two of the book of Genesis."

Everyone was surprised that the Actor-Robot would voice this line of reasoning and, of course, the most startled of all was Buck Alice. "You led us to believe (1f22-r-5jb-v6) that you wanted revenge," said the flabbergasted writer

"And so I did," said the emissary, "but like all of you I must abide by the decision of the committee."

"I demand that the committee be publicly polled," read Buck from his hastily illuminated note paper.

"SSSSSCCCCCHHHHHHHHHHHHHH," shushed the entire colony, relieved that the popular Robbie had been reprieved.

"Don't be a poor sport!" said Titheria threateningly. "After all, you're the one who said that the committee should decide." Buck, fearful lest additional protest result in further loss of status, tucked his head deeper into his shoulders and, cursing to himself about the perfidy and collusion of all life forces, snapped shut his briefcase.

"As determined by sacred article seven of the original Pathfinder Constitution, the Committee has deemed that Robbie be rewarded for his conscientiousness and be designated chief of the Commission for Order Protection and Selection."

"Hurrah," everyone said, dismissing in their enthusiasm the unfamiliar ring of the identified organization.

At last Titheria spoke up. "Where did the right to invent new committees come from?" she demanded.

"From the Bureau for Omnipresent Security and Safety," the Actor-Robot diffidently replied.

"The Bureau of what?!" shouted Titheria curling her upper lip over her long yellow teeth.

"The anonymous committee voted, independently of course, to give itself a name."

"That's just great," retorted Titheria sarcastically, while regretting that she herself had not volunteered for a position on the council.

"It's a small thing really," soothed the Actor-Robot.

"But its work is done. We found out why Claude was killed," continued the Cro-Magnon cousin jealously, as her low brow seemed to sink still deeper and further reduce the distance between her hairline and eyes.

"We have???" said Robbie and the murderer as one.

"The committee . . . I mean the Bureau agreed that as long as Isobel can have babies every means available must be used to secure her safety against other possible dangers." Before Titheria could protest again, the Actor-

Robot continued. "And the Bureau also decided that you, Titheria, should be the first woman ever to be second in command of the Commission for Order Protection and Selection."

"Hurrah," everybody obediently shouted again. Titheria, with perhaps the applause of her university triumph still thumping in her ears, wept openly in response to this second great honor in her lifetime. The Actor-Robot then tied everything neatly together by adding the name of Titheria's husband, Gardner, to the commission.

"Grumble," said Buck, always the writer, under his breath.

Isobel's mother had left Isobel's hashslinging father in short order but only after eighteen years when she discovered he had misrepresented the facts concerning his extended buying trips in pursuit of U.S. Choice "flanks" and "rumps." Isobel's mother celebrated her discovery by absconding to Miami Beach with the family car. Much to her chagrin she also discovered, after a few hundred miles, that Isobel had stowed away in the trunk. To spite her husband, Isobel's mother dedicated herself to sleeping with the first Floridian who indicated an inclination.

After a short six months, the despondent exiled owner of a Cuban sugar plantation invited both mother and daughter aboard his sumptuous yacht. No sooner had the ship left port than Isobel's mother (who, after one hundred and eighty deprived days, was quite beside herself) raced fore and aft, topside and downside in search of a brig, an apple barrel, a mackerel net or anything at all into which the interfering Isobel might be safely stowed away. After a brief struggle, the child was secured inside an old foot locker and the mother, who was a faded copy of the daughter, raced fore and aft, topside and downside with visions of a Cuban's sugar cane dancing in her head.

All she ever found was a document attesting to the plantation owner's watery suicide and a note of thanks to both mother and daughter for providing him with the inspiration to end it all. The yacht drifted aimlessly before breaking up on some rocks. Fortunately, the rocks were within wading distance of land and a two-day walk from the site of the newly formed settlement.

As they disappeared into the underbrush, mother and daughter looked up and saw a fleet of silvery spaceships of a singularly foreign design streaking through the sky.

When Claude had been excluded from Isobel's stud list, a feeling of uneasiness had crept through some New Hope tents. "Who next would be legislated against and to what degree?" their creased foreheads silently asked. The stirring momentarily grew more agitated with the formation of the Bureau and the appointment of the Commission because their existence seemed to imply the implementation of additional controls. However, when Robbie was exonerated by the Bureau and it was made clear that the Commission was to interfere only in Isobel's life, there was a general unfurrowing of brows. The following weeks of calm and quiet lent support to the belief that normalcy still reigned in New Hope.

During this period, Isobel's mother's tent became the most frequented hangout for inconsequential chatter. People were forever dropping in for nothing important and discussing things that didn't matter. The exchange of conversation between the guests and the hostess was always a great trial, particularly since Isobel's mother, being only a faded copy of her daughter, operated with the additional handicap of appearing drab and colorless.

Undaunted, however, they continued to come and fill the tent to brimming. Isobel suspected that the real reason for the chit-chat was to see her and, of course, she was right. If the child had the qualities of a troll and indeed she had, not the least to be faulted was the way she was received by the community. "Nice weather to start a garden," they would say to Isobel's mother, while hoping she would read between the banalities the question, "When will Isobel be ripe?"

The mother also surmised that the real interest of the villagers was in the child's impending maturity, but she feigned ignorance of their intentions and of the knowledge that the frog-girl had already come into heat in the hope of milking the neighborly visits a while longer. She reasoned that once the settlement knew that Isobel was pregnable, they would stop making inquiries and mother and child would be left to their own counsel. The thought of being left alone with Isobel in this isolated society send shivers up the poor woman's curved spine.

The community would learn in good time the reason Isobel herself withheld the information of her recently arrived pubescence.

In the weeks that followed the appointment of the Commission, the settlement seemed to be floating along in the most tranquil of seas. The peaceful times might have continued indefinitely had not Isobel's increasing irritability begun to generate what in time would become a distinctly violent ripple.

The undulation began faintly enough with Isobel's growing nervousness. Her mother noticed that she had chewed her rapier-long fingernails to the quick and had developed a tick or two not previously part of her inventory. The parent wrote off the symptoms as rites of fertility, however, and was only concerned lest someone else make the observation and draw the same conclusion. Isobel had tried to explain to her mother about the hairy lady with the low-slung arms and low-slung forehead who had been shadowing her every move and who was the cause of her anxiety, but the older woman closed her mind to the complaints with an admonition about the girl's vivid imagination. The Commission had been directed to safeguard Isobel and Titheria meant to live up to it even if her hot breath gave the child the chills. When Isobel found that there was no place she could go without the silent simian hovering above her, she began to show signs of a breakdown.

"Leavemealone, leavemealone, leavemealone!!!" she would cajole, threaten and implore. Titheria, in response, would pick for cooties between her toes.

Concentric circles began to form in the placid waters when Isobel finally had to give up her afternoon atrocity announcements. She rightly reasoned that any of her made-up stories could be denied by the omnipresent primitive. The waters really became troubled when the child finally decided to take matters into her own hands and personally discourage Titheria's constant hounding. As she did every mid-day, Isobel wandered off into the surrounding woods. This time, however, she bolted ahead and hid behind a sheltering palm. The moment Titheria crashed past, Isobel let fly with a mud bomb that caught the gorilla-girl smack where her tail ought to have been. Reverting to type, Titheria threw back her head, pounded her chest and screamed.

The Actor-Robot again lay in his tent munching on his oil-slick lip. Earlier in the day Robbie had informed him of the events following Titheria's blood-curdling scream and now late that night he was still chewing on the possibilities. "Despite the appearance of things, there is a silver lining here . . . somewhere. The thing to remember is," he said, whispering confidentially to himself, "I am not programmed to panic; consequently, I shall be able to turn this situation into one of advantage and successfully complete my mission to get Buck Alice. In the meantime I better stall." Saying that, the fusebox lever in his head tripped itself and the Actor-Robot fell asleep.

The following morning, the Bureau for Omnipresent Safety and Security issued a statement advising that Isobel was Safe and Secure but being held out of sight for her own protection. "Someone or something may or may not be after Isobel," said the Bureau representative, "and until we can be sure what or who it is or isn't, Isobel will be fully protected by the Commission for Order Protection and Safety."

"But I'm worried about my daughter," said Isobel's mother, worried about not having any visitors while the child was absent. "The Bureau also proposes," said the Actor-Robot, prepared for the maternal instinct, "that Isobel's mother be given special commendation for delivering Isobel into the world."

"Now wait a minute," began Buck Alice, suspiciously, writing and talking at the same time. "Isobel belongs to us all and we have a right to see her."

There was a long pause while a small explosion occurred in the Actor-Robot's head. He generally reacted poorly anyway to any comment by Buck Alice and this time the trauma was compounded by his failure to anticipate the confrontation and produce a reasonable reply. "I am not programed to panic," he told himself, as his eyes went vacant and his tapes began the countdown for "self-destruct." In another moment he would topple forward and break into a thousand pieces. Just then, Isobel's beaming mother came to the rescue. Out of gratitude for the honor bestowed upon her, she impetuously revealed that Isobel had come into "season." A great hurrah went up. "Babies or Bust" baroomed Hank Hank and everybody dashed for their tents. The Actor-Robot had been saved.

Hank Hank peeked out from behind the flap of his tent as he crossed and uncrossed his legs. "I have tactical maneuvers to go on," he complained, petting the whispy remnant of his former pride, "but I'm stuck here until those bastards retreat to their tents." Major Hank was alluding to the two figures still standing in the town square. Every other settlement male, by now, was safely holed up.

"Whirl-hum-click," went the Actor-Robot as the shutters over his eyes unwound and he looked narrowly at Buck Alice. "Press-snap-pop," repeatedly went Buck Alice, as he nervously opened and closed his briefcase and stared back at the Actor-Robot. The thought had come to Buck Alice first but the Actor-Robot had read it there and made it his own. "ISOBEL WAS THE ONE IRREVERSIBLE RALLYING POINT FOR THE ENTIRE COMMUNITY AND HE WHO HAD HER, HAD THE SETTLEMENT FIGURATIVELY AND LITERALLY BY THE BALLS." "Of course," said the science fictionalist to himself, "Robbie has convinced the Bureau into using Isobel as a weapon to take control and that is why they are keeping her from us." "Of course," said the thespian-android to himself, "why didn't I think of it sooner?"

Five hundred yards from the settlement, an improvised stockade had been erected on a newly cleared site. Inside sat a badly battered Isobel with eyes crossed and tongue extended. The decision to keep her there until her bruises healed was made immediately after the pounding inflicted by Titheria. It was fortunate indeed that she was now alive at all. Had not Robbie and Gardner been following close behind, Titheria (who once said, "generally speaking, I am a gentle, sensitive girl but whenever I am struck on the ass with a mud bomb I am transformed into a raging homicidal primitive") would surely have throttled the last breath from the child's gills. Once recovered from her wounds, the Commission members reasoned, it would be their word against the acknowledged "wolf crier" as to the reality of her beating.

As soon as he was able to safely slip away from Buck Alice, the Bureau representative went to the secret hideout and conferred at length with the contrary child. After several hours of apologies and the blood-sworn promise that Titheria would cease bothering her, the Actor-Robot concluded a pact with Isobel aimed at finally revenging himself on the Polish epistler.

The Actor-Robot didn't munch on his lip that night.

In a kind of poetic tribute to Isobel and her penchant for three o'clock pronouncements, mid-afternoon of the following day was deemed the most appropriate time for getting her debauchment under way. At precisely three, the Bureau deputy, with Isobel at his side, strode to the center of the town square. Everyone stopped what they were doing and raced for an up-front view of the proceedings.

"I fell in the woods and hurt myself all over," obediently began the visibly bruised girl. "I wish to thank the Commission for rescuing me from untold dangers. They saved my life."

"The brat's been brainwashed," thought Buck to himself, guessing the real source of her injuries but for the wrong reason. "They've tortured her into making false statements." Alice knew he couldn't make himself believed over the roar of approval that went up from the crowd and so prudently held his tongue. The Actor-Robot then took over and addressed the colony.

"In the light of the new knowledge about Isobel, the Bureau has ordered me to issue the following directive. The young lady" (with exaggerated emphasis on "lady" to the oohh's and aahh's of the proud audience) "shall be courted" (with telling emphasis on "courted" to the oohh's and aahh's of the libidinous audience) "by each of the volunteers in alphabetical order, as previously determined, for a period of sixty days" (with significant emphasis on "sixty" to the oohh's and aahh's of the gynecologically oriented audience) "until there is no further need. With this in mind the Bureau wishes Buck and Isobel Godspeed and asks all of you to join in Christian prayer for their fruitful union."

Everyone then dropped to their knees, bowed their heads and clasped their hands together. "It don't count," said the ex-Jewish moustached mother to herself, "if I keep my fingers crossed."

When the minute was over, the gallery rose and solemnly filed past the Buck and Isobel receiving line. They each kissed Isobel's right cheek and shook Buck's left hand (the right one had a firm grip on his briefcase). The matched couple then turned and slowly walked toward the specially erected mating tent. They turned once more before entering and waved "farewell."

"We salute you," the Actor-Robot called after them.

"We salute you," the crowd repeated ceremoniously.

Then something extraordinary happened. Just as Buck and Isobel slipped from view, the whole settlement, very nearly the entire population of the world, simultaneously but independently, spontaneously but reverently, broke into song with the first verse of "Tumblin' Tumbleweeds."

A miracle was about to occur in New Hope Settlement.

"Take off your clothes."

"No."

"Take off your clothes."

"You don't have a neck."

"What?"

"You don't have a neck and you always carry that case and you speak funny."

"I don't. . . ."

"I ain't going to do it with somebody who does all those things."

"I have a neck."

"You do not."

"I do."

"You do not."

"I do."

"Where?"

"Where everyone has one."

"Point to it . . . I still don't see it. Make it come out."

"There."

"Where?"

"Can't you see it now?"

"Is that all there is? I ain't going to do it with somebody with such a little neck."

"My neck isn't little."

"Then I'm not going to do it with you because of what my mother told me."

"She told you . . . ?"

"Never trust anybody who hunches his shoulders."

"Why?"

"He's hiding something."

"I'm not hiding anything."

"Then you've got a little neck."

"MY NECK ISN'T LITTLE!"

"Prove it."

"Huh?"

"Take off your shirt."

"Take off my shirt?"

"So I can see your whole neck."

"No."

Thus with Buck refusing to take off his clothes, and Isobel refusing to take off her clothes, things got off to a bad start.

In time it got worse.

For ninety-six heroic hours, Buck fought the good fight on three fronts, the first of which was Isobel's mind. In anticipation of some intellectual resistance, he had cleverly fortified himself with an extensive catalog of index cards that eloquently argued her surrender. When she at last tired of her opening evasive tactics, Buck took the offensive. With his loaded briefcase, he moved in for the kill. Isobel countered by tearing up all his notes and throwing his pencils to the wind. He then parried by deftly manipulating tone and inflection to wheedle, bully, flatter and arouse. The effort was Herculean but in the end, Isobel won by default. No matter how passionately proclaimed or with what subtle nuances expressed, lists of numbers and letters simply left the child cold.

The second front was his own wilting enthusiasm. The girl's supine unresisting body was only part of the objective. Buck also had to look to his own physical condition. Isobel might give in at any moment and he could not risk missing the opportunity by being less than firmly at attention at all times. To accomplish this, in the face of the face before him, he had to conjure up visions of ascending rockets, blasting rayguns and streaming jet exhausts in an inexhaustible supply.

The third front was Isobel's frontal front. Besides the manufacture of soothing gibberish and science fiction fantasies, he was called upon to generate a powerhouse of physical energy to combat all the various expressions of resistance that the disavowed daughter of Mongo's evil Ming could devise. (Days later, Buck would point to his throat and the enduring impression of her teeth.)

It was obvious to the initiated that he had failed on all fronts when he stumbled out of the tent four days later.

"Congratulations, congratulations," said the Actor-Robot, rushing to Buck and pumping his hand before anyone else could reach him.

"For what?" Buck asked.

"For the successful completion of your responsibility to the human race," lied the Actor-Robot, knowing full well from Buck's expression that Isobel had not broken their pact.

"But, but. . .," said Buck as his larynx became a beaded string. "Hip, hip, hurrah," said the multitude, descending on Buck and elevating him to their shoulders. "Hail Buck Alice, the father of our country," they chanted, anticipating a fertile union where there had been no union at all.

"I have been instructed by the Bureau," said the Actor-Robot grandly, "to bestow upon you our greatest award, The Eagle Merit Badge for Good Citizenship."

The roar of acclamation was deafening. Tears streamed from eyes and hands reached out to touch him. All about him Buck could see beaming faces of gratitude. A great weight lifted from his shoulders as his neck sleepily rose from the musty cavern in his chest and carried his head up, up to new and dizzying heights. "We love you, Buck, we love you. Speech-speech-speech," they implored. The temptation was too great. They admired him and were proud of him and he could not disappoint them. He could not admit his failure.

The crowd hushed to silence as he moved over to the improvised platform and began to speak. Not once did he look to his briefcase for help. "My fellow Americans, my heart is full. All my life I have been battling evil and now it appears that the merit in my fight has been recognized. I am deeply touched. Although I was not an original Pathfinder and can't really know what the Eagle Badge for Good Citizenship means to you, I can guess. And if it means half as much as I think it means, then it means twice as much as anything else has *ever* meant to me."

It was like apple-bobbing at a Halloween party the way the crowd kept nodding their approval and eating up everything he had to say. Of course they didn't quite understand the reference to the "fight against evil," but then they couldn't have guessed that Buck's address was really his well-rehearsed inauguration speech for the time when he would take over New Hope and become its leader.

"The Alice name has always been synonymous with American know-how and get-up-and-go. I can remember the time when, as a child, my father took me on his knee and explained my responsibilities to my country." The crowd burst into applause again and in the process missed several references to Paul Revere, Walt Disney and J. Edgar Hoover. ". . . so my dear friends I just wanted to say thank you . . . thank you . . . thank you."

The congregation, sensing he was finished, leaped forward and lifted Buck to their shoulders. They had just begun to parade him around the settlement when the ear-quaking sound of fifty exploding cannons in a wind tunnel registered behind them. "FOR WHAT?" shot the voice a second time. "THANK YOU FOR WHAT?" Buck felt his shoulders rising past his temples as his body was lowered to the ground by the chastened group. Isobel stood facing them with her fists on her hips, her legs spread and her jowls full of the venomous truth.

"Thank you for what?" she repeated again. "Nothing happened. Absolutely nothing happened!"

Buck was suddenly nine years old again and his father was in his customary pose. This time, however, he had twenty pair of naked feet and forty pair of callused hands and the skin on Buck's head was being squished into ridges and rills wherever the old man's fingers made contact. "HE WASN'T ANY GOOD AT ALL" was the last thing Buck heard or imagined before he fainted from the pain all over his head. The Actor-Robot had his revenge.

Buck Alice awoke sick and helpless. There were people milling in the background but they seemed to be pretending he wasn't there. At last he dragged himself from the ground and managed to find his feet. He stood wavering back and forth, trying to bring himself into focus. In the space of the few seconds it had taken Isobel to make her appearance and speak her part, his mind had undergone a severe emotional bipolarization. One moment he had been ecstatically happy and the next moment he was in the grip of a terrifying panic. His confusion persisted even now. He had the distinct feeling that he was coexisting in two different worlds and would either soon come all together or fall away forever into a million separate atoms.

"What happened, what really happened?" he asked himself. "Did I imagine that they gave me the Eagle Badge or did I imagine that Isobel told them the truth?" It seemed incomprehensible to Buck Alice that the two situations with their accompanying emotional extremes could have occurred so nearly continuously. Buck Alice crawled off to his tent and for many days worked at putting the pieces together.

Shortly after Buck's retreat, the Actor-Robot issued a Bureau directive censuring the writer for failure of a stated mission and for misrepresentation of facts. It forbade him further voice in settlement affairs and threatened corporal punishment and exile as sanctions for succeeding violations. The Actor-Robot should have left well enough alone.

The next day the number two man on the volunteer list took Isobel to the mating bed. He was followed in quick succession by numbers three, four, five, all the way through the letter ''T'' and number twelve, the last man on the list. It now became apparent why Isobel had not revealed the fact of her coming of age and why she was willing to agree with the Actor-Robot against Buck Alice.

Isobel just didn't wanna do it with nobody.

Since Isobel was also inviolate to criticism, the Bureau found itself in the uncomfortable position of either rescinding at least part of its censure of Buck Alice or condemning the other eleven to an equal fate. At that point, the Actor-Robert remembered the professional reasons why he hated the science fiction writer.

Thus it came to pass that the ''unfriendly twelve'' came to be.

FOURTEEN

THE sound of one hundred thousand little girls catching their breath while applying one hand to their mouths in a kind of general recrimination against all that isn't starched and frilly, accompanied the appearance of the Swoop Craft and its gasping turbojet rockets.

"Where there is a tractor there must have been a man," said Imhor the pragmatic pilot, setting his craft at 'hover' a scant seventy-five yards above the ground. Imhor guessed correctly that the tractor was abandoned when its fuel supply ran out, but he had no way of knowing when that event occurred or whether its operator was still alive and in these parts. He had located the farm machine fifty miles to the north and was slowly inching his way south when he arrived at this particular location. "This must have been a populated area," thought Imhor, noting that the white landscape was full of powdery pimples and bumps where structures and living things once stood. Imhor didn't stay long. He saw nothing that resembled a thriving spleen or a healthy heart value and was convinced that he would have to continue his search elsewhere. Without further delay, he double-pressed the propulsion system engage button. As the ship jumped forward and away, leaving in its wake a heavy blanket of swirling dust, all of the bumps and most of the pimples collapsed from the force of the activated jet exhausts. Imhor looked back at the mostly leveled plain and sighed. The vision of a smooth uniform surface evoked in him a faint joy; in a life in which few pleasures remained, neatness still counted for something.

A curious thing happened as the ship began to fade into the horizon. The earth stirred. A pimple not leveled by the jet blast erupted into self-propelled movement and suddenly stood out in relief against the rest of the white dust. Since the invasion the world had been just white but now, on this one isolated spot, it had become white-on-white. The match was so close that Imhor, in his hovering craft, had missed the distinction. It also helped, of course, that the alien was not looking for a human who could blend so closely with his surroundings.

The naked man who know rose shakily to his feet had a vastly different appearance from the pre-invasion Jewish insurance salesman.

Joshua's metamorphosis had started three weeks before, just after the tractor had run out of gas and he laid himself down to die for the third time. There wasn't much to do while waiting, so after several hours he took to examining his fingers. He discovered he wasn't able to distinguish the little half-moons at the base of his nails. At first he suspected that they had just gone away. He concluded later that the whole nail had turned a solid opaque white. Finally he realized that it was the skin beneath the nail that had changed color. He traced the finger up into the hand and found that his palm was as white as his fingers. He turned his hand over and discovered that he could only see the hairs on his wrist by holding his arm up to the light. "What's this?" rhetorically asked the pale Jew. "I guess this time I really am dying," he mumbled under his tongue. "I REALLY AM DYING," he repeated clearly. "It must be so because I'm not sleepy."

He fell back, not knowing whether he should feel relieved or depressed. "One thing, it doesn't hurt. That's something." Eventually, he shed a few tears, not because he was so overcome, but because he felt it appropriate for the occasion. "I am dying, it's that simple. *I am dying*," he told himself like a first-grade teacher explaining how Peter Rabbit got caught in the farmer's cabbage patch. "I-am-dying-and-that's-all-there-is-to-it." He spread himself out before himself and waited with growing interest. The blue veins in his calves disappeared and the color drained from his pupils. Fascination replaced curiosity. He felt no different physically. Where was the rot and the stench and the kind of iridescent purplish sheen that comes to the skin with death and decay? Consternation replaced fascination. "This is too much," he piqued on the second day; "by now at least I should have turned stiff and cold, and all I feel is hungry." The white became more intense and more complete. Joshua suddenly realized he couldn't tell where the earth left off and the bare parts of his body began.

Jubilation replaced consternation. "Holy shit," he said, jumping to his feet. "I'm not dying, I'm adapting. But why? Who knows, maybe it's God's will . . . or maybe it's something to do with the after effects of the invasion." Joshua didn't know too much about genetic predispositions to biological change as a consequence of radiation poisoning and was glad for it. "I'll choose god," he declared. "God did it. I mean why not, who's to say no? I'm his last remaining son and it has been ordained that I should set things right. Let's see then," he said, taking stock of the situation, "not only am I a hero but I'm also divinely inspired. This can only mean one thing—I'm supposed to save the world. I mean, why else would He make me practically invisible to the invaders?" Joshua would have been more than happy to bounce the idea off somebody else and get a reaction. Unfortunately, there was no one else around and hadn't been for two hundred days. As a result of this situation and his already highly developed penchant for daydreaming, Joshua's perspective had predictably gone awry. "What do you know about that," he said, feeling for his long white robes. "I'm God's kid."

Later, much much later, when he received yet another sign, the course of history changed. But, now, just three weeks after his initial religious discovery, Joshua stood shaking his fist after Imhor's fast-vanishing spacecraft. "Screw you, monsters," he cried out saintedly while putting on his clothes. "I've got your number now!"

At precisely the moment that Joshua was threatening Imhor from afar, the alien was reversing direction on his Swoop Craft. "*Most* of the pimples collapsed, the earth was *mostly* smooth." He had been reflecting on the previous scene, and now decided to double-check his initial findings. Seconds later Joshua was himself deep in reflection. "How can a spaceship that's going farther away be getting bigger? Maybe it has something to do with heat waves and the curvature of the Earth, or some law of physics regarding illusion based on the juxtaposition of the stars, or the properties of the International Dateline in relation to time and space . . . or maybe the son of a bitch is coming back?" For a moment there,

Joshua saw a big-ass kid in a raglan sleeve overcoat soaring through the air six stories above the ground. "No, damn it, I will not run. Come on, you Mick," he shouted under his breath as the ship loomed on the horizon. No sooner had he assumed a fighting stance than he had second thoughts. "I may be God's last remaining son," he told himself, "but I'm not crazy." Once again he threw off the telltale clothes, lay down and disappeared into the earth.

Like a beachcomber with a geiger counter looking for coins in the sand, the returning ship passed over the area in small, overlapping circles. Pretty soon it came close to where Joshua was holding his breath. Imhor adjusted his controls and dropped down one hundred feet. The spacecraft was now close enough to scorch the earth with the heat from its rockets. This fact did not escape Joshua. Any moment he would change from chalk white to ash grey and be captured in an urn. "Fight fair, prick!" he screamed, jumping to his feet and starting to run. He didn't have a chance. The trapnets ensnarled him before he made a dozen feet. As he felt himself lifted into the air, he looked out from between the net binding and saw below him the evidence of his betrayal. He had taken off his raggedy clothes all right but he had neglected to bury them. There they still lay a few inches from the impression of his body.

Imhor was tired, so tired that despite harboring a question or two concerning his pale captive, he hadn't the energy to leave his post and satisfy his curiosity. A check of his panel reassured him that the hoist had gone without a hitch and the human was properly secured in the hold. "That's all that's really important anyway," one of his voices told him. He quickly activated the propulsion system and set his sights for the mother craft.

"If you can only get some sleep," sympathetically speculated another of his voices.

"I know, I know," he returned in irritation; "a little sleep will inspire me to devise a good plan to return home. I've been saying that very thing for weeks."

Meanwhile, back in the hold, the eventual source of Imhor's inspiration had his own problems. "The best I can hope for," said Joshua, trying to evaluate the situation with his limited knowledge of extraplanetary literature, "is that they'll put me in a zoo."

Thirty minutes later they landed. Joshua surmised as much despite being cramped up in the net when the low-pitched hum that accompanied them in flight ceased and the lights in his compartment went out. For a minute or two, nothing happened. He began to like it there in the dark. "So far it isn't much different from my closet." Involuntarily, Joshua's mind skipped back twenty-three years to a happy time when he would crawl into his dark closet and fondle his collection of bottle caps. Just then he heard the alien disembark and the door to the pilot's cabin close behind him. There were another twenty seconds of silence. "Maybe he's forgotten me, maybe. . . ." A panel behind him suddenly slid open and the first Milliginian Joshua had ever seen stood revealed. "For heaven's sake he's. . . ." Joshua didn't have time to finish the blue thought.

"Hello, my name is Imhor. I'm your Cobalt Blue Swoop Craft operator. I hope you had a pleasant trip. If anyone asks, please tell them that it was Imhor, I-m-h-o-r, who . . . found you. Also, tell them, please, that you were fairly treated and suffered no bruises, cuts or other tissue damage at my hands. I get certain . . . credit points for . . . conducting humans safely into the ship. I hope you will enjoy your stay with us. Thank you."

With that Joshua was released from the net and waved from the hold into a large hangar. He no sooner found his feet than he was ushered through a small door and promptly fell fifty feet down a shaft. Six feet from the bottom, his fall was cushioned by a high-velocity blast of a compressed heavy gas and he floated down the remaining distance in reasonable comfort. As he landed, a door in front of him automatically opened. The walls, ceiling and floor of the corridor into which he stepped were painted an ultimate black. The contrast of his stark whiteness against the pitch blackness looked like the trick of an assembly line painter attempting to achieve a three-dimensional look to his artless work.

Joshua was expecting to hear something behind him and as he collected his wits he realized what it was— another blast of the compressed gas accompanying his captor's descent. Nothing happened. It didn't come. He was alone. It was then that Joshua remembered he wasn't wearing any clothes. Nerve impulses began synapsing all over his head. "My God, I'm naked!" The way a starving man dreams of crepe suzettes he began having visions of raglan sleeve overcoats. He wanted to hide. He turned and pressed his body up against the wall. He was suddenly struck by a dreadful insight. His cheeks blushed scarlet and just as quickly he turned around the other way. "Now I know, now I know, and how cruel to find out here in this place and like this," he said in a panic that distorted his reason. Self-pityingly he clutched at himself. *There* was the problem, *there* was the reason for all his mediocrity, for all his failure. It was his nether face as it always had been. Never 'good athlete', 'sharp kid' or 'sensitive child', just 'Big ass'. And now, God have mercy, it was adding insult to injury, ridicule on top of betrayal. The Milliginians would come and kill him all right, but before they did they would point to his rear end and laugh. Lord, the embarrassment, the mortification.

He started to bolt but as his jelly behind bounced up and down, he felt the creases where the fat layered on his buttocks insanely twist back and forth. He just knew that with each step they were sketching mocking smirks and scowls of disgust all over his posterior in a kind of manic-depressive testimonial to self-debasement. "I've got the kind of fat ass that scares the pants off people," he sardonically thought, and here it was right out back for all the Milliginians to see. He was immobilized by his humiliation.

For a long time, he just stood there with his back against the wall. At last he had a thought. "Maybe if I start walking I'll find a room that has some clothes." Slowly he began sliding sideways down the hall. It was a long corridor and being so intensely black it was hard to tell whether it cul-de-sac'd or had a crossing passageway at its end. With ten feet to go, he realized that the wall did in fact turn a corner. Still hugging it from behind, he approached the junction. He took one look up the section of the intersecting passageway that faced him and saw nothing. He then navigated the turn only to fall back in horror. The sound of a punctured billows came from his throat. The new passageway, like the old, was as deep as the eye could see, but unlike the old, deep as the eye could see stood row upon row of somber, silent Milliginians dying on their feet. They made no move toward him and uttered not a sound; it seemed as if they weren't even breathing. Joshua had no way of knowing what a healthy alien looked like, but he guessed correctly that these weren't it.

Imhor had looked sick but not like the apparitions before him. The skin on their faces had shrunk and tightened and pulled away. Eyeballs and teeth like the headlights and grill of a worn-out '57 Cadillac stood out in rusty chrome relief. Their bodies, or what was left of them, rattled in triple time to the rhythm of a different bongo drummer. In all the sea of faces the only expression Joshua could identify was a feverish hunger. Still no one moved and Joshua's composure began to return. His fear made room for incredulity. "We gave up the world to you?" He had no time for a follow-up thought. At last some of them feebly stepped forward, feebly took his arm and still without a sound, gently led him away. "Up yours, Imhor," Joshua said to himself, feeling vaguely that the alien's absence was a double-cross. "Just see if I help you get any extra credit points."

Joshua was carefully and silently led through a maze of galleries. He counted six in his entourage. Two held him by the wrists, two at the elbows and the remaining two, flanking him from behind, gripped at his waist with each of their hands. "Cackle-growl, cackle-growl" went his buttocks but ironic as it may seem, the Milliginians were too preoccupied to notice. The trip was a long one. Joshua began to suspect that the aliens' initimacy reflected less the fear of an escape and more a fear that without his support they would all fall down from fatigue. As it was, marching in such tight formation probably tripled the length of the journey. In order to grip him at the waist with both hands, the two rear guards were forced to cross over their inside arms. As a result of this alignment, they kept bumping heads and tripping over each other's feet and in an exercise of the domino theory sent the entire squad careening into first one wall and then another along the myriad passageways. Joshua shut his eyes and let his imagination expand on the idea of himself as a prospective groom out for a last fling with his drunken bachelor buddies, all of whom coincidentally happened to be deaf mutes. At last a door opened and he was led into his new 'home'.

The first impression to register on his senses was the aromatic smell of a hearty but mellow, outdoorsy but indoorsy, exotic but familiar cherry-nut-pine-rum mixture of burning tobacco. His knees grew unsteady. The pipe itself was a thing of beauty, all laminated and shiny with carvings of little hermaphroditic Dutch boys dancing around windmills. Beside the pipe was a pair of maroon crushed velvet, worn-at-the-toe, slightly down-at-the-back slippers. Both articles rested on a lion-paw-legged victorian night table of deepest mahogany. Also sharing the table and illuminating part of the room with a new-day warmth while casting homey shadows over the rest was a 'Colonial'-style lamp dripping cunning curlicues. Joshua felt a great heaviness lift from his stomach and begin to creep into his chest.

The desk was large and sturdy and loaded with Mediterranean influences. On it rested a handsomely jacketed copy of *Leaves of Grass*, appropriately dogeared and opened to "Crossing Brooklyn Ferry." Beside it napped a Herman Melville opus with just a hint of cobweb. A genuine Naugahyde easy chair delicately fissured from comfortable wear with a million little blood vessels occupied one corner. Beside it stood the couch, deep and soft and plush with throw pillows. A red and blue bathrobe resplendent with papoose-carrying squaws and necklace-stringing braves hung from a hook near the library wall. The books on the shelves were of uniform size and dimension, and formed, in color and attitude, a perfect complement to the flowered drapes and oriental throw rug.

Even if he had wanted to, Joshua couldn't have helped himself. He sighed heavily. Up from his chest, past his bobbing adam's apple, nostalgia and sweet melancholy rose. They found an opening in his eyes and condensed to liquid when they hit the air. To describe the room as a *caricature* of the American dream is to be excessive in description. Never mind the exaggeration of effect, never mind that Joshua didn't smoke a pipe or flop about in slippers, that he personally preferred wicker chairs and rattan lounges; never mind that the room was inspired by the confiscated tape of a Winston cigarette commercial, never mind all that—it still struck a responsive chord and in awe Joshua muttered aloud, "My God, how did they know?"

"We like you," said the first of his jailers.

"We really do," reassured the second.

"Have a good time," tossed in a third.

"Don't get overheated," cautioned a fourth.

"Or fall down," worried a fifth.

"Or anything . . . ," included the last jailer, intending to stop there. But suddenly deceived by his lust (which was probably the reason he was only the sixth jailer), he blurted out, "and for goodness sake, evacuate those precious kidneys just as often as you have to."

"Crack-crunch" went the elbow of the fifth and the rib of the sixth as the latter was peremptorily shoved from the room in advance of the other rapidly exiting Milliginians. "Bye, bye," they chorused to him from behind the locked door.

Joshua didn't feel the least bit alone, not in this beautiful room. He was like a child again, less than twelve, before his father had gone away for the last time and died. He had come in from the snow, reluctant to leave the game but full of pee and too timid to relieve himself in the bush. "Hurry up," he called impatiently, ringing the doorbell to his apartment, "I gotta go!" The door flew open and the first thing he saw was the foyer piled high with boxes of every size and color. "Is dad back?" he asked hopefully.

"No, but he sent you these. They're all presents for you." As Joshua stood surveying the bookcase, the oriental rug, the night table and all the rest, he remembered his reaction to all those long-ago presents. It had been one of the happiest moments in his life—all those marvelous packages packed full of his father's love.

"Aren't you going to unwrap them?" his mother asked.

"I will, I will," said the child reluctantly, knowing full well that there was more in those boxes than met the eye and that once they were opened he would not be able to see it.

That's the way Joshua felt now as he looked around the room. He wanted to go and touch everything, to sit at the desk and the chair, to rest on the couch. But he knew too that once he did, reality would intrude, imagination would wither and happiness, though still warm, would no longer be greater than the sum of the parts. Eventually he did anyway. He put on the slippers and the bathrobe, puffed on the pipe and sunk himself deep into the easy chair.

"My old man . . . ," he thought, "my old man who died when I was twelve . . . maybe things would have been different. Maybe I would have grown up into somebody else. Maybe I wouldn't have flown from roof tops and had a fat ass. Who knows? How little I've thought about him these last few months . . . oh well." Like a Queen dismissing her subjects, Joshua clapped his hands together to erase his memory. Immediately he heard the medium-pitched sound of a machine whirling into activity. The oak-paneled wall had looked solid enough, but as he turned to locate the noise, he noticed that at least one section was actually transparent. He stepped closer and discovered, recessed in the wall, a six-inch disc-shaped object rotating at a speed that seemed to double with every revolution. A grey light spilling from the machine brightened in intensity as the speed of the spinning disc increased. Faster and faster, louder and louder, brighter and brighter went the contraption. Joshua backed away. He was sure that at any moment it would come bursting through the wall and lop off his head. Just as he was preparing to dive for cover, however, it seemed to exhaust itself. The noise cut out and the blinding light vanished. A soft 'poof' in tandem with a whispy curl of smoke saluted the return to normalcy.

"It's dead," Joshua thought, catching his breath and edging toward the window. He was wrong. The whirling plate was still revolving but at such an incredible velocity that it was very nearly invisible. Joshua guessed correctly that the light and sound waves it emitted were now traveling so fast that he was no longer aware of them. He whistled his admiration. Suddenly some books on a shelf in the library wall parted and exposed another whirling plate. Over the next thirty minutes the scene was repeated again and again as Joshua discovered that anything from a sneeze to a racing pulse could turn the walls on. Apparently the pitch of the sound and the color of the light were modulated by the density of the activating noise. When he realized this, Joshua took to playing the room the way one would a set of Swiss bells. Here a snap of the fingers, there a deep breath and behold, a synthesized music and light show of infinite variety. However, because the increasing speed of the revolving discs decreased their effectiveness after a few seconds, Joshua was forced to furiously gallop up and down clicking his teeth, clucking his tongue, and batting his eyes in a mad race against those deadly lapses that are the bane of every great composer. Once again he was the brilliant soccer player with one leg or the comic on the telethon for paranoid schizophrenics. "I'm a hero," he said out loud, "and I'm God's son on earth, and what's more," he concluded triumphantly, "I'm *Leonard Bernstein!*"

A group of culturally deprived Milliginians burst in upon him then and tried to interrupt the concert. "Please, please," they shouted, "calm yourself, calm yourself. Those devices are not playthings," they yelled above the din. "They are only meant to test the condition of your vital organs. They are sensitive and easily destructible. Your adrenal gland is pumping so hard it's going to break the machine. PLEASE."

But by now Joshua was deep into the second movement of the "War of the Worlds" suite and had transcended mortal time and space. The aliens might have tried to overpower the human but they were fearful lest they damage his body, as well as their own, irreparably.

"It must be the female then," the leader concluded at last, and the word rapidly spread through the ranks. She arrived in an instant and the rest quickly shuffled out. Joshua had not seen her enter and only became aware of her when she stepped in front of his next lunge across the room. The first thing he noticed was that she was a pastel shade of aquamarine, then that she was gorgeous and, finally, that she was stark naked.

"My name is Loinine," she cooed. "What's yours?"

For a moment, he forgot. Joshua had never seen anyone so soft to look at. She lowered her eyes and rested her chin against her chest. Her arms hung loosely at her sides. Her ankles touched.

"My name is Loinine and you can do with me whatever you wish."

"I see. . . ." The only thing Joshua really saw was her breasts. They were perfect, with nipples like a puppy's wet nose searching the air for a warm cradle. "Snuggle me, please?"

"I beg your pardon?" Joshua asked and then caught himself. Breasts do not speak, at least not out loud and certainly not in English. He made a mental note to watch that kind of thing.

She slowly raised her head and looked at him. He thought he might never recover from the experience.

"How defenseless, how eternally defenseless she is." There was a look in her eyes that told him she had always been hurt. It asked silently whether he would hurt her too. God, how he wanted to . . . what? Beat her? Yes, beat her and make her cry out, but no blood, no injuries, no cuts and bruises. Then how to hurt her without hurting her? Break her heart? Yes, break her heart, walk away into the sunset and have her cry forever. Sacrifice himself to a solitary existence for just that moment of parting when her sadness would be most supreme. And why? So that he would actually feel— taste—her love for him. So that he could know quantitatively just how many gallons he was capable of being loved. So that he could drink it all down and satisfy the thirst for self-love. He *could* be God's son. He *could* save the world if he could believe in himself the way this beautiful girl with her love believed in him.

"My God, a tear." She had begun to cry.

"Don't leave me, please."

She had said it, she had actually said it. He was suddenly rocked by rage and jealousy. Rage at all those who had made her the wounded, delicate creature she was and jealousy that it hadn't been him. It passed when she stepped closer to him. It was a strange move, full of hesitancy and diffidence and yet somehow compulsive, as if she had been gently pushed from behind. Now he saw that her vulnerability was not only to the outside world but to her own body. Those breasts again, they were making her come to him, and now her stomach too. How could he have overlooked her stomach—her belly, her tummy, her tum-tum—how could he have missed that the first time around? He had an almost overpowering urge to bury his face in it and wrap it around his ears. She kept coming. "She has no will, no choice, her body is making her come to me . . . like little Italian women who hate American G.I.'s but love their candy bars? No, no . . . because . . . Yes! Because although her body does compel her, Loinine *wants* to come, *wants* me, *wants* me to hold her, to protect her—*to do anything I wish with her.* Closer still. My God, those breasts, that tummy, so near. And now the thighs. The deep of the thighs, the feel of *that* against me, *Jesus*! What, still more? Some yet undiscovered ultimate wonder more than the breasts and the tummy and the thighs? Some final ultimate wonder . . . oh yes, OH YES!

> She stepped into his arms and embraced him
> still standing
> And he remembered poems never recited
> and drank from a vessel long forgotten
> as down all of her back his hands traveled
> and rested still roving
> beside still waters yet rushing
> while all of the stars,
> all but one,
> disappeared from the Heavens.

Incredible yes, but better, better than everything that went before. "Boy, oh boy, Loinine, do you have great buns," he whispered in her ear. And of course he should know.

Then like a sequence of lap dissolves in a motion picture, Loinine sunk slowly to the oriental throw rug.

Like a series of still life photographs from a Brownie camera, Joshua stood still. At last, like a new-born tadpole uttering its first sound, Joshua croaked:

"It's just that you're so greenish blue. I've never slept with a greenish blue person before."

In defense of her position, she merely elaborated on it and gently parted her thighs. Just like that, Joshua transcended five thousand years of human racism. He lowered himself onto her and experienced the unendurable ecstasy of a prepubescent being bathed by a libidinous young aunt in a tub of warm water. She enveloped him in an embrace that unfolded the last page in the story of the eternal quest for perfection and he entered her with a joy that formed the preface to the sequel. With that first thrust he loosened the shackles of Earth's gravity and floated away to a new land where the women all have beautiful behinds and the men don't have any.

Little wonder, extraterrestrial as he was, that the humming sound in the ceiling, initiated with that first memorable plunge, was less than the distant rattle of a Milliginian's bones.

Imhor had left Joshua at the 'drop shaft' door in order to get some much-needed rest. He dispatched the Earthling from his mind with a thought or two concerning the cell into which he was to be settled. It had been nicknamed the 'incubator' with good reason. The purpose in its design was first, to record and second, to stabilize all vital function chemistry. Imhor vehemently opposed the latter part of the concept. By providing a warm, sentimentally familiar environment, the subject was in fact being fattened for the kill. Imhor believed that such coldly impersonal calculations were beneath the dignity of his species, and he seized upon his distaste to vindicate his own murderous intentions. "They're no brothers of mine," he corrected, self-righteously laying himself down on his cot. "How low, how really low they have sunk," he sighed, sinking into a deep sleep that passed into a coma from which he awoke on the operating table.

Joshua's father lay stretched across the kitchen table. His head lay turned to the wall and Joshua couldn't see his face. In fact, all that Joshua could see was the great paunch that rested below his father's chest and one hand that dangled over the near side of the table. The hand was warm. Hopefully, the grief-stricken child looked up into his mommy's face. "Aren't dead people supposed to be cold?" he asked, but his mother burst into tears and led him from the room. The father he had seen so little of when alive was dead all right, and no amount of wishing could make it undone.

The dream was a recurring one. Only semi-conscious, the ten-year-old child climbed from his bed and made his way toward the kitchen. He stopped short at the sight of his long-absent father eating bagels and lox.

"Hi," said Joshua in a small voice. The older man turned and opened his arms.

"Hello, my darling son," he replied. . . .

The child's mother then called and the child awoke from his second dream knowing that his father was not dead but neither had he come home.

Joshua was now slowly awakening in the incubator. He lay very still with his eyes closed.

After the Milliginian attack had abated, those few who had survived, like Joshua, crawled from under cover and wandered out alone into a blank world. They came out separately, widely scattered across the earth, and saw a world so completely leveled that in all directions they could see the horizon, and so completely white that there was no direction in which turning would relieve the glare from the sun's reflection. In the effort to turn from madness they mistakenly sought some recognizable thing—some object, some familiar sound or sight or smell that would tell them who they were. In the course of searching and not finding it, they turned back the other way. In the presence of unremitting sameness, white might just as well be black, for the lack of orientation that comes after hours in the dark seized these few pitiful humans as well. Those that were not caught by the aliens stuffed their mouths full with the dust of taxi cabs and outdoor cafes and children playing. It was different for Joshua. When he understood that there was nothing left—no reminder, no memorabilia that he could hold up to his face and through touch or sight or smell identify and thereby reidentify himself—he simply turned from the real world to the world of his imagination. It was not a difficult adjustment; he had always lived there more comfortably anyway.

Joshua lay very still with his eyes closed. His fantasies had been good to him. They had always been good to him. They had saved him in the pre-invasion days and they had saved him in the post-invasion days. They gave him companionship and filled in most of the empty places. They gave him prestige and honor and respect. They gave him credit and merit and worth. They gave him and they gave him and they gave him. He never ceased to take because of the one thing they could not give: love. Not mother love which is candy-striped and prefabricated and assembles itself with the pull of a string, but the kind of love that breeds self-love and makes daydreaming unimportant and unnecessary: the love of a woman. Joshua had found that kind of love at last. He found it in this marvelous room with this unimaginable girl.

Joshua lay very still with his eyes closed because he was in love with Loinine and was fearful lest the reality of the new day give the lie to his feelings. Was the Milliginian holocaust, like the dreams of his childhood, only a bad dream? Was Loinine, whom he loved, just another trick of his subconscious? Perhaps Loinine was real and the other only a nightmare. But Loinine was Milliginian and if she existed, so must all the rest. Father is not dead but neither is he here. The world is dead but not entirely if Loinine lives beyond my imagination.

Joshua could bear the game no longer and at last opened his eyes and found the beautiful girl asleep at his side.

Again the pain came, played the length of his abdomen like a child with a stick across a wooden fence, and then abated. Imhor no longer waited for the agony to come and go. Anticipation of it was as bad as the actual hurt so he did not acknowledge to himself the moments of respite. Instead, he constantly kept his eyes clenched, his teeth gritted, and repeated "It hurts, it hurts" to drown out the message that the pain had momentarily left him. He remembered how they were, the doctors, when they opened him up. He remembered how their eyes went narrow as they exchanged cryptic looks. "They have found something bad," he told himself, something more than a sealed sphinctor. Why didn't they say so? Why didn't they tell him? "You're going to be fine now," the chief had said, but he had busied himself with a chart and averted his eyes. The policy had always been to tell the patient the worst: "The following bodily functions have been impaired and need repair but don't

despair,'' and the list would be ticked off. No matter
how serious no one ever gave up hope, but then why
had he averted his eyes?

It had been four days since the operation. Curiously,
Imhor had not been without visitors. A steady stream of
Cobalt Blues had passed through his room. The heavy
traffic was all the more peculiar since Imhor, always
more comfortable around machines than in circles of
people, had not made a single friend aboard ship. His
bewilderment grew as did their warmth and intimacy.
They sat at the foot of his bed and talked quite personally about themselves and their feelings concerning Earth.

"Can you believe it, Imhor, that human of yours, that
ridiculously white primitive, had the nerve to shrink
from us."

"Shrink . . . ?"

"Yes, *we* appalled him. Can you believe that?"

"We . . . ?"

". . . Because of our sickness. I tell you, Imhor, this
species has no compassion. They are worthless."

"Worthless . . . ?"

"Well, Imhor, what do you think, has it been worth
it?"

"Worth it . . . ?"

"The conquering of Earth at the cost of so many,
many lives. The useless, senseless murder of so many
innocent living beings. And I don't mean only the three
hundred and six Cobalt Blues, no sir, the Aquamarines
too. Yes sir, over four hundred and twenty Aquamarines
have also passed on, have just had their lives snuffed
out. Well, Imhor, what do you think, has it been worth
it?"

"Worth it . . . ?"

"Yes, worth it."

"Worth . . . what . . . ?"

"But of course, how could you know. You've been so sick this last week. The new chief scientist has announced a cure for electrocution. A soon as we find the new humans we are going back. . . ."

"New humans . . . ?"

"Yes, the one you captured was on his way to a colony of them. If we can only hold out until we have them located, we'll be able to build up our strength for the trip back . . . ."

"How many?"

"A very rich vein, close to one hundred and twenty. Enough to go around if we can only hold out until we find them. Some little girl your human met told him about a settlement and he was on his way there when you caught him. Once we find the colony we'll be on our way back. . . ."

"My . . . human . . . ?"

"Yes, of course, the credit point system—you found him, you get first dibs."

The last reply came in a voice so fraught with anxiety that Imhor imagined the sound of a splitting seam and furtively checked for rents in his visitors' stretched cellophane faces. "Lots of furrows, but no tears," said Imhor to himself, making a mental note about the resilience of cellulose.

". . . and of course, once we get our strength built back up, we will be able to go back home and spread the word. Before long, Earth will be habitable and many more of us will return here."

"HOME": the word squeezed through a dropped stitch in Imhor's crocheted-over mind. "Now I understand. Now I understand why you've been coming to see me. Now I understand your interest. My human must be the only new one that's been captured since before I left. You're afraid I'll live and take all the good parts and leave nothing for you. With going home now suddenly possible, you've panicked and shown your true colors. You're afraid that without my Earthling you'll die before you can find the other ones. All that talk about how shocked he looked when he saw how sick you were— that wasn't innermost soul-baring or the 'joy of old friendship rekindled'. No, that was a deceitful gambit aimed at catching me off guard. Hypocrites, sniveling, diseased hypocrites! Avant, avant!''

"Well, take care of yourself and you'll soon be up and around," they concluded, shaking his ligaments good-bye and slithering craftily from the room like escaping intestinal odors.

"The next time, tomorrow when they come to visit me again, I really am going to tell them off," said Imhor, still silently talking to himself.

"*I* would if *I* were *you* and I am," said one of his voices. "After all, they're practically trying to kill you."

"Us."

"Me," they corrected each other and he corrected them.

"But they haven't succeeded, have they?"

"Not on your life!"

"My?"

"Our," he corrected them and they corrected him.

For the first time since his operation he rose from his bed. Painfully, he made his way toward the dresser mirror.

"No wonder my human blanched when he saw them in the corridor," said Imhor, chuckling to himselves. "You would have to say that they do look pretty awful, wouldn't you?"

"We."

"I," they improved upon and he amended.

Then Imhor looked at his reflection.

"Oh!" He honked "oh" just once. He lurched back toward his bed. The vision of Joshua turning a corner and discovering the decaying enemy came unsolicited to his mind. When he pictured the look of revulsion that must have crossed the human's face, he buried his grill in the pillow and wept openly. Imhor was now as sick as the others.

"How mortifying," he thought, "to look revolting, to induce disgust." He wallowed in the muck. "Like open sores or excrement. Something ugly, reprehensible. How humiliating. No wonder they shared their confidences with me." He plunged in over his head. "After all, vomit is thicker than blood!" He filled his lungs with it. "Look what they've done to us, look at the grotesque thing we've become," he called to his voices.

"You."

"You," they repeated slightly detached, setting the record straight.

"*They* did this to you."

"That's right."

"*They* did this to you."

"That's right."

"*They* mustn't get away with it."

"You're right."

"*They* mustn't get away with it."

"You're right, too."

"*They* mustn't get away with it."

"So are you. I never wanted to come, I begged not to be included, but they insisted and now look, look, I'm this loathsome, hideous creature. Do they think they can get away with this? Do this to me and then just go home?" Imhor stopped short and suddenly raised his hands for silence. Only the dried-out marrow rattling around in his wrists defied him. "That's it, that's it. I'll kill them all and take the ship home myself. That'll show them. And now I know the way, now I have the plan. I must find my human.''

"Our.''

"Our,'' volunteered his voices with renewed camaraderie.

After the first twenty-four hours alone with Loinine, Joshua began to have visitors. The aliens came just after breakfast and then again intermittently throughout the day. They didn't so much enter the room as seep into it. Once inside they gave no feeling of having come from any place. One might think that they had always been there, swaying in the air, as if suspended on wall hooks. Only the burning eyes and the occasional screech of a whispered exchange hinted at a purpose for their presence.

They looked so much like ghosts in their sickness and so ghostly in their alikeness that after the day's third visit, Joshua began to imagine himself as the keeper of a rest stop for a phantom passenger train on a self-repeating track going nowhere. When he was able to penetrate beneath the most obvious physical characteristics and discovered that while the guide remained the same, the group behind him was in reality different each time, he began to feel less detached and more the subject of the proceedings. When he discovered that his whispered name produced among the unwelcome guests a Pavlovian trickle of stringy saliva, and when he realized that the burning headlight eyes were set on high beam and directed at him, he began to feel less like a custodian and more like an axeless axe murderer released into the custody of an opportunistic landlord with a thriving tourist business on the side among Joshua's former homicide victims.

The most disturbing thing of all was that these inter-

ruptions reduced his time with Loinine. She disappeared
with the first knock and didn't return until the door had
shut behind them. Worse even than her absence to his
sight at these times was the void created by the lack of
her tactile presence. His agitation grew as the minutes
ticked away and she was not there to touch. God, how
he needed to touch her, to hold her, to caress her. Then
at last she would return and suddenly it was as if she
had never gone. They meant so much to each other, had
become so much 'one' that when she stood before him,
he couldn't imagine her ever not being where he was.
As before the interruption, she would step into his arms
and, as before, the hours would go by without a word
passing between them. There simply was no need. He
knew her and wanted to know her only in terms of how
she related to him—to his pleasure—and that she told
him with her eyes and body far better than ever she
could by speaking.

It was the ultimate in physical relationships. She did
not so much become part of him as *a* part of him—a
part of his sex—an extension of all the nerve endings
that made his heart pound and race. He touched her
breast (his breast) and she smiled "how good it feels."
He kissed her stomach (his stomach) and her hands in
his hair told him "how good it feels." She raised
herself to her knees and her mouth (his mouth) went
wide and soft and their fluttering eyelids tapped out
"how good it feels." The glorious thing was that she
still, at the same time, had form and shape and substance apart from his own, and so was something in
addition to being a part of him. She was something new,
something totally unique to his frame of reference. She
was . . . she was. . . . Yes, she was *not* a daydream.
She was a person, a living, breathing, adoring, beautiful
woman person, and the love he had been denied when

he alone stroked himself lovingly was now in her arms, his to have. Joshua had found the love of a woman and through that love had found self-love.

"If only I was twelve years old and on my way to that dance class *now*!" he thought, as knots formed in the muscles of his jaws.

"He doesn't recognize me," thought Imhor. "How dare he not recognize me!" It was the fourth evening of Joshua's stay aboard the ship. "I am the one who found you," Imhor said aloud with studied patience.

"Thank you."

"How's that?" said Imhor disconcertedly, thinking, "What does he mean by that?"

"Thank you for finding me."

"Oh, *that*," said Imhor, barely acknowledging the masked reference to Loinine. "Look, I have something really important to tell you."

"Can she stay?"

"Who? Oh, her. Yes, yes."

"Thank you."

"How's that?" said Imhor suspiciously, thinking, "Is he trying to make fun of me?"

"Thank you for letting her stay."

"Yes, yes, never mind, never mind that. The thing is this. Tomorrow I am going to help you escape."

"How's that?" said Joshua confusedly, thinking, "There's a spatula in my head making flapjacks with my brain."

"Escape-escape, you have heard of escape?"

"Yes, but somehow I never thought about it in connection with me."

"You do want to leave here, don't you—be among your own kind?"

"I wonder what is one's own kind," Joshua returned, absently putting his arm around Loinine.

"How's that?" said Imhor rhetorically, thinking, "I wish I was with my bright lights and button downs right now." And then, out loud, "Never mind, never mind. The point is that they're not going to let you live much longer—they're going to kill you.'"

"I can't believe that."

"How's that?" said Imhor menacingly, thinking, "How dare this impudent albino take that condescending tone with me." And then, out loud, "Furthermore, they're going to destroy that colony of humans you were on your way to. . . ."

"How did you . . . ?"

"How else? We read your mind. You do realize that we are superior to you, that we are a more advanced society? After all, we have destroyed nearly your entire population."

"How's that?" said Joshua incredulously, thinking, "He can't really mean to make the two things appear synonymous."

"How's that? How's that . . . ," said Imhor sarcastically, barely thinking at all because of the pain. "With our apex gain zenith laser 'bang-bangs', that's how!" Then, in a more conciliatory tone, "Look, if I can prove that they intend to kill you, will you please escape and save what's left of your mankind?"

"Of course . . . sure . . . I mean . . . yeah . . . I guess so."

"All right then, I'll call for you in the morning before breakfast when everybody is still checking to see whether he has survived the night." And with that Imhor was gone.

"I can't really believe it," said Joshua to Loinine. "I don't really believe they mean to take me away from

you and kill me." But then Joshua heard his words echo
in his ears. "Just the same, we had better be prepared to
leave when he comes."

Loinine smiled.

Joshua was at the point of ascending to a new peak of
self-gratification with the part of himself that was Loinine
when Imhor slipped into the room early the next morning.

"For Christ sakes, you could have knocked."

"Never mind, never mind, come."

"Are you trying to be funny?"

But Imhor had already pulled the door open and was
on his way out. Joshua knew he was supposed to follow, but when he beckoned to Loinine she only smiled
sadly and would not take his hand. He gestured to her
again but she did not respond. Without a backward
glance, Imhor had started shuffling down the corridor.
Joshua looked after him and began to feel apprehensive.
It didn't seem to matter much whether or not he went
with the alien when there was nothing to stand in his
way, but now he suddenly was faced with a conflict:
Loinine, apparently, did not intend to go with him. He
looked out into the passageway and saw that Imhor was
about to turn a corner. Without warning, full-blown
panic burst upon Joshua.

"I've got to stay alive, I've got to stay alive to save
mankind. I'm a hero and I'm God's son. I can't quit
now." He looked back at Loinine. "Or can I?" He
rushed to her side and tried to collect her in his arms and
carry her with him. She slipped from his grasp like
mercury and, smiling her sensuous smile, settled to the
floor in degrees like a pack of playing cards fluttering
between the hands of a dealer. He stood transfixed as
she moved her hips and placed one lovely hand between

her legs and gently rested it there. "I can't leave without Loinine, without myself." Joshua began to think that maybe Imhor didn't really expect him to follow. "Perhaps this isn't the time—maybe it's tomorrow or the day after. Maybe they're only testing my worthiness, my devotion, my faithfulness to my woman." How good that sounded. "My woman." To have a woman, to be so sure, so confident, so strong as to be able to say 'my woman' and to know without reservation that she did indeed belong to him.

"Maybe it could be some kind of character test hopefully. I can't leave, I can't leave Loinine. I'd rather die, yes die." Imhor was nowhere to be seen. "To hell with mankind." Joshua fell to his knees before her. "All the months of staying alive." He touched her lips. "All the years of staying alive." He pressed his cheek against her inner thigh. "The reason for it all, for my existence. . . ." He kissed beneath her hand. "This beautiful Loinine . . ." He buried his face. ". . . the courage she has given me. . . ."

Imhor was there, thank God. Joshua had blindly stumbled down a maze of corridors and somehow found the Milliginian heavily pushing against a foreboding steel door. Joshua reached Imhor's side and smiled triumphantly. Imhor took no notice. Joshua thought, "I just won the greatest battle of my life and the bastard doesn't even shake my hand."

"Lend a hand," Imhor rattled, still struggling with the door.

"I just decided to put the salvation of mankind above my own needs, a thing of great courage, of greater courage even, because in order to do so I had to leave behind my Loinine, my woman, the very inspiration for that courage, and now the blue son of a bitch won't even stop to compose even just a shitty little ballad about it."

At last the door flew open and Joshua half fell into the lab. In horror, he turned back to Imhor. From somewhere in his scrambled mind Joshua had a flash of a comic strip black man wearing a brightly checkered, heavily padded sports coat and a wide-brimmed porkpie hat and twirling a gold keychain. "Heeeey, Baabeeee, how you like my new auto-*mo*-bile?" Imhor stood just outside the room; Joshua stood just inside it. Outside, Joshua saw the worn-out '57 Caddy; inside, he saw the spare parts: human heads and torsos and limbs, human hearts and brains and bowels, all floating in a purple liquid like toy boats in glass vats (ten feet square) with names printed along one side—and his, Joshua Chaplin —at the bottom.

"You're scheduled to be dissected tomorrow."

"Why?" asked Joshua, barely finding his voice.

"Transplants. We can't tolerate the electricity in your atmosphere. Our bodies break down. Human organs keep us going a while longer. We need you and that colony of yours for the strength to return home."

And that was it. No further explanation, no apology. Not even embarrassment. Joshua forced himself to look again. A slight vibration caused one of the heads to bob and turn in his direction. Joshua rocked back on his heels. "Wait a minute, isn't that Herman what's-his-face from my old neighborhood? No, no, I must be going nuts, he was bigger, much bigger. Wait another minute, what am I talking about, what am I talking about? I *am* going nuts!" Joshua again recoiled. "What am I doing here, what am I doing aboard this ship, what am I doing aboard this life? I don't belong here. I don't belong here," he repeated aloud.

"That's just what I've been trying to tell you."

For the first time in several minutes, Joshua became aware of Imhor at his side. "If he's trying to help me

escape, then why does he look like the others—the
monsters, the vampires, who put Herman's head in
there? My God, I've thrown my lot in with a ghoul who
isn't even human!'' Then he had another thought. It is
curious how the order of things can change in their
importance. In his concern over being parted from
Loinine, it had never occurred to him to ask, until now.
"By the way," he inquired, "why are you helping me
to escape?"

"I have my reasons."

"I don't trust you."

Imhor grew nervous. He couldn't risk a last-second
hitch. What if some early-rising Milliginian should come
upon him while he was out here arguing with the human? Not only would his plans go awry but he might
even face some kind of punishment. They might, for
example, order him to remain on dreaded Earth! With
his remaining strength he marshalled his concentration
and focused in on a plausible story.

"Well?" demanded Joshua.

"Because. . . ."

"Because what?"

"Just because. . . ."

"Just because what?"

"Just because . . . because." Imhor released his breath
and looked hopefully at the human. If this explanation
didn't work he was in real trouble. Already he could
feel his strength wrinkle, turn yellow and curl at the
edges.

"*Not-good-enough*. NOT GOOD ENOUGH!!" Joshua
folded his arms and firmly planted his feet. It was
obvious he did not intend to move until he received a
more satisfactory answer.

This time the pain started in Imhor's feet. It fit over
his calves as tightly as stretch socks and threatened to

envelop his body as completely as winter underwear. He wasn't sure he could stand up much longer. He decided to get it over with and tell the truth.

"An electric storm is coming here . . . it will arrive in three days. It's a small trick to harness that electricity and create a high-energy field. I need to get the entire crew outside the ship and into that field. To accomplish that I must have a lure. The one thing they will come out for is humans, enough humans to make the prospect attractive. Only in this way can we prevent them from returning home with the news that they've found a way to survive on Earth. If they do that, you realize others will come back here in their place and finish off the rest of you."

Joshua remembered the five-time daily visits from the other Milliginians with their burning eyes and saliva-spun lips.

"The electricity level will not harm your people. Also, machine weapons destroy tissue so they probably will try to overpower you by hand. It will take me twelve minutes to funnel the atmospheric currents. In that short time only one or two of your people at most might have to . . . succumb. A small sacrifice to save an entire race. You must bring this message to your colony and have them return here to bait the trap."

Joshua had been so involved in the contents of Imhor's explanation that he totally missed the three subtle changes in inflection and pitch that accompanied the progress of the story. The fact is that the alien could never have gotten through so long-winded a dissertation without the assistance of his other voices.

Joshua was still playing back what he had just heard. Finally, he reached a decision.

"I don't think you answered the question."

A string of double-edged razor blades was being shuttled in through one ear of Imhor's head and out the other as he fought to remain conscious.

"I did, I did."

"No. *Why* are you willing to help us? Why are you willing to kill your own people?"

"My business."

"No."

"My business, my business, my business!!!"

"No, no, damn it, no! You son of a bitch prick bastard, *no*. I saw what was in those vats—and I want to know why." Joshua wasn't making too much sense himself but he had never been so overcome by rage and horror. He hadn't been given a say when a handful of these dying creatures had murdered millions upon millions of his people and now, when this diseased, leaky sack of splayed marbles was going to murder the murderers, he still wasn't supposed to have a say. For a moment there as he protested on behalf of all those who had been turned to white dust, he really was God's son on Earth.

"Come on, you shit, you motherfucker, tell me!"

"I don't have to, I don't have to," shrieked Imhor, "and besides, you'll bring them down on us with all that shrieking."

"God damn it, God damn it, I'll take them all on right here. I don't want you to sing songs about me. I've got *two* legs and a big ass and I never made anyone laugh on purpose in my entire life. But God damn it, I saw what I saw in there. You aren't going to make me into *a* shoulder, *a* neck, *a* ball. I'll go down fighting and I won't go down until there's not enough left of me to make even *a chopped* liver." Joshua was working himself up into a fine hysteria and found it positively exhilarating. (Even the boy on the roof stopped, stooped, picked up the metal clothes-line pole and turned on his pursuers.)

Imhor watched the fire in Joshua's eyes. He was envious of his indignation, of the fact that he stood for something. The Earthling had felt the degradation of the vats no more strongly than he did, but whereas he had only experienced repulsion, the human had become angry—fighting mad. Faced with the unfavorable comparison, Imhor now desperately grappled for a self-righteous thought of his own.

"Maybe in destroying all of my kind I am purging myself of this debasement. Maybe in this way I am standing up against the invasion and the incubator and the lab. Maybe in my own way I am lifting my voice and crying forth for all to hear: THEY MUST BE PUNISHED FOR MAKING ME COME HERE!" That's not what Imhor meant to think or say out loud but the pain took him from his blind side and that's what came out. Imhor cringed as Joshua turned toward him. "Contempt? Contempt from this human, from this bleached-out primitive?" Against his will Imhor lifted his eyes and looked into Joshua's face and saw something—something even worse than contempt. "Let them have him, let them skin him, let them flush away the stringy parts. We'll all die right here on stinking Earth. I don't care anymore. How dare he, HOW DARE HE!"

Joshua, who a moment before had decided that the Milliginians were beyond human feelings, had just heard Imhor's childlike wail. Turning to him, he expressed with his eyes what the alien had accurately read there—not contempt but pity. Imhor tried to lunge at the human but the effort was so weak that Joshua thought that the other, on the verge of passing out, had reached out to him for support. Joshua lowered him to the floor and started to loosen his tunic. Imhor slapped his hands away peevishly.

"Will you not understand?"

"What?"

"I hate you," Imhor wanted to say, but knew it would come out girlish and ineffectual. Then what? What epithet, what villification, what calumny would impeach the character of this condescending albino with his super-ordinate attitudes?

"You . . . you . . . you . . ."

"Yes, yes." Joshua thought that the creature was about to expire and leaned closer for some rare pearl.

"You . . . you . . . you . . ."

"Yes? Yes? Yes?"

"You . . . you . . . you . . . *masturbator!* Imhor heard himself accuse Joshua and, reacting as if to a self-administered cathartic, leaped to his feet, relieved and revived. Joshua, on the other hand, as if hearing again the gurgling of the gaggle of toilets from all the Saturday evenings of his lonely adolescence, reacted to the accusation with a guilty flush.

"Not me . . . not me!"

"Oh yes, YOU, you MASTURBATOR, you SELF-MANIPULATOR, you AUTO-EROTIC, you . . . you . . . PLAYER-WITH-YOURSELFER!!!"

"What? What are you talking about?" ("The last stages of Milliginian sickness: the brain tissue is degenerating," Joshua hoped.)

"I'm not crazy," Imhor screamed, "you are. Where is your beautiful Loinine?" Imhor singsonged. "Where is she? Why is her body so beautiful, so perfect, when all the rest of us like me are so disgusting to look at?"

Joshua stood openmouthed. He knew he was about to hear something terrible, something true, something that would hurt him, and the fear of that hurt held a death grip on his larynx. (The boy on the roof wavered. The size of the enemy force was far greater than he had imagined. His grip on the metal pole began to loosen.)

"Well, well?"

"I don't know." (The gang descended.)

"Because she doesn't exist. There was no one in there with you. There is no Loinine. We helped you to imagine her, just as we did with the other humans—to keep you quiet and happy. We can do that, you know, with our machines. We can obscure reality because we are more advanced than you, because we are superior to you!"

("Hello, my darling son"—"Wake up, Joshua"—"Then daddy isn't here after all. He's still away?" "No, Joshua, daddy is dead, he died in the night. The telegram came while you slept.")

"All those wonderful sensations you felt, all that loving—you did it to yourself, by yourself, with your own hands."

"I don't . . . believe it . . ." (The boy on the roof suddenly realized how defenseless, how hopelessly alone he was.)

". . . I . . . don't . . . I . . . don't. . . ." (The boy turned and raced to the roof's edge.)

"I'VE GOT TO GET OUT OF HERE, I'VE GOT TO GET OUT OF HERE!!"

"Wait, wait for me," called Imhor, trying to keep up with the out-of-control human racing insanely down the corridor.

FIFTEEN

"THE new middleweight 'champeen' of the world," the announcer bellowed and the crowd responded accordingly. Sam jogged in place with his right hand raised high in victory. His admirers surged through the ropes and hoisted him to their shoulders. For an eternity of seconds he stood above the crowd at the top of a high mountain. Sure of their firm support, he let himself relax in their arms. His head fell back and he caught sight of the arena ceiling. An enormous crack along one of the supporting beams appeared and spread like a lighted fuse. In a moment, the roof would collapse and bury them all. He tried to warn them, but couldn't make himself heard above the din. He tried to wrestle free but their embrace tightened with every frenzied effort. Too late, too late, the ring buckled as everything started to cave in. He felt himself falling, falling down from his mountain, and at last felt real pain as his body smashed to the ground.

John stood above him, fists clenched and trembling.

"Next time I ask you something, you answer me, hear? *Hear?*"

Samatoba swept together the pieces of himself and attacked. Battling for the resurrection of his fantasies, he set his teeth for mortal combat. John, slow and clumsy in his prime, had not improved with disuse, but exhilarated with the success of the initial engagement, he charged swiftly into murderous battle. The death of one or the other was avoided only by the fast thinking of Mobawamba who, slashing at both with a branch, parted them long enough to propose that the issue be settled in a ring with gloves in the manner of their profession.

Thus a simple lapse in communication on a sweltering day in an otherwise good time provided the circumstances for the final defeat of the tribe.

The same industry and enthusiasm that had been recently applied to building new dwellings was now directed toward fashioning a boxing arena. A quarter-ton of mud baked dry in the sun was packed down over a twenty-foot square area leveled of brush and trees. Corner posts hewn from saplings were shaped to match and hammered into place while ropes laboriously woven from vines were stretched and strung around the perimeter.

After the recent storm had abated and Mobawamba had abdicated, the members of the tribe had remained frozen before the dying day weighing the alternatives to dying with it. At last they found the courage to do battle with the future when they remembered that golden past during which they had stood toe to toe and slugged it out with human opponents no less formidable in their time-dimmed eyes than was the challenge of 'tomorrow'. The project of the boxing match was an updating of all their memories and a further reinforcement for their thriving will.

It was understandable, then, that everyone partici-
pated in the week-long training sessions as if they themselves were going to step through the ropes on the
culminating day. Raymon and Damon acted as handlers
but they slept apart and watched their diets and were up
early. Arnoldumbo was the referee but he did wind
sprints twice daily and calisthenics every evening.
Mobawamba was the timekeeper but he parried and
feinted and shadowboxed for much of each morning.
Consequently, when the day finally arrived and Sam and
John put on their beaverskin gloves, they did so less as
individuals and more as probasic extensions of the con-
gregate tribal body. The tight-lipped, tight-eyed concern
on that fateful morning was not so much who might win
or lose but how well the contest would be fought. A
good bout reflected back on the tribe as an affidavit of
worth; a poorly fought match would open to question
their memories as valiant gladiators and challenge the
source material for their self-esteem (the same source
material, incidentally, from which they had drawn the
courage to build the future).

All in all it looked like a good bet.

The odds were certainly on their side.

The fight was a disaster anyway.

From start to finish, only a dozen punches missed
their mark. Unfortunately, from start to finish, only half
again that many were ever thrown. By the fifth round,
John had thrown up over three different cornerposts and
could do little else but wait stolidly for Samatoba to
come within lunging range. By the fourth round, Samatoba
had misplaced the name of his adversary and conducted
his fight by jabbing and parrying and right-crossing near
the center of the ring . . . alone.

Curiously, one of the twin brothers broke the silence
at last and screamed: "For the love of Christ, fight!

Fight, damn you, fight! Kill each other, kill each other!''
pleaded Raymon, suddenly remembering that he had
been a bad fighter and a coward in the ring and remembering, too, that he was a homosexual and altogether a
thing of ridicule and that the insulation of his brother's
love had only succeeded in suppressing the news. "Fuck
you, you bitch," he screamed again. It was difficult to
ascertain whether he was jargoning as a queer or lashing
out at the progenitor of all his woes.

"Bitch, bitch," he repeated, injecting himself with a
full vial of insulin. "Bitch," he tried again, forgetting
perhaps and injecting himself a second time from the
very last insulin capsule in the world. "Bitch," he
trembled once more as he broke into a cold sweat and
his arms and legs took leave of his body and danced
insanely across the packed earth. "Bitch," he gagged
one last time as he swallowed his tongue and suddenly
lay still. "My brother is dead," wept Damon, looking
up.

As fate would have it, it was Mobawamba who was
standing before him. "My brother is dead," he said,
looking into Mobawamba's eyes.

"It was because of the fight," said Celestealulu (still
trying to see the red cape and the blue uniform and the
yellow lightning bolt).

"Yeah, who thought up having this fight anyway?"
said Pearl spitefully (as her gold tooth tarnished in the
sun).

"It's not my fault," came the strangled reply from
Mobawamba (as Akut, the great ape, tearfully dropped
leaves on the jungle lord's grave).

"It wasn't my fault . . . ('Hi Mo'/'Hey, remember
the time I. . . .'/'Oh yeah, that' / 'That wasn't my fault,
was it?' / 'Sure it was.' / 'But it was war' /'It was
murder man, for once in your life face up to it.' / 'Are

you sure?' / 'I was there, wasn't I?') It wasn't my fault, it wasn't,'' and now he was shaking Celestealulu hard by the shoulders.

"Leave her alone, you punk," cried Samatoba, dropping out of the air and the ring to save Celeste from all the 'screamin' an' the bugs'. "You can't make a fool out of me," he said, swinging wildly and losing his balance and stumbling against Mo as they both fell to the earth and landed hard. "I am the leader now," said John, standing over the prostrate forms on the ground. "I am what counts now, and what counts is what I say."

Morris saw no reason to get up ever again and Sam could not bear to rise and see, still, the look of love in Celeste's eyes. Everyone else turned to John . . . and waited.

"I'll show them," he thought, trying to think of a way to show them. "I'll show them who I am."

"I am the leader, that's who," he clarified.

Everyone stared at John and waited.

"I am the leader and the leader says. . . ."

"You are nothing," whispered rotting twigs.

"And the leader says. . . ."

"You are nothing," whispered wormy bark.

"And the leader says . . . and the leader says . . . we will build a fire and burn all the dead wood around here."

"A fire!" said Pearl, reaching with tweaking fingers for John's ear. "On a hot sweltering day like this?"

"Yes, damn it," he cursed, shoving her from him so that she tripped and fell. "A fire. Arnoldumbo, get us firewood."

Arnold didn't understand the excitement he felt, didn't understand why he scampered off so quickly to complete the task, didn't yet realize why he was laughing to himself.

"Now light it, light the God damn fire and let it burn and burn." John stood solidly before the blaze even after everyone had edged far back. "I'll show you, I'll show you," he said, talking more to the fire than to the others.

The fire grew more intense but John did not budge. He continued staring into the face of it even after his eyes welled with tears and his lungs choked with smoke because he simply didn't know what else to do. "I know why I am!" he said, gasping for air and collapsing in a heap.

Arnold rushed to his side and dragged him safely away. Then Arnold turned back to the group. "I am the King," he called, standing on his toes to look over the flames. "Long live the King," he whispered to himself, understanding now what before he had only suspected— that he would in short order succeed John to the throne.

"The king of what?" said Louella simply, looking around at all the fallen bodies.

"Let's find another place," said Celeste.

"Why not?" said Louella.

"Glicki," said Maytag.

Slowly they rose and slowly, like toys on a string dragged behind by a small child, they followed their women and again vanished into the swamp.

Raymon was buried in a shallow grave.

SIXTEEN

THE home of the woolly Venusians ("the touch of whose finger-like tentacles," Buck once wrote, "resulted in the mirror image reorientation of a human being aufgaba") still twinkled modestly in the sky as Alice's fist struck the soft earth. "This secret meeting is hereby convened," he whispered an octave above comfortable hearing. "All those present raise their hands."

The first convention of the Unfriendly Twelve was in session. The chairman shuffled his notes nervously.

"I know how these things work," he insisted, "today chastisement, tomorrow second-class citizenship, and the day after, kangaroo courts and sudden mysterious disappearances. The day after that," he reasoned with Orwellian clarity, "the ledger is revised and the record of our existence is lost to history."

As one, the Unfriendly Twelve sucked its breath and bit its lower lip. Rosy-fingered dawn began to display her cuticles; Venus showed less brightly. Identifiable faces began to appear from the small group of shadowy figures.

"What to do, what to do," they implored, huddling close. Buck was prepared. "How," he asked, showing off his writing skill just a little, "were the Super Phi on the planet Phi-Delta Six in the quadrant Epsilon Gamma Two in the galaxy Beta Beta Beta able to overthrow the Sub-Phi with their superior arsenal of Lunge guns?"

Fortunately, no one knew. "By stealing the sarcophagus of the legendary Boris Taos in whose name all evil by the Sub-Phi was committed. Once the corpse of Boris Taos was removed, the Norm-Phi were able to see the Sub-Phi for what they were and quickly rallied to the side of the Super-Phi and together subdued the Sub-Phi without a single gun being lunged!"

"So?" The question hung heavily in the air alongside the pall.

"So, just as on Phi-Delta Six, we must capture the one symbol the state relies upon to justify all its dastardly deeds. Only in this way can we destroy the Bureau and return true private enterprise to our beloved village. Our target, gentlemen, is Isobel."

Buck had used the time since his fall from grace to lick his wounds and collect his wits. Unfortunately, as sometimes happens after severe psychological trauma, some of his wits were collected in a colander and not all of his wounds had healed properly. In effect, he had confusedly concluded that if he was to learn from the events succeeding his failure with Isobel, he must achieve a position that was beyond the indignities of criticism; he must become President of the United States. It wasn't so much the dizzy heights to which he aspired that suggested an incomplete convalescence as it was the qualities he ascribed to the office itself. It therefore followed that the light burning in Buck's eyes when he at last emerged from his tent was as much the result of a high fever as it was a new determination.

Thus it was understandable that when the eleven limp lotharios left Buck's early morning conclave, they did so still unconvinced that stealing Isobel was an entirely sound idea. Later that afternoon they had a change of heart.

No one, it seemed, had been paying any attention to Isobel, at least not since she had kicked the last suitor from her boudoir. The lay of the land being who and what it was, the responsibility for the failure of "Operation Impregnation" was of course officially deposited at the door of the twelve woeful wooers. Nevertheless, and despite itself, the community unconsciously did aim a certain measure of its disappointment in the direction of the petulant pubescent. The message finally got through to Isobel when she realized that even in the absence of hulking Titheria, the fun had gone out of her three o'clock brutality bulletins. The ground still trembled where she rumbled and great rents in the sky still appeared near where she ranted, but the crowd reaction of her pre-adolescent salad days was missing; no one even *pretended* to be frightened anymore.

Thus on the afternoon following the morning of Buck's clandestine convention, Isobel made an altogether different kind of announcement. "For the good of the human race I have decided to do 'IT'. Starting tomorrow I will interview everyone in the camp until I find 'Mr. Right'." Isobel, of course, had no intention of doing 'IT', but she figured what with holidays, postponements, and call-backs she could continue to stall indefinitely. At the moment, however, a great cheer went up and Hank Hank's booming basso could be heard initiating the charge for the tents.

"Wait!" cried Titheria, planting herself directly in the line of fire. "As the only female ever to be second in command of the Commission for Order, Protection and Selection, I must warn the twelve censored volunteers that it might be against the law for them to participate in a community private enterprise orgy."

"On what grounds?" yelled one of the dozen.

"On the grounds that you have been punished for disobeying the law and this might be part of your penalty."

"Who says?" demanded another of the twelve.

"That's up to the Bureau but until they meet and decide, I feel it's my duty to warn you."

The Actor-Robot wanted to intervene. He hadn't meant for the Bureau edict to be carried so far. On the other hand, without the weight of an 'official' Bureau directive, which required calling a meeting, he felt unprepared for a confrontation. He decided to remain silent.

"Well, then, have the representative convene a Bureau meeting right now," suggested one of the Unfriendlies.

"Not now, not now," boomed Hank, panting hard. "Now we must have the orgy."

"Well, then," said another spokesman for the rejected roués, "since everything is private in New Hope Settlement including the orgy, in the privacy of our tents we intend to be part of it."

A second layer of hair began to grow on Titheria's arms. "I'm warning you," she growled, "this is a *private*, private enterprise orgy and you're not invited."

"It's our private business when and where we perform our business," protested another.

"As long as it doesn't interfere with the settlement

business of privacy,'' chattered Titheria as her knuckles scraped the ground.

"How can our private business interfere with settlement business if we are carrying out the settlement business of being private?" The hair turned to fur. "It is the difference between public private and private private," shot back the law enforcer. "What you do privately is private unless it's publicly private; when it's privately publicly private as in the present case and you're not invited, then any effort on your part to join in is an infraction of the laws of privacy."

"It is an infraction of the laws of privacy for you to interfere with our privacy and . . . ," continued another of the rebuffed rakes looking around at the large crowd, ". . . in public yet."

"The public be damned," cried Hank, changing the subject. "Onward and *upward*," he bellowed, and with much jostling and bumping, everyone, including the Unfriendly Twelve, raced for their tents.

Titheria stopped them once more. "Ok, ok," she shouted after them, "but when the account of this orgy is written into the history of New Hope Settlement, the Unfriendly Twelve will not be included!"

In another instant everybody had disappeared into his tent.

As it turned out, Titheria had won the battle after all. Once her parting exhortation had sunk in, not one of the dour dozen had the heart for reveling. Buck Alice's dire warning about the ledger being revised and the record of their existence being lost came back to them like a ricocheting bullet that strikes deep into the gut.

The following afternoon Isobel was kidnapped.

"Monsters, monsters," she screamed as usual. The crowd was even bigger than she anticipated. "Horrible pus-filled monsters," she amplified. "I just saw them."

"Oh my goodness, oh my goodness" came the obedient reply from the now tractable troupe. "Where? Where?" asked a few select others disregarding the recommended script.

"Huh?" said Isobel, caught off base.

"Show us, show us," said the 'Where? Where's?.'

"Huh?" said Isobel's mouth, disappearing into the folds of her cheeks.

"Quick, quick, show us the monsters, show us the monsters." In another moment they had her by the elbows and were whisking her off into the surrounding swamp. The others in the crowd, although surprised by the unusual turn of events, decided to mind their own business.

"Show us, show us," continued her enthusiastic supporters, continuing to encourage her.

It didn't take much for the child to get caught up in her own ghoulish story. "This way, this way," she shouted, racing ahead. "This way to the pus-filled monsters."

Three hours elapsed and Isobel had not returned. Since Titheria had been ordered from the girl's side, Robbie appointed Gardner, the other member of the commission, to the task of tracking her down. Dusk was settling over the jungle when he started out and before long he was making his way in the dark. As always happens at least once, a pit of quicksand loomed in his path. With some last flickering thoughts about aphids and soil reclamation, Gardner the gardner disappeared forever.

Three hours more elapsed. At last Robbie ran to the Actor-Robot with the strange story of the double disappearance. As evidenced by the clank of several screws that immediately worked themselves loose and were rolling around inside his head, the Actor-Robot observed to himself that things were getting out of hand.

Without quite being sure how it happened, he was a few seconds later standing in the center of the compound calling everybody out of the tents for a town meeting. The stragglers had barely slipped from between the sheets when he commenced in full voice to issue a blanket indictment. On behalf of the Bureau he denounced Gardner (despite Titheria's objections) for abducting or murdering Isobel, denounced unknown but suspected criminals for abducting or killing Gardner, and/or denounced unknown but suspected subversives for abducting or killing Isobel. Before the eyewitnesses who had earlier seen her romp off into the woods could volunteer any information, Buck Alice stepped forward as emissary for a new organization called the "Guardians of the Unfriendly Twelve." He revealed that Isobel was now in its possession safe and unharmed and denounced the Bureau for the vicious tactic of laying the blame elsewhere when it was obviously Robbie, an already convicted murderer, who had done in the vanished Gardner for permitting Isobel to be liberated.

Slowly Titheria turned and looked at Robbie.

Buck Alice stated further that until such time as sanity was restored to New Hope Settlement and all twelve of Isobel's "volunteers" were completely vindicated, Isobel would not be returned to the colony. "I will consult with the Bureau," violently vibrated the Actor-Robot, turning on his castors and rumbling off.

Sensing victory close at hand, the Actor-Robot's retreat was met with a great cheer from Buck and his cohorts.

"Actor-Robots never panic," said the Actor-Robot to himself later that night, trying to replug his hopelessly tangled cables. "They do, however, become a little bit hysterical once in a while."

Robbie was also up late that night. He kept hearing, he thought, a crashing in the bush outside his tent.

"I have been instructed to issue the following proclamation," said the Bureau spokesman the following morning. "The Guardians of the Unfriendly Twelve is an illegal gang of mobsters and must return Isobel to the settlement at once."

Buck Alice smirked. If that was all Robbie and the Bureau could come up with, the take-over of New Hope was going to be duck soup. He stepped forward confidently. "The Guardians declare that the use of the words 'gang of mobsters' is a clever but thinly disguised paraphrasing of the commie invective, 'a capitalist mob of gangsters,' and cautions that New Hope Settlement may now be under siege by fifth columnists and saboteurs masquerading as the official government."

The insulation melted from one of the relays in the Actor-Robot's brain and sparks began to light up his head. The word 'KILL' flashed repeatedly before him. "You're no father of mine," he suddenly screamed, grasping for Buck's absent neck but locking on only to his chin.

"Father?" mused the science fiction writer, rubbing his jaw after being liberated from the Actor-Robot's hands. "What the hell did he mean by that?"

Robbie in the meantime had begun to develop the same kind of nervous ticks that Isobel had earlier exhibited.

The Actor-Robot had momentarily fallen victim to a decreased state of non-panic and almost spoiled his own plan. Fortunately, however, the ex-Jewish mother remembered her assignment and now leapt forward with her news.

"Guess what?"

"What?" came the well-rehearsed reply from the quickly recovered metal man.

"All of a sudden, just like that, I noticed it and I didn't cut myself or sit on a tack or anything."

"You mean . . . ?"

"Sure, all of a sudden just like that I can have babies."

"Hurrah," said everyone, hardly believing their ears.

"We must all celebrate," said the Actor-Robot, "that is, of course, all but the previously named aforementioned felons."

"Who says?" bullied six of the 'twelvers' on the move.

"You can't stop us," added another half dozen close behind.

"Up hers!" came the rallying cry from Hank Hank as the rest of the colony entered the race for the tents.

In the hope of pumping some life into the community, the town square was soon as quiet as a morgue. Buck Alice, however, suspected a trick.

"With no one around like this, someone may try to steal Isobel back." Stealthily he slipped out the back end of his tent and scampered off into the swamp. Too bad for his cause that he only suspected half the trick. The Actor-Robot, on the other hand, had guessed one hundred percent correctly. He figured that the mateless Buck would smell a rat and run off to guard his captive. The duty of trailing him to the lair was assigned to Major Hank. (He had been a Boy Scout long before he had been a soldier and consequently was considered eminently qualified.) Sacrificing his 'undercover' duties on this one occasion, Hank was soon in hot pursuit of Buck.

Buck Alice breathed a sigh of relief. Isobel was still safely tied up inside the recently constructed barricade. He had no sooner checked her bindings, however, when Hank came crashing through the brush.

"In the name of all that is decent and holy, I demand in the name of God and Country that you give us back our little mother in the name of what is only right."

"Come another step closer (381-7tb-0) and I'll blast you (7y-2wd-xa)," replied Buck, hiding one hand behind his back.

"With what?" scoffed the retired soldier, stopping all the same.

"I have a high (6t-8i-kqc2) powered weapon behind my back."

"Let me see."

"It's a secret device and (m7-620h-f-14) no one who sees it (a-b-c) may live. If I show (8-jjkj5) it to you I'll have (3w4e5r) to kill you as well."

A long pause followed during which the old war horse mulled over several tales of his own to explain the failure of the mission to the Actor-Robot. Misjudging the silence, Buck decided he had better elaborate on his story. Taking advantage of the lapse, he whipped out some paper with his free hand and made some clinching notes.

"I can tell you this much . . . ," he read, ". . . this secret weapon, with its hair-pin trigger, that I have in my possession is a 'shock' gun. It causes the victim to experience the physiological reactions that accompany sudden death, such as kidney, bowel and gonadal evacuations, to a heightened degree. You will therefore and in effect stew in your own juices as you die and that doesn't even include all the bleeding you will do."

Still no comment from Hank.

". . . And it is called an Electrosowaspitup."

"Charge," screamed Hank suddenly coming to life, bowling Buck over and releasing Isobel from her shackles.

"God Bless America!" he sang out with Isobel firmly cradled under his arm in a crotch hold. "As soon as I heard the foreign-sounding name of that weapon," he said, clucking to himself, "I figured that the odds were at least two to one the thing would misfire."

Later that day the Actor-Robot explained to an assembly of New Hopers the particulars of the plan that returned Isobel to their midst. For her part in the proceedings the still (alas) sterile ex-Jewish mother was embraced warmly and rewarded with a 'Green Certificate of Lesser Merit'. As for the Unfriendly Twelve, the Bureau saw no alternative other than to banish them forever from New Hope. With Buck in the lead, the besieged bevy packed up their belongings and their wives and moved their tents a hundred and fifty yards up the street to a position just outside the established camp grounds.

"We shall not rest," Buck called back, waving his note paper, "until Isobel is again in our possession."

Shortly thereafter, the standard of a new community rose in the swamp. Still frail, still wobbly, but all the same, filled with the enthusiasm and courage that fortify faint beginnings and one day turn them into mighty endings, the birth of *Newer* Hope Settlement had come to pass.

It was about this time that Robbie started walking backwards a lot.

The series of raids and counter-raids that took place between New Hope and Newer Hope was aimed at securing total rights to Isobel and her reproductive system. The fear in New Hope, quite naturally, was that

Isobel might be raped by the rabble rousers to the north before she could be screwed by the good guys in the south. During the first week alone she was kidnapped and rescued back nine times. Not only were the New Hopers fearful for the child's chastity while she was in the hands of the marauders, but they were frustrated in equal part by Isobel's refusal to do anything but interview prospective beaus when safely in the hands of the defenders. Tension over the matter so distorted the proceedings that before long the girl was being ushered directly from the battleground of her latest successful rescue into the interview tent in the hope that she would make a choice and slip into the mating bed before the next abduction occurred.

"Tell me something about yourself," she'd begin, still trying to catch her breath. "What do you think of angelfish? What's your best color and what is the ickiest thing that's ever happened to you? Do you like rock and roll and what do you think monster pus tastes like? What's your favorite food and was your little brother a brat? How tall are you and how big are you? Do you believe in love at first sight and do you like dogs or cats better? What's the most unforgettable thing that's ever happened to you and in a scoring system from one to ten, how badly do you want to do 'IT' with me? What do you look for first in a girl and what do you think of angelfish?"

On the bleak side, it appeared that Isobel could go on asking questions forever; on the bright side, however, it started to look as if the outnumbered forces of Newer Hope Settlement could not. It was taking them longer and longer to recover from the stick-wielding and rock-throwing exchanges of each battle. Talk of giving up even began creeping into the conversation of some "Unfriendlies" of lesser character.

Fate, however, has a way of intervening on such occasions and did so admirably on this one. Just as New Hope was preparing for its first-ever act of aggression against Newer Hope with the objective of leveling it and chasing its inhabitants off into the jungle forever, Just Call Me Robbie started screaming: "Leave me alone, leave me alone, LEAVE ME ALONE!" As it had been with Isobel, the subject of his cajoling-threatening-imploring cry was Titheria.

Buck Alice's accusation involving Robbie in Gardner's disappearance had not been lost on the hirsute hominid and the conviction of his guilt had grown stronger with each passing day. "After all," she concluded with fur-brained reasoning, "how different, really, was Gardner with his flowers from Claude with his invisible staircase?" Apparently not very much for as Robbie had suspected, Titheria was at the very moment about to exact vengeance and murder him.

"LEAVEMEALONE!" he screamed again, backing away as Titheria crawled toward him on all fours. Already partially paralyzed by fear, he was further incapacitated by a mind-blocking confusion stemming from her hands and knees approach. She *had* to know that he knew she was there, just five feet away in an unobstructed clearing with nothing between them but his perspiration, and he found it extremely unnerving that she would still try to sneak up on him under such circumstances.

"Help, Help!" he cried, as everyone once again poured from their tents.

"I did it, I admit it, I did it. I killed Claude!"

This didn't seem to come as a surprise to anyone since each had long ago accepted Buck's planted shovel as conclusive evidence of guilt. What's more, it was old news. They started to return to their bunks.

Terrified of being left alone with the throwback, Robbie continued: "He was working on a new pantomime . . . about me. He found my badge, yes, my badge, and discovered I was a private detective. Yes, a private detective. You didn't know that about me, did you?"

They had to admit that he was right there. They turned to him with renewed interest.

"I saw him rehearsing the way I walk and pretending to carry a magnifying glass. I was afraid someone would guess that I made my living snooping on people, interfering with their private affairs, making a mockery of the beloved private enterprise system. I was afraid someone would find out and I would be banished from the settlement."

"And you killed Gardner, too," roared Titheria, springing on him.

"No, no, not Gardner," protested Robbie, kicking Titheria in the throat and running pell-mell for Newer Hope Settlement.

"I'm sorry," he called back. "I'm sorry it had to end this way."

Buck Alice had heard everything from his location in the new neighborhood and was, of course, dumbfounded. He had pinned Claude's murder on Robbie only as a means of stopping his evil plans for power and now, as it turned out, he *was* the murderer but nothing more.

"Then who," asked Buck to himself for the first time, "really is the power behind the throne?" He hardly had a chance to examine the possibilities. "Sanctuary, sanctuary," Robbie gasped, collapsing at Buck's feet.

During the night, nineteen pairs of Pathfinders who remembered the good things about Robbie—his classes in Suppressing Cries of Agony and his devotion and loyalty to the settlement—packed up their tents and followed Robbie into Newer Hope Settlement. Thus on the very eve of Newer Hope's demise, a new balance of power was struck and the two communities faced each other on more equal terms.

After learning of the defections, the Actor-Robot proceeded to make the only adjustment he felt reasonable under the circumstances. While the remaining villagers crowded around the town square and somberly watched, an enormous stake was driven deep into the earth. While the remaining villagers gravely nodded, Isobel was dragged to the spot and chained to the post. While the remaining villagers stood around, several of them were picked to perform sentry duty and watch her on a rotating twelve-hour-a-day basis. The Actor-Robot was making sure that even a reinforced Newer Hope army would not easily steal the child again. The interviews were carried on as usual.

The stalemate was finally broken on the day that the bush parted and the tribe stepped out of the surrounding bog.

Actually, it looked more like the bog had stepped out of itself. To perceive any resemblance between the creatures who now appeared and the ex-pug, ex-bookie runners, ex-gang, ex-tribe, required an extraordinary perceptivity. It was as if the jungle had sensed that these strange wanderers had given up hope and rushed in to take advantage of their condition. From the look of them, it appeared that its goal was more than just their destruction; from the look of them, it appeared that the jungle meant to absorb them and make them part of it. From head to toe they were packed in mud and clay. The first impression to strike was that of a breaded veal cutlet ready for the spit—until, that is, one drew closer and observed that there was vegetation, 'honest-to-Gardner' jungle growth sprouting from the rich soil that covered their bodies. Incredible as it seemed, tropical flowers in hues of violet, magenta and golden orange had cautiously begun to open their petals alongside their arms and chests and even on top of their heads. More incredible still were the insects that constantly swarmed about them and, dear God, the little pink striated worms that had adjusted to a mobile home and could be observed peeking out from between dirt-encased shoulder blades. Most incredible of all was that these garden-variety humans didn't seem to care.

It had rained on the fourth day of their aimless two-week march and the mud from dripping branches and brush and shallow pools had settled on their bodies. After they had some sleep, they told themselves, they would scrape it off with their fingernails and maybe wash their faces in a nearby stream. During the night it had rained again and they had lain awake wondering if the ground under them would become so soft that they would sink beneath the surface and be swallowed up. In their despair the idea began to have some appeal. They discovered on the following morning that although the ground had not parted for them, it had done more than its level best. It had risen up and covered them over. The soft popping sound of a baby's lips parting from the breast accompanied their efforts to rise from Mother Earth. They turned and looked at each other and saw their reflection in each other's mud. Before they could fan their senses into a repulsion that would motivate action, their will flickered and died, extinguished by the suffocating weight of their incrustations. They had at last found an insulation against the pain of living. After that they could even look at each other without turning away.

*　　*　　*

When they materialized in the compound it was, as fate would have it, at the north end. There was a rapping on his tent and Buck's head quickly emerged and followed the pointing finger to the strange group collected at the perimeter of the camp. Just as quickly, his head disappeared again. "They've come, Isobel's monsters have come," he said, trying to hide inside his chest. After several moments he peeked again. The monsters had not moved. Already it seemed one could see root fingers inching from their bodies and tentatively probing the ground for a foothold. Again Buck ducked back in. Frantically, he grabbed for his briefcase, turned it upside down, and for the first time in his life shook out every index card, piece of notepaper and pencil. Like a man who has awakened in the middle of an operation to discover his organs hanging on the outside, he experienced a moment of emptiness as the contents of his case free-fell to the ground. Never mind, never mind, in another second he was on his hands and knees. Nowhere, nowhere in all the galaxy, in all the galaxies, in all the universe, in all the universes, could he find a reference to creatures even remotely similar to the ones hanging around outside. Then suddenly fist hit palm and insight momentarily vanquished pendantry. Amidst an avalanche of numbers and letters the answer and a solution to all his problems came to him simultaneously.

"(H8m-t-5elcc2) human beings! Human beings that look (7j3g66) scary enough to be aliens!" In another second he had dashed from his tent and was racing toward the intruders.

"WELCOME," he cried loud enough for everyone in old New Hope Settlement to hear, "WELCOME, OH GREAT SPACE BEASTS." With much tugging and pushing, he managed to crowd them into his tent and out of sight.

The effect had not been lost on the New Hopers across the way. The creatures looked even more ferocious from their vantage point than they did up close. It seemed reasonable to assume, as many in the older community did, that their fate had been sealed. Either the Newer Hope group would conclude a pact with the intergalactic interlopers and they, the Actor-Robot contingent, would shortly be eaten for dinner, or the rebel colony would fail to reach an agreement with the aliens, and they, Buck's bunch, would be eaten for dinner, and they, the New Hopers, would be eaten for breakfast. Compounding their apprehension was the fact that for three days following the monsters' initial appearance, neither hide nor hair was seen of any Newer Hoper.

Secreted as he was inside his tent, Buck could only guess that his plan was working. The 'ghost town' quiet of the older fellowship, however, was definitely a reassuring sign.

"They don't know what's happening here and they're scared stiff," he told himself. "Another twenty-four hours and they'll be ready to believe anything. Then, at last, the human race again will have a future. Then at last we can start to build a new heritage. Then at last a new patriotism and loyalty will spring forth upon the earth and all men will be equal in the eyes of the law and I can become President." Buck began to glow. All around him the darkness melted away. He felt for his corona. Yes, yes, it was there all right, burning brightly on the gases of his humanitarianism. Soon, very soon, he would step forward and light the way for all men.

"To make it work, all I've got to do now," he said, looking coolly at his nearly catatonic guests, "is to convince this bunch of weirdos."

Buck didn't know who the ex-tribe was or where it
had come from. When he learned with relief that its
members had no desire to scrape off the clay and wash
themselves clean, he also learned with chagrin that neither had they any desire to answer any of his questions.
Sensing that their silence was a personal matter unrelated to the present situation, he held out hope of eventually being accepted by them. On the other hand, time
was of the utmost. He realized that it was a calculated
risk to ask their cooperation before he was assured of
their friendship—"A reversal now might be irreversible," he told himself—but he finally decided that he
had no choice. Although he believed that the Bureau
had by now worked up a good deal of anxiety, he felt a
protracted delay might take the edge off its fear. Then,
too, he wasn't sure how long he could contain his own
people. 'Old town' had seen nothing of the new guard
because Buck had ordered his followers to venture forth
only after dark. Buck knew he trespassed on private
property when he took away self-determination, even
temporarily, and feared that before long he would hear
angry murmurings from his own quarter. Seeing no
alternative, Buck shuffled his index cards and began to
outline his plan to the visitors. He concluded by saying
that he would leave them alone to discuss it among
themselves.

"Listen to your consciences," he said, stepping from
the tent, not knowing from their dead eyes and caked
countenances whether, in fact, they had even been listening to *him*.

Most of them hadn't.

Damon was one. A fearful thing had happened to him
after his brother's death: he lost his personal orientation.
The imposed character of effeminacy in whose skirts he
had pranced these many years turned to tatters and

unraveled at his feet. He was suddenly left exposed and vulnerable, a ganglion of nerve endings without a protective sheath, an incomplete organism throbbing in the cold night air. He didn't know why it happened.

As children, Raymon and Damon turned to each other to find the courage and love with which to battle mother and world. The older they grew, the more insulated that love became, the less willing they were to reach out to others and the more tightly they were drawn to each other. The love became sexual when their bodies matured. They became 'homosexuals' when life demanded they place themselves in the order of things. They became effeminate to strengthen the identification and to shape their self-images. They were happy in their life-style because being so close, each was all the other needed to assuage any doubts. In the last analysis, the whole thing worked for them because they were not so much two different people as twin parts of one person. By the same token, as Damon discovered, in the absence of the reinforcing presence of the one, the other became less than half the man he was originally. Damon stopped being his brother's lover when Raymon died. When that relationship ceased to exist, so did all that had been built upon it, including the labels by which he had learned to identify himself. What was left in the rubble was not even a 'thing', only a 'something'. With a sense of relief, Damon awoke from that rainy night and found himself covered like the others. "For all they know," he told himself, "disguised like this, I could be one of them, one of the mud people."

Damon had guessed that the mud people weren't listening to Buck and so he didn't either.

Sam was also one who wasn't listening. Instead, he was living one of the tortures of hell. His mind had become a conveyor belt. It kept making the same trip in the same direction, looping under and back, and then making the same trip over again. Each time the journey it took was his memory of the fight with John: how he had bobbed and weaved and gracefully slipped off the ropes; how he had jabbed like a riveter's gun and counter-punched in telling combinations; how he had escaped near disaster to finally wing home the blow that sent his adversary crashing to the canvas. It was beautiful, except that always, always just *before* his victory was announced, just *before* the exaltation set in and the cameras popped and the microphones were thrust in his face and the word 'Champion' was whispered in his ear, the fight would begin again and he would parry and dance and jab and counter-punch. . . .

Sam did not know that the earth had grown thick on his body nor that anyone was trying to talk to him.

Celeste was another who hadn't heard. She had become gravely ill from exposure and fatigue and was taxed beyond endurance by thoughts other than those relating to Sam's welfare. She pulled the mud up around her ears to keep out the chill.

Maytag had not been listening either. On her, the filth was a terrible punishment. Even after the others had lost sight of the need to be clean, she had not. She perceived, however, that she could not take care of herself alone and consequently bowed to their superior wisdom for the disposition of her conduct. Vainly, she struggled to understand why they must remain dirty when the only meaningful thing in her life besides Arnold was to be always thoroughly washed. She went along at last, but the sense of her mortification filled her up and left no room for other thoughts and other voices.

Neither had Pearl been listening. Resolutely, she shut her mind to everything outside her frame of reference.

"Beats me what that white boy was talking about," she said, polishing the mud to a high luster.

And neither had Arnold who, earlier, had peeked through the tent flap and saw to the south the meaning for his existence. "This is one secret I ain't telling nobody," he whispered into his cupped hands the whole time Buck had been speaking.

Louella had heard and so had Morris, so the conversation in the tent started with them where they huddled close in a corner.

"I love you, Louella, I really do. I can tell you that now."

"You . . . love . . . me?"

"Yes."

"You love me? You really do?"

"Do you want to know why?"

"Oh dear God, I love you too. But you know that, you've always known that."

"Do you want to know why?"

"Everything is going to be all right now. We'll get out of this somehow, I can feel it. You love me and everything is going to be all right now."

"Do you want to know why?"

"I don't care why. You don't have to tell me. If you're really sure, then it's enough for me."

"I want to tell you. You should know. I . . . once killed a man . . . an enemy soldier . . . when I was in the army. We were in a foxhole and he charged . . ."

"But that was war."

"It was murder."

"It wasn't, it wasn't. You're too hard on yourself, my darling. Is that what you've been carrying with yourself all these years? And it wasn't even your fault— never your fault."

"It was my fault."

"No, no . . ."

"Yes. But at last I have accepted it, at last I can live with it. You must believe that. . . ."

"I think I can understand now. Any death is a murder. Is that what you're saying?"

". . . and now at last I am free of that guilt and do you know why? Do you know why, Louella?"

"Because you've come to realize that in war . . ."

"No. I've already told you it was murder."

"Because . . . because. . . . I don't know."

"Because, my darling Louella, whom I love so dearly. . . ."

"Oh, my darling, I love you too. . . ."

"Because, my darling, I have at last figured it out that I have been sufficiently punished."

". . . Punished?"

"Punished for my sin of murder. The failure of everything that we have done from the beginning has been my fault. The failure of the tribe to make it was my fault. The failure of Raymon's life was my fault and the weight of all those failures is my punishment for murder. This mud, the heaviness of it on my body, is the embodiment of my sin. It is my 'cross' to bear. Every day I feel it growing crustier, harder. Soon it will crack and begin to fall from me. When that happens, it will be like I was new-born, a blank tablet, free from the memory of my crime. I have finally come to understand this. When we awoke after the rain, it started. Slowly, very slowly, a piece of an idea at a time until now—yesterday—at last—the pain in my head stopped and I took a deep breath and understood everything."

A terrible thing happened to Louella at the moment: she backed away. Just a step, not even enough for Morris to notice, but enough for her to realize that she had become frightened and that the man before her was suddenly different. She knew that if she asked the next question, a butcher's cleaver would cut through what was left between them and they would become something even less than strangers. She would never again be able to see him clearly. The little things that had never before mattered would suddenly obscure her vision. She did not even know what his answer would be, but from the tone of his voice—the sound of serenity, and the look in his face—the sense of peace, in this time of devastation and decay and ultimate degeneration—she knew she would no longer be able to see Morris, see Mobawamba; she would see only a black man. She could not help herself. She asked it anyway.

"Everything?"

"The invasion was a judgment. The human race was found wanting and was destroyed. All but a few, all but us, the tribe and these people here. Think, Louella, what does that mean? Why were we kept alive and not the others? Because we are more worthy? No, we are less worthy. Our punishment is greatest of all—to stay alive, to start it all over again, to burn not in hell but on earth. Then why? I will tell you. It is because he who has sinned the greatest and suffered the most knows the greatest pain and consequently the greatest compassion, knows better than the rest the meaning of love, is most qualified to do it right the second time around when the world is young again."

There was a silence, but Louella knew that Morris wasn't finished. She now knew what he was going to say. Only the telling of it was missing, but not for long.

"And of all of us who have sinned and suffered, who among us is the greatest sinner, who among us has suffered the most? It came to me a piece of an idea at a time until now—yesterday—at last I figured it out. I am the one who murdered and I am the one who must lead.

I have not dropped from the sky, Louella, but I didn't start on a street in Detroit either. I am new, fresh-born, clean, without sin, filled only with love and peace."

"Say it!" The words came from her lips like the crack of a whip. Responding as if the lash had cut deep into his flesh, he smiled.

"I am the teacher. I am the son of God."

"Daddy, who am I?"

"A fine boy."

"But who am I?"

"Yourself."

"They won't let me be myself."

"Dance between the raindrops."

"I'm soaked, pop."

"Sit awhile in the sun."

Morris Laverne Tate had at last found his piece of sun.

Louella was wrong—she still loved him. Now at last she did know what he was thinking, where his mind was. How she wished she didn't, but even that didn't matter.

"I don't care, I don't care," she told herself. "He loves me, he said so, and I love him and that is all that is important." The little things had not gotten in the way.

"And, of course," said Morris, that is why we cannot play any part in Buck Alice's plan."

John also had been listening. In the light of past events, it was an extraordinary achievement.

First, there had been the boxing match with Sam. The results of that fight had once more proven to John that he was a fool in this life to seek a better station. All he remembered from the combat was hanging onto the corner ropes and convulsively throwing up down his legs. He recalled that the vomit was not what he had eaten but what he was, part of his insides, and the stink of it spilling down his legs was the memorial to his ignominy.

Then there was the aftermath to the fight and now, still, he could hear in his mind's ear the burning twigs cackle as they crackled.

Then, finally, there was the rain and the mud. From this point on he remembered most clearly. How he had used the clay first to stop up his face so that he wouldn't hear the whispering jungle and had heard it anyway. How he had applied it next to plug his pores but still the truth had found an opening. How finally the last of his will had died when shoots and stalks had begun to grow and the truth had changed:

"*Now* you belong," the jungle had said then.

All the same, John had heard Buck's oratory and now climbed to his feet. Like soldiers whose hearts have been shot through with bullets but who keep their feet to complete their charge, John rose on the momentum of his past life's struggle and broke from the tent toward the figure hunched over the stack of index cards.

Buck Alice was trying to put things right in his head: If Robbie wasn't the evil genius behind the Bureau, then which of the evil New Hopers was? Was it Hank? Possibly, but not likely. Hank and Buck had faced each other in the jungle over Isobel and mad dog leaders never have personal confrontations with the powers of good until the last chapter. No, the chances were that Hank was an expendable underling . . . unless he was such an evil genius that to throw Buck off the scent he had risked personal safety by appearing himself. And what of Gardner? Was he really dead and planted or was he just pretending so that Buck would look for the mastermind in another direction? After all, Satan-worshiping leaders often cultivate innocuous hobbies like gardening so that, in contrast to themselves, they will look even more fearsome to their duped henchmen. And what of Titheria? A woman is never a crime over-lord unless she has high cheekbones, a pointed chin and inverted V-shaped eyebrows. That is, unless she is even more warped than he imagined and would purposely appoint herself number one to confuse him. Then too, what about Robbie *really*? Wasn't it possible that Buck had been right the first time around, that Robbie's entire performance with Titheria was in reality a sly means of insinuating himself into Buck's good graces so as to attack him from within? Wouldn't it then follow that the nineteen pairs of New Hopers who trailed after him were actually paid outside activists, imported to stir up trouble? Buck chuckled to himself.

"And to think," he thought, "that all this scheming and diabolical planning, all this masterminding and evil geniusing was all part of their blood-sworn, crazed brain-inspired oath to get little me, to do away with little, short-necked, little me, to assassinate little, short-necked, thick-tongued, little me, to sneak up behind little, short-necked, thick-tongued, little me when I'm not looking and pinch me on the back of the head! And what about the Bureau representative? Why did he say I wasn't his father? What was the hidden meaning there? Was he calling out to me in some kind of code? Was it some kind of pitiful message asking for help? Was he trying to tell me who really. . . ."

"OK," said John.

"Huh?" said Buck, struggling to uncover the signifi-cance of the black man in his paranoiac peregrinations.

"I'm ready to do what you said."

"Oh yes, yes, of course. Good. Good! And the others?"

"No, just me."

Buck nodded. He had more than taxed the extent of his impromptu delivery and wasn't confident he could say more without a sprinkling of numbers and letters that would, he realized in fairness to the slow-thinking John, be confusing to any Negro.

Buck was disappointed in the failure of the others to agree to his plan, but he reasoned that it could still work if it was to appear that this one was the spokesman for all the rest. In any event, he knew he musn't let his disappointment show lest John lose confidence and decide he wasn't up to carrying on alone.

Buck reached for his briefcase and found his tongue. "The first thing that must be done is to design some kind of costume for you that will augment your natural appearance and underscore the impression that you have come from another planet. It must inspire awe and fear in the hearts of the enemy and bring home to them the fact that you are invincible. Dig me?" added Buck to establish lines of communication.

"Yeah," replied John, all the while thinking that despite being white, Buck Alice was a perfect candidate for his 'why is he alive' game.

Buck continued, "The next part is most difficult and requires great acting. We must carry off this fantastic bluff. You must walk straight into their camp and address the Bureau spokesman, saying, 'In the name of private enterprise, capitalism and the welfare of the human race, which I and the rest of my horde have been sent here to protect, you must tell the Bureau that if it doesn't surrender control of Isobel and New Hope Settlement for good, it shall be destroyed?' "

"And they'll believe this?" said John incredulously.

The science fiction writer looked at John with penetrating irritation. "They always do!" he snapped.

"But what if they don't?"

"Then," sighed Buck tragically, "you will have to destroy the Bureau for Omnipresent Safety and Security."

"How many are these omnipresent guys?"

"We don't know."

"Two—three?"

"We don't know."

"Nineteen—twenty . . . ?" asked John, throwing out an absurdly large number with the expectation that an emphatic negative reply would fortify his resolve.

"We don't know," repeated Buck, "but don't worry, the entire army of Newer Hope will be behind you . . . General." On this occasion Buck's instinct was flawless and John gobbled the bait.

"General": the word echoed silently in John's head. "General." He could do anything if he were "General." Inexplicably he was coming back to life. With difficulty, he suppressed the strange new sensation exploding within his breast and worked at mimicking Buck's taut upper lip. From somewhere deep beneath the garbage pile of anonymity that was his existence, from beneath the stench of vacuity and the slough of meaninglessness, from beneath the disease of selflessness, he scavenged for a lost bit of pleasure that marred the desolation and found it: a movie about the Foreign Legion he had seen when he was ten and which, for the only time in his life, made him forget who he wasn't. There was a sergeant in that picture who was English and black and who, when the time came to answer the call to duty, looked his commanding officer straight in the eye and answered simply but with majesty . . .

"Righto," John said, looking the other straight in the

eye while a faint smile played across his face. The smile said, "We are more than men. We are *soldiers*."

Buck Alice smiled back and never knew that for a moment there his turtle shell body had been washed out to sea and in its place had emerged a whole new set of physical characteristics, including a dapper mouth, a nice neck and a cunning moustache. Buck's whole life might have been different had he known that it was possible for someone to look at him and see, if only for a few brief seconds, a charming, resourceful, determined David Niven.

"When?" John asked.

"Tomorrow." On the eve of combat, questions and answers were always terse and to the point. Buck, catching the flavor if not the text of John's fantasy, responded in kind.

"Good," said John, who abruptly spun on his heel and marched off in the direction of his camel.

Early the next morning. . .

"These people here depend on me, they never gonna be free from the Bureau unless I do the freeing. I gotta knock some heads."

"You won't do it."

"How you gonna stop me?"

"John, we're starting over. The world is young again. All the bad times are gone. The good in your life is all ahead of you."

"I know what's good for me. Good for me is that they're afraid of me. Good for me is that when they see me comin' they step aside."

"What they are afraid of is the way we look, the mud on our bodies."

"*So?*"

"Well, that isn't us."

"Who says?"

"We're more than that, you're more than that. You're something good, something beautiful. You have so much to give the world, the new world, so much . . ."

"Bullshit!"

"John, John, hold on please. For my sake, hold on just a little while longer."

"For your sake?!"

"Don't you see how important it is, how far I've come—the meaning for everything. I wasn't born on a Detroit street. Don't you see that tomorrow is really coming, that tomorrow, tomorrow will really be here? The rebirth . . ."

"To hell with tomorrow. There isn't any tomorrow, there's never been. There's never been no past neither—or now—until now. Now I gotta now. Now I got something to do, something to be. I'm one of the mud beasts from outer space, man, and I'm gonna free the human race. I'VE GOT A REASON!"

"John, I know, I'm telling you I know, that you won't do this. You won't go out of here and make war. You won't go out of here and kill or get killed. At the last moment, you'll realize that we've started over again and that the world is peace and love."

"You're right, Mo. It suddenly came to me listening to you speak. You're absolutely right. There is only one way for us. It's the only way. It is the way of peace and love. Listening to you speak, I knew it was so. I will never doubt again."

John had been long gone before John finished saying in Morris' mind the things Morris needed to hear.

There's no denying that the outer space costume designed by Buck and put together by several motor-defective Newer Hopers had true organic reference to the rest of John's appearance: a collection of weeds sewn into a mango sprung from atop John's head. The mango was fastened to the straps of a bra and firmly held in place by the nestling of his chin in one tautly stretched cup. Woven into the cup were two long creepers that hung down his body like a stringy beard and tied at his ankles. Pliable bark strippings were knotted together into two long pieces. The end of one circled the left shoulder and tied under the left arm while the end of the other did the same on the other side. Each piece then snaked around his body in figure-eight fashion and fastened across the opposite leg. In this way, the bark cuttings intersected at John's chest and again low on his hips, further emphasizing his already imposing stomach. Across the clay on this latter surface were painted strange and mysterious symbols. For the rest, several very large banana peels, disguised with lipstick coloring, were strung across and tied flush to his groin. One housed the evidence of his manhood while the others were stuffed with leaves and the like. All looked relatively similar and indistinguishable. It was here that Buck felt his genius had truly shown. The craters were full of intergalactic gargoyles with three eyes and four heads and five arms, but when had one ever before been created with six phallic appendages!

"If that doesn't intimidate those commie bastards . . . ," thought Buck.

Buck and John put their heads together for a last-minute strategy talk. The 'Generals' and 'Rightos' flew thick and fast. Achieving at last a fever pitch peak, John bolted from his commander's side and made for enemy territory.

Buck Alice could hardly believe his own brilliance. He had accomplished that which no science fiction writer had done before. He had injected blood into a creature of his imagination and brought it to terrifying life. "Now I know a little of what God must have felt," Buck thought to himself with a tingle of reverence and a shudder of awe for his own powers of creation. Just then, however, Buck noticed that not all the wrinkles in his monster had apparently been ironed out. Instead of stately marching into the enemy quarters, John was charging like a herd of Frankensteins.

"How can he possibly ask for an unconditional surrender with dignity when he is conveying with all that running the false impression that he is running amok?" thought Buck, not yet comprehending.

John, his mango spinning recklessly on his head and his banana skins fluttering coquettishly in the breeze, had changed the battle plan in the middle of the battle. With his first step away from Buck's side, he suddenly became aware that all eyes in both settlements were upon him. He was the center of attention. He was everybody's 'now'. He was important, he was special, he was almost real. He was on the verge of knowing why he was alive. A wave of exhilaration swept over him and Buck's carefully conceived strategy was washed away in the undertow. Like a boy doing cartwheels for an admiring audience of girls, he felt a sudden and implacable urge to show off to the world just who he was. He would not simply tell the enemy to surrender, he would *make* them surrender. He would divide and conquer and lay desolate the terrain. Halfway across the field, he yelled "Geronimo," broke into a gallop and charged.

"Charge," cried Hank Hank, pointing the way into the jungle behind them and leading the retreat of New Hopers into the swamp.

Like a woman left panting one thrust from completion, John found himself 'combatus interruptus' by the total withdrawal of the enemy. Isobel was still hitched to the post nearby but his need to realize himself required bigger game. He stood in the middle of the compound bellowing inarticulately, demanding and pleading in turn that the forces of evil return to the arena.

"This is my last chance," he wailed. He began to cry with rage. He had been so close to being total and complete, so close to finding a reason why he was alive. Ironically, it was he, himself, their fear of him, that had stolen that chance from him. How could he ever prove to the world and himself that he had meaning and significance if he could not feel his fists against their heads and see their bodies beneath his feet? With no one else to assault, he turned his frustration inward and began raising welts over the length of his body. 'Squash' went the mango, 'split' went the bark, 'peal' went the banana skins. After a while the self-inflicted violence became less spontaneous and more deliberate.

"I'll have to kill myself, there's no other way. There's nothing else to do. I can't go back. I'll have to kill myself." He looked around for a weapon more deadly than his fists and at last saw Isobel or rather the stake to which she was shackled. He would unearth the post and run the sharp end through his body. He made for it.

The missing link in the evolution from ape to man may never be discovered, and yet what might be said of the noise that at that moment shattered the air like exploding cannons and troubled the prehistoric graves of forgotten dinosaurs.

"PPPPPPEEEEEE."

"As surely as that long-ago creature had a voice," wheezed the suddenly plummeting birds, "so must the current feather-stripping sound have been its means of communication."

Even John stopped and listened.

"PPPPPPPEEEEEEEEEERRRRRRRRR," it came again, as two parrots and a mynah bird landed on their heads.

"PPPPPEEEEEEEEEERRRRRRRRRRVVVVVEEEE," it rose a third time in the afternoon air, and with the repetition this time began the beginning of understanding. The sound was definitely a word.

As several woodpeckers buried their beaks to the hilt for support, it came once more and at last the world and John in particular got the message. From a leafy knoll on the edge of the compound, a figure nearly as grotesque as the sound it emitted suddenly emerged and charged. It was Titheria. As she bore down on John stationed near Isobel's young body, there was no mistaking the implication in her rallying cry.

"PPPPEEEERRRRVVVVEEEERRRRTTTT," she thundered with lightning in her eyes. Shorn of his phallic crown and reduced to the measure of a man, John's mud-encased presence did not seem to Titheria nearly as sinister as was his objective in approaching Isobel. In another second, they were on top of each other. Over and over they rolled in the dust, John using his fists like anvils hammering away at Titheria's stone-age head and Titheria in turn pinching and twisting and pulling to great advantage.

"You son of a bitch," cried John.

"Me—you—sky—fire," grunted Titheria, now totally regressed to a bygone era. So it went, the ground now scarlet, now crimson, with no sign of a victor in sight. Then it happened. With one mighty claw sunk deep into his chest, Titheria tore loose six inches of packed clay. The weakened foundation then cracked in several other places and in another second the body underneath stood revealed. Titheria next leapt at his head and scratched the mud free from his face.

"Why, you're a. . . ."

"Outer Space Nigger," chorused the gang of New Hopers, bolting from their hiding places.

It didn't take four repetitions for John to decipher this epithet. New will coursed through his veins. With a dispatching kick to Titheria's brain, he whirled triumphantly on his new adversaries. The blood spilled in puddles as from a child's melting ice cream cone and before long the combatants were wading ankle-deep in the sticky stuff. Still John kept his feet. The ranks swelled as more and more of the old guard number jumped into the fray.

"Outer Space Nigger," shouted one and the rest took up the cry. In response, John fought all the more furiously.

'Splish' went life-preserving bodily fluid, 'splash' went some more of it, and still John's knees would not buckle.

"Outer Space Nigger, Outer Space Nigger"—it was now more a chant than a cry. John chuckled to himself in rebuttal. Thoughts soared in his mind as all about him bodies came to an abrupt halt.

"A reason, man. A reason at last. Not 'nigger', man, because nigger is nothing—just a black hole—but *'Outer Space Nigger'*! A concession, a recognition, a thing different, an admission, an acceptance, more even: Outer Space-like Superman—'faster than a speeding shiv, more powerful than a ghetto merchant,' look up in the sky, man, 'cause I'm a thing to look up to. I have made these people move, all of them," as the mob surged forward and clutched at his body. "I have controlled their thoughts," as a tree limb crushed his ribcage. "I have occupied their lives," as an axe buried itself in his scalp. "I AM ALIVE, THAT'S WHY I AM!" as his eyes rolled to the back of his head and he died standing with no room to fall. "Hack-hack-hack" went the axe. "Crunch-crunch-crunch" went the sticks and stones.

"Beat him into butter," screamed someone, para-

phrasing the old fable. "Back where you came from,"
came the topper from another.

No one seemed to notice or care that John was long
since beyond abuse. And then, just as it all started, it
ended with a piercing scream. This time it came from
Isobel. In all the excitement someone had again made
off with the troll child.

Arnold had stopped talking into his hands long enough
to put them into action elsewhere. While John's body
was being disassembled, Isobel's ropes were being untied. The child's freedom was fleeting, however, for she
found herself quickly hoisted to the little man's back
and carried at a canter toward the forest thicket. The
Isobelian scream was the last anyone heard of the little
girl that day.

With a reluctant sigh, John's carcass was abandoned
to the pedestrian birds and the mob's attention turned
toward pursuit.

Back in Newer Hope Settlement, Buck had seized
upon Arnold's act as a testimonial of loyalty to the rebel
brigade. Embittered the moment before by John's failure
to carry out his assignment, he was now suddenly thrilled
beyond words (which for him was easy) and, throwing
caution to the winds, was a second later leading a
charge at the disorganized and wilting mob at the other
end of the compound.

"Lj-8-fr5w-6vy-t," he cried at the top of his lungs
and his followers, catching his enthusiasm, raged back,
"Lj-8-fr5w-6vy-t." Confused by the ever-changing direction of events, nearly exhausted from the assault on
John's body and overwhelmed by an enemy strategy that
used equations in its deployment, New Hope Settlement
promptly fell to its knees. In no time at all, Buck and
his cohorts had taken prisoner every one of its inhabitants with the exception of mole-like Isobel who, very

much in the hands of mole-like Arnold, was by then long gone deep into the woods.

Morris, sitting all this time quietly inside his tent, did not know the details of the war being waged to the south. At the beginning when John stood in the middle of the camp beseeching his enemies to come out and fight, Morris thought he could make out John's voice. From that distance, however, he sounded exactly like a new-foaled lamb bleating away inside a stuffy cardboard box. The image danced in Morris' head and finally took center stage: a wet, sticky, matted hair-thing crying, "Where's my momma, where's my momma?"

"How wild," he thought; "there are the creases and wrinkles where its little hooves jab and scrape at its prison walls. There are its first droppings, loose and pungent, already smeared over the floor in a kind of modern art design. What about this? Its kicking is getting stronger, more violent . . . and it's no longer just born . . . it's all fluffy white and soft and pretty and bigger, much bigger . . . and now there are great gashes in the box. Looking at it from the outside and hearing the pounding on the walls and suddenly seeing this black hoof thing come crashing through the cardboard, why man, if you didn't ever see a lamb before and know what its feet looked like, this black-hoofed thing coming through the wall could really scare you. But from the inside it's just this pretty lamb frantically trying to break free. 'Let me out, let me out,' it's demanding. If someone doesn't help it soon, it's going to suffocate in its own leavings. Why, the stuff is up to its chest now . . . Now what? . . . Hey, where did those horns come from? Look at that, he's butting those walls with his head. That's a full-grown sheep in there and I just don't see how that cardboard box can hold him in much longer. He's breaking through! He's out, he's free! He's gonna go frolic in that pasture and eat all that clover. Come on, sheep, go frolic, frolic, you poor bastard. No, no, no, not that way, not *that* way,'' but by then the words 'Outer Space Nigger' were full in Morris' ears and he suddenly realized he had never seen a sheep, not one, in his whole life.

Buck came in and told him about John. Halfway through the description, Morris' mind's eye closed and he shut out the rest. He felt himself sinking beneath the waves and offered no resistance. He felt himself come to rest against coral and sponge and hemp, felt the air bubble out of him and still heard nothing and had no thoughts—other than fragments that briefly shimmered high above him on the surface. "Thou shalt" and "He whosoever," they said, but their light did not penetrate to the deep, placid waters in which he slept.

It was a long rest but at last he awoke and frog-kicked and began the long ascent. *Stroke:* "I am Morris, I am new, I am peace and love." *Stroke:* "Don't take up their fight, John, leave it be." *Stroke:* John is dead, and I was right, but John is dead. What good is Morris if John is dead. Morris is words and words won't put John's head back together." *Stroke:* "I should have tried harder." 'Stroke: "I failed again." *Stroke:* "I should at least have been at his side fighting along with him." *Stroke:* "No, *No!* Morris starts with words, but it is more; it is a way, it lives, it grows, and next time it will be strong enough to stop John from getting killed. Next time it will be strong enough to stop all killing. I am Morris, I am new, the world is young." Morris ascended into consciousness and opened his eyes and for the twentieth time heard Buck ask him when Arnold would return with Isobel.

Several paces up the trail of Buck's growing anxiety over Isobel's protracted absence was corroborating evidence that he was on the right path. Already there and lying in wait with murder on her mind was Maytagagawa. If anyone should have known what Arnold was up to, it would be her. "Glicki-glicki," she muttered aloud while in her brain a vision of Arnold and Isobel in unholy consort ejaculated itself over and over again.

On the third day of the long wait, Maytagagawa shed her mud and her clothes, took a bath and went hunting for Arnold.

The glory of God is the creation of man. The glory of man is the development of himself as an individual, the glory of being different. It is a tragedy of 'civilization' that often the difference does not emerge. An infinite variety of people clawing out an existence on a finite variety of prescriptions dictates the suppression of differences, the consequent subjugation of the individual and the deglorification of the species.

John went searching for his glory and died in the quest. Maytag's underdeveloped mind made no demands for glory. She lived only to be clean and to be near Arnold. However, when she was deprived of the latter after already being deprived of the former, the compounded trauma tore from her back the trappings of inhibiting civilization. In the civilized world, the world of formulae, she would merely have chosen procedure 'F-127' to express her loss and run blindly into the street to be hit by a car. In the jungle world, unencumbered, free, naked and on all fours, she unwittingly found her difference:

She licked her lips and growled with pleasure;
The wind brought her the news that
Ten miles to the east in a dark cave. . . .

She stopped and wrinkled her nose again
Yes, Ten miles to the east in a dark cave
Arnold would be there.
Unsolicited her glory had emerged
Unbeknownst she was already in its care.
She relaxed her expanded nostrils
His scent was heavy in the air.

Isobel had been remembering her angelfish. The small aquarium had been given to her on her seventh birthday. As she had done with all her presents, her first impulses were to shove her foot through it and watch the water splash all over the newly polished floors. She had decided from the first that the sea shells were dumb, the green-colored pebbles were dumb, and the guy in the diving suit was dumb. But then her father opened up a small bottle and dropped into the tank the first angelfish Isobel had ever seen. The little fish flopped over a couple of times, found its bearings and swam straight to Isobel, or at least to the aquarium wall in front of which she sat. She then commanded that the aquarium be placed on Isobel's table, called for Isobel's lamp to be lighted, ordered Isobel's chair to be brought forth, lost her patience momentarily when Isobel's cushion was found missing, and excused Isobel's parents from the room. At last, propped up on her throne with her hands buried deep in the folds of her cheeks, she proceeded to establish the first meaningful relationship in her life.

The world had always marshaled its forces to defeat Isobel. A hot pavement, a stuffy nose, a tardy ice cream peddler were all manifestations of the plan to make life as nasty as possible for her. Then the angelfish, which never left its tank and always swam back to her and always blew her a big kiss, appeared and she became lost in the world of her fish and herself the way other kids do in the fantasies that envelop them on the TV screen. Her parents, sharp as tacks, were quick to draw the analogy and concluded quicker than you could change channels that the aquarium had become a surrogate television set. As all parents have since "Uncle Milty," they realized that at last they had a weapon to hold over her head.

The commission of the smallest infraction soon resulted in the withdrawal of all aquarium privileges. Isobel's already low frustration tolerance collapsed under the weight of several such episodes. Instinctively, she reverted to type. She broke off the lock on the closed door, tore the extension cord from its socket and peremptorily gave in to her first impulses. The angelfish poured through the shattered glass along with the cascading water. Its fossil-like imprint decorated several places on the newly polished floor where it flipped and flopped before suffocating in the vapid atmosphere of the family apartment. Isobel then cried, possibly for the last time.

The sleeping form beside her reminded Isobel of her angelfish. They had 'fought' several times since her abduction and Arnold had won the best three out of five. Looking down now at the funny-looking man, Isobel tried to decide whether she had not after all thrown the last contest. He had taken her by surprise the first time and finished so quickly that she had only the pain to remind her of the assault. They had traded victories since then, with physical exhaustion on the part of one or the other being the deciding factor in each case. Except perhaps for the last time when by her own reckoning, surrender had come before fatigue.

"Yes," she concluded at last, "I let him the last time on purpose." But why? Was it because Arnold, asleep with his mouth stretched wide to gulp air, looked even more like her angelfish unconscious than he did awake? Or was it because that with the last 'rape', she discarded forever the stuffed bear she sometimes smuggled between the sheets? At last she made a decision and turned to Arnold with a carefree mind. She listened lovingly to his adenoidal snore and then smoothed the ground in preparation for her own nap. She made herself into a tight little ball at his side and almost immediately fell asleep. Just as she was drifting off, her hand, on its own, reached out and patted Arnold on his right fin, proving, in the last analysis, that even dreadful little Isobel, under extraordinary circumstances, was capable of a spiritual experience.

Arnold in the meantime dreamed on of one day becoming king.

Just past dusk, Maytag's nostrils flared. Anger, humiliation, joy and lugubriousness drained through her brain pan as she espied the lovers. Either the holes in her sifter were too large or the contradictory emotions too similar in size and intensity because her subsequent rush on the cave was without a specific objective. She found herself upon the sleeping couple without a notion as to how to proceed. A moment of high theater ensued during which the groggy Arnold stared up at Maytag and the confused Maytag stared down at Arnold. Isobel's scream, coming as it did after what seemed an age or two, released the hypnotic hold one had on the other. Pushing Maytag from him, Arnold tried to climb upright. What transpired next was a direct reflection on his amatory habits. As always with Arnold, sleep befell him shortly after sex did, and in the drowsy aftermath to his last tryst with Isobel, he remained conscious only long enough to raise but not secure his trousers. This negligence now cost him dearly. He bounded to his feet but immediately fell flat again as his pants, dropping to his ankles, trapped him with his first step. The sight of the exposed Arnold lying on his back and trying mightily to kick off his trousers gave Maytag the inspiration she desperately required. Tearing a tatter from his tattered trappings, she descended with full steam onto Arnold's stomach, spitting voluminously (parched though she was from the long jungle haul). His groin was soon awash with her saliva.

"Glicki-glicki," she cried but once and set about with her improvised washrag to clean the offending organ. Back and forth she rubbed and scrubbed until, despite his howls of real pain, the servant of his libido was again tumescent. Seeing Arnold thus equipped, Maytag pounced. Seeing Maytag thus acquitted, Isobel pounced. Seeing the two females pouncing, Arnold closed his eyes and prayed.

Buck Alice sat in his tent rubbing his hands. Everything was almost perfect. He could hardly believe his notes. With the exception of the still absent Isobel, things had really worked out the way he had planned. He was now in total control of both hands of the compound and before long would organize an election to have himself named President of the United States. He was so pleased that he even permitted himself a little indulgent reflection.

"I never thought I could do it, not really, not come this far— not as far as President. But then of course I always knew I had the capacity, always was aware of the injustice of my modest beginnings. But the strength, the courage, to break the mold, to destroy the pattern, to rise beyond my station in life, to defeat the forces of communism and other evilness sworn to hold me down, sworn to deny me anything more than the talents of a gifted writer—that, that *I* didn't even know I had in me. 'President of the United States'!'' he said aloud in a trembling voice, and then to himself, ''I feel so humble'' (now there were enough splashing tears to make turtle soup), ''so deeply humble and grateful. The first thing I must do, even before entering office,'' he said, applying his handkerchief liberally, ''is to perform some noteworthy act of leadership like executing all the members of the Bureau.'' With that in mind, he shortly convened a tribunal with himself as chief magistrate.

Titheria was the first witness. Her body, battered from her battle with John, was borne to the hearing on a stretcher. ''Me-you-sky-water,'' she repeated to every question, taking the fifth, and was finally excused.

After Titheria came Robbie who reiterated his earlier confession but had nothing new to add except to say that the 'emissary' was the only person tied to the Bureau with whom he had ever conferred. This was the moment Buck had been waiting for. Now, at last, all would be revealed to him; now at last he would know who had the bare feet in the group. Eagerly he called the Actor-Robot to the stand.

''If you refuse to bear witness,'' cautioned Buck, reading from a card which was also his ace, ''we will have to assume that you are the leader of the Bureau and responsible for all its actions. If, on the other hand, you reveal here and now the names of each and every member of the 'Brain Trust,' we will assume that you were an innocent if naive dupe, and will recommend amnesty.''

''Recommend?''

''All right, then, guarantee, *guarantee* complete amnesty.'' Buck wasn't about to quibble. He was too eager to pin his adversaries to the wall with their own thumbs and index fingers.

''Click-click, whirl-whirl'' went the Actor-Robot's

mouth. "Tic-tic-tic" went Buck Alice's face as he listened to the unbelievable testimony: "There are *no* members of the Bureau, there never were. No one ever volunteered. Everybody was busy minding their own business."

"Hurrah," shouted all the Pathfinders, happy for the strength of their character and the integrity of their lifestyle.

"Flop-flop, pad-pad" came the imagined sound behind Buck. He felt himself crowded into a corner with no way to turn. Instinctively, he knew that the Actor-Robot wasn't lying. He failed to recognize the truth before only because he was too good a writer to believe that the butler had done it. Now, however, with the Actor-Robot having everything to gain and nothing to lose, it became abundantly clear that pulp still played a part in life. Nevertheless, he still would have gone back on his word and demanded the mechanical man's head if he could have struck from the record his next statement.

"If you go back on your word and demand my head, then you must also execute everyone else for failing to become involved enough to intercede. It is called guilt by omission."

"You're innocent, you're innocent," everyone naturally cried at once. There was a hollow ring to Buck's voice as his head sunk deeper into his chest. "Why did you pretend (i8j-Or-2) there was a Bureau? Why (4-fgv-186) did you plot against me?"

The Actor-Robot had expected this moment, had actually longed for it. At last he would let the science fiction writer know the reason for his overwhelming hate, the reason he tried so desperately to get even. "Actor-Robots do not panic," he told himself as he coolly stepped forward. "Because I don't like you— never have. Not since from long before the invasion; not since you began writing and never gave the androids and robots good parts in your stories. What kind of a father are you anyway, to play favorites among the people you bring to life in your fantasies?'' He stopped for a moment and fixed his face into a smile. He wasn't about to let Buck Alice know how he really felt. ''I've played a lot of robots and they have feelings too, you know. In your stories, my people were always being dented or melted or going berserk, and anyone who knows the slightest thing about machine men knows they never panic.''

Despite himself, some feeling began to creep into his tone. ''(whirl-hum) and then you wrote an episode of the TV series I was on and you wrote out the robot and I didn't get a residual on the rerun.'' The clanging of years of pent-up frustration could now be heard vibrating through his speaking mechanism. ''(clang-clang-clang) and then you wrote again for my show (clang-rattle-bang) and you had the robot fall in love with an airplane motor (bang-rattle-clang) and try to fly away with her by jumping off the roof of a ball-bearing factory (crash-bang-knock-ping).'' The Actor-Robot was now too choked with emotion to continue; already he could feel the paint flaking from around his joints.

The sci-fi writer stared back at him in disbelief, but not without compassion. ''The commies must be after him too,'' he thought. ''But, but (7a-4fv8w-Om) I saw the robot. It (s562-li-8i) was made of tin.''

Poor Actor-Robot, poor Actor-Robot, warning signals were flashing all through his circuits. ''Overload, overload,'' they blinked. Too late, too late, he was building toward a power failure. He could no longer control himself. ''BUT DON'T YOU SEE, DON'T YOU SEE, I WAS INSIDE!''

Despite the superiority of the blueprint, despite the

durability of the parts, despite the meticulous crafting, a crack appeared just above his left temple, traveled, grew larger, and finally split open his face. Triggered by a photoelectric cell sensitive to exposed feelings, a small recessed sack of tears long ago hidden away and forgotten now burst with a mighty 'boo-hoo' and inundated all his working parts. "Ssssszzzzz" went the hot wires as steam poured from his ears and he blacked out. *Inconceivably, the Actor-Robot had panicked*. After a while, they wheeled him away and propped him up against a tree.

Buck felt that he was definitely in a predicament. He could, he supposed, still execute the entire population of New Hope Settlement, but that would defeat the purpose of conquering it. The idea, after all, was to enlarge his influence, not reduce it. On the other hand, how solid could his victory and his performance as a leader be if there was no enemy that could be brought to its knees? In his need to live up to the conviction that he had beaten the odds and become a great man, Buck finally put logic aside and arrived at a solution.

"Hear ye, hear ye, hear ye," he ranted as his pencil raced. "It is my decision that the body of the Bureau be executed until dead . . . in abstentia. In this way we are forever after and far and wide letting it be known that good triumphs over evil."

There was some weeping, of course, but mostly it was courage and bravery that prevailed as the entire community gathered around the chopping block in the town square. At high noon, a black-hooded figure who was stripped to the waist and cradling an axe stepped out of the shadows. Behind him stood Buck carrying a thick paper scroll which he shortly proceeded to unravel. "Let the execution commence," he intoned, as the masked man spit on his hands and squeezed his missing testicle for good luck.

"Number one," Buck read, and the hooded knight of death brought the axe smashing down into the wood block with a resounding crash. Everyone either lowered his eyes or fought the impulse and stared straight ahead— except for Buck who, several times, could be seen faintly bobbing his head as if tracing the course of the severed (albeit imaginary) top bouncing and rolling before clunking to a rest. Twenty-five times Buck called out a number and twenty-five times the merchant of doom wielded his blade until in the end the ground was a veritable sea of wood chips. Finally, it was over and there was silence. It was the kind of magic moment when each man stops the breakneck, helter-skelter pace of his life and pauses to reflect inwardly about the really important issues: the reasons he was truly set upon the earth. Then faintly, very faintly at first, the singing started. No one ever really knew with whom it began and everyone afterwards agreed that it didn't matter. The important thing was that God had entered their lives and brought two-part harmony with him.

". . . Where seldom is heard
a discouraging word
and the skies are not cloudy all day.
Home, home on the range. . . ."

Imhor was in the vicinity. He knew he was close to the settlement because of the presence of three semi-human figures below him.

"What have we done?"
  "What have we done?"
    "What have we done?" he wailed in a round

with his other voices. He had never seen humans look
and act like this and could only imagine that they had
somehow become victims of the invasion.

Actually, the scene in progress was a reenactment of
the age-old eternal triangle with Isobel and Maytag com-
peting for Arnold's favors. As a result of repeated dis-
charge, Arnold's favors were pretty well shot, so what
Imhor saw was the two still unsatisfied women butting
each other with their heads while holding fast to Arnold's flaccid musket.

"Still no sign of Joshua," thought Imhor, changing
the subject. Immediately after Imhor had revealed the
real nature of Loinine, the human had run screaming
down the corridor. Somehow, he had managed to reach
the hangar and activate one of the Swoop Craft without
being halted. Hard on his heels, Imhor had arrived in
time to see the ship disappearing in the distance. Hardly
stopping for a breath, he climbed aboard another vessel
and was soon in hot pursuit. He lost his trail in dense
fog but after determining from Joshua's initial heading
that he was going south towards the suspected colony,
he set his own ship on that course. Imhor knew that
without Joshua's help he could never get these other
humans to go along with his plan. Consequently, he
would have to wait for Joshua to show up and recon-
vince him, if it took that, to act as his mouthpiece in the
settlement.

"How else," he said to himselves, "can I ever get
back at those who made me come to this horrible planet?"

"Right," said his voices while withholding from him
the knowledge that he had managed to hang on to life
this long only because his will would not let him die
without first gaining revenge. Imhor meant to push the
lift button and climb above the sheltering tree tops, but
suddenly he felt his stomach being bent and folded and

stapled together in eighths. Reflexively he clutched at his side. "There is less time than I supposed," he thought, doubling up and blacking out and inadvertently hitting the descent button as he toppled forward into unconsciousness.

There wasn't much question about Arnold falling asleep this time. The Swoop Craft deftly gauged the distance to solid earth with its automatic radar control system and engaged all components for a gentle vertical landing within spitting distance of Maytag and the ménage-a-trois. Isobel, given a second chance to save her 'angel-fish' by rescuing Arnold from Maytag's clutches, had a moment before sworn to fight until death. However, all thoughts of changing history vanished with the appearance of the alien spaceship and its unconscious blue pilot. Her hysteria was quickly transmitted to the other two. Terrified beyond discriminating action, they raced round and round the craft, unable to dislodge themselves from the pull of a magnetic field they themselves had imposed. Desperately, they tried to flee but with Arnold following Maytag, and Maytag following Isobel and Isobel following Arnold, they were a trio of babbling monkeys caught with each other's tails in their mouths. They would surely have died like that, perpetually running in circles, had not Imhor started to revive.

"My name is Imhor."

"So is mine."

"Mine too," said three of his voices, meaning to soothe the ruffled maypolers.

"Glicki-glicki," screamed Maytag, introducing herself.

Arnold, who in the past might have found fault with his girlfriend's limited vocabulary, now inexplicably took up the cry. "Glicki-glicki," he yelled at the top of his lungs while forgetting to bow.

"Glicki-glicki!" cried Isobel louder than the other

two, not to be outdone. Miraculously, the next jetti-soned 'glicki' did the trick. Just like that the afterburn-ers on the monkey ship ignited, and with Isobel in the lead, the trio blasted out of orbit and rocketed back toward the settlement.

After the final chorus had been sung, Buck raised the scroll high above his head and with great solemnity, tore it into little pieces. Without lowering his arms he opened his hands, and while rotating his body clockwise, let the scraps drift away with the breeze. No less a vision than "Atlas taking a Breather" was called to mind when Buck at last dropped his hands to his sides and his chin to his chest. Equaled only by Buck's own, the crowd let out a mighty sigh. Slowly, the future President of the United States composed himself. Fortified with the im-age of Joan of Arc he then proceeded to undertake the long, lonely trek back to his tent.

Needless to say, the crowd wept. It was a marvelous performance and Buck, in the seclusion of his teepee, had just begun to savor it when the terrified yelping of Isobel shattered the aura.

"The monsters are here, the monsters are here," she cried insanely, while deftly knocking the underpinnings from the two nearest tents. "Oh my goodness, oh my goodness," obediently replied the crowd, overjoyed at her safe return.

"It's true, it's true, it's true," she implored, leveling another tent in the full heat of her tantrum. "Of course, of course," they soothed, puckering their lips and strok-ing her face and wiping their hands of the bubbling saliva that gushed from the frothing child like a Yellow-stone geyser.

"YYYYYYAAAAAHHIIIIGGGGGSSSSHHHHHH-HHHAAAAADDDDDUUUUUPPPPP"

screamed Isobel, beseeching them to listen to reason. "And *we're* happy to have *you* back," they replied politely, misreading her meaning.

Uppermost in Isobel's mind at this point was the vision of a poisoned spike being thrust through the heart of each member in the group.

"All right then, all right then," she screamed, remembering by way of the penetrating rod a way to get through to the crowd. "I WENT AND DID 'IT'!" The reaction was different from what she expected. Instead of commanding a stunned silence, the news brought a resounding cheer. Arnold, nearby, was a trifle upset. The plan had been to make that announcement as well as the rest at a more reasonable time and here Isobel had gone and jumped the gun. The rest of the crowd was not so critical, however. Before she could catch her breath, a ring formed around the woman-child and an impromptu folk dance began. Infecting several people in the process, Isobel bit through the encircling chain and made a break for freedom. She didn't quite succeed. A hand hooked into her tu-tu and the circle became a snake with the girl in the lead. Happily committed to any direction Isobel chose, it slithered merrily across the camp.

"Let go, let go!" she screamed, trying to shake loose of the scaly thing. "Who-who-who" spit back the serpent, more interested in knowing the name of the lucky mate.

The body grew longer and longer as more and more people attached themselves. Almost the entire colony was accounted for, including Arnold who was, in the end, pressed into service at the tip of the tail. Having by then vented some of her hysteria, Isobel at last stopped, turned abruptly and screeched, "Arnold, Arnold is the one!" The reptile's vertebrae, as if individually marked by bull's-eyes and hit simultaneously by as many marks-

men in a shooting gallery, about-faced as one and came
smack dab up against the rattling telltale tail tip. There
stood Arnold, shaking with the vision of John's violent
end before him.

"You?! You?! You?!" exclaimed the snake archly,
preparing to strike.

"Wait!" cried Isobel, throwing herself at his feet, "I
love him!"

Strung out by the 'flash', the backbone hung limply
back as Isobel, warming to her role, stepped to the
front. "He has opened the sky to me and the earth. He
has made me see the simple joy of the animals and the
trees on the ground and the smell of the birds and the
angelfish that swim around." A spark ignited in Isobel's
head as she caught the ring of a rhyme in her rhetoric.
In the subsequent attempt to nurture the gift, she lowered the quality of the recitation deep into the minus
numbers.

"If together we don't mount the throne
I will plainly moan and groan
Until I die.
And then there won't be anyone left on Earth to
     survi(ve)."

"Awful, awful," hissed the snake (referring in equal
part to both the ultimatum implied in the text and the
skill of its construction), now dismembered and running
twitchingly in every direction at once.

"What shall we do, what shall we do?" pleaded the
mob, congregating around Buck Alice. "Must we make
Isobel queen? Must we make Arnold king?"

"Relax," said Buck, about to collapse from shock.
"Leave everything to me."

Already collapsed at the moment was the memory of

the two lovers. Totally forgotten by Isobel and Arnold in the heat of new excitement was the old excitement of Imhor's appearance. Fortunately, their failure to communicate his arrival was not to be an immediate problem for the settlement since Imhor was content to remain hidden until Joshua showed up.

Maytag, the other eyewitness to the alien's appearance, could not have conveyed the news even if she had been able to speak. Her thoughts were totally wrapped up in choosing the most suitable means by which to murder her rival.

Buck's plan was simple. He would explain to Arnold (obviously the less obdurate of the lovebirds) the impossibility of establishing a kingdom in the United States of America. If that should fail, unlikely though it seemed, he would then have Arnold killed. Isobel, he was sure, would retreat from her lofty ambition if her mate was not at her side. Armed with his sharpest pencils, he called Arnold into his tent.

"Well, what have you to say for yourself?"

"What do you mean?"

"Why did you do it?"

"Do what?"

"Steal our freshest flower and tear her petals."

"I thought you wanted to talk about the kid with the fat cheeks."

"I am."

"Oh, well, because I wanted to be king."

"No, no, the real reason—I mean, the reason you had at the beginning."

"That's it."

"But that's ridiculous . . . how could you think . . . I mean, where's the president . . . I mean, the precedent?"

"The what?"

"We've never had kings in this country—that's for

dictatorships—here everybody rules himself. What made you think we would let *you* become king?''

''Well, for one thing, Isobel and I got this suicide pact where she kills herself if I don't become king. She loves me, see. And then I figured that since everybody around here is supposed to mind their own business, nobody would mind if we wanted to be queen and king. And then there is this secret reason . . .''

''Well, what is it, what is it?''

''What's what?''

''The secret reason.''

''Oh yeah, that.''

Buck was beginning to experience an acute sense of anxiety. He wasn't sure anymore that he could convince Arnold of the absurdity of his plan. Arnold was obviously a dunce but that very fact seemed to work to his advantage. He didn't understand the ground rules and fought with a kind of 'guerilla' logic that threw Buck off balance. It was like battling a soft banana with a bazooka. On the one hand, the enemy is hopelessly overmatched, and on the other, he is capable of slipping you up.

''Well . . . ?''

''Well, you see, I always dreamed of being king of this certain realm and the people around here always look and act the way I dreamed they would in this certain realm, except that they don't look the way I dreamed they would.''

''Well,'' said Buck, with renewed confidence, ''if they don't look the way you always dreamed they would, then this isn't the realm you always dreamed about.''

''Yeah, I know what you mean. . . .''

''So. . . .''

''That bothered me at first too, but I think I've figured it out. See, the people around here are doing things

backwards from the way they should, like doing everything apart when, like Mo told us, you gotta stick
together to stay alive. Since the people around here are
doing things opposite to the way they should, they do
think the way I always guessed they would in my realm.
And since they do think that way, even though they
don't *look* like they'd think that way, maybe you can't
tell a book from its cover and maybe they really do look
that way."

"Snap" went the pencil point as it wedged itself
between a wisdom (thinking) tooth and an eye (looking)
tooth in Buck's head.

"What way, what way are people supposed to look
and think in your realm?"

"Ugly and stupid."

"You're crazy. I'm not going to be president of the
ugly and stupid. There are no ugly and stupid here!"

"Ok, then you be president of them and I'll be king
of the others."

It was about this time that Buck, in a fit, ate most of
his notes and got a bad cramp, which still was nothing
compared to what happened to him the next day after
handing the vengeance-bent Maytag an axe and pointing
in the direction of Arnold.

Immediately he saw his error as Maytag with her
all-purpose war cry bore down on Isobel instead. "No,
no, the wrong one, the wrong one," he called, leaping
in front of the gnome-girl and catching the full brunt of
the axe heel on the top of his frontal lobe.

"B-4-p-mc2. . . . s," said Buck, no longer troubled
by the conflict between intelligible words and numbers
and letters. "B4p-m-c2. . . . . s," he repeated from
underneath his dangling tongue. B-4-pm-c-2. . . . . s,"
he intoned endlessly, now a full-fledged member of
Arnold's realm.

Then, as if it were a morning unlike all others except one in the annals of recorded history, a truly miraculous thing happened to Buck. The gathering crowd gasped and pointed to beneath Buck's chin and said in a hushed whisper, "Look, look," and lo, they had spoken not one single false word.

From out of the crypt of his chest
did arise
Buck's neck,
A full foot from his shoulders
And resting on top
A face with a smile
A head unafraid
No longer on trial
At peace with the world
with commies and pinks
no longer thc president
no longer a fink.

"B4-p-mc2. . . . . . . s," said Buck, grinning from ear to ear.

No one had ever remembered seeing Buck like this, so relaxed, so comfortable, so happy. It was a truly awesome sight. "B4pmc-2. . . . s," cooed Buck again from his position on the ground.

At last someone broke the spell. "What's he saying, what's he trying to tell us? It must be about Isobel, about making her queen. Is that right, Buck?"

"B4-pm-c-2. . . . . s."

"Before p.m. see to . . . what?" interrupted another, reading a meaning into the gibberish. "Before p.m. see to . . . what, see to the coronation?" inquired Robbie excitedly with his hand in Damon's.

"See to making Isobel queen?" jumped in the queen mother.

"See to the *marriage*?" added the ex-Jewish mother, ethnically.

"Bfpmc2. . . ."

"Is that what you're trying to tell us?" interrupted everybody, breathing hard in Buck's face. Before p.m., see to. . . ."

". . . s," finished Buck, interrupting the interrupters.

" 'Yes,' he said 'yes!' Hip, hip, hurrah!"

At 11:37 a.m., twenty-three minutes before the p.m., Isobel and Arnold were married and crowned in that order. Everyone remarked on how mature Isobel had become and with what royal bearing Arnold carried himself.

No one, of course, understood why Buck had insisted that the double ceremony be carried out before noon, but then again, neither did they fully understand why he had twenty-five non-existent people executed.

"No one had not benefited by the first decision," they reasoned, "so why not abide by the second as well," they stopped reasoning. Actually, as usual, there were a few malcontents bent on finding flaws. In the face of the midday deadline, however, they found themselves with only the meanest of opportunities to outline their objections.

The fact was that for the first time since the invasion, the members of the settlement had been furnished a common, immediate and accessible objective behind which they could throw their weight. The interpretation given to Buck's nonsense mutterings was no accident. The people were looking for a chance, needed a chance, to engage in some task, some goal that required harmony of action. Left panting at the door of self-determination was the genetic demand for cooperation—to share, to exchange, to reestablish the unique ties that in the past had distinguished man from other animals. Thus was explained the alacrity and dispatch with which the ground was cleared, a royal alcove constructed, two thrones built, crowns shaped, scepters hewn, and a song (inspired by Isobel's 'throne-groan-moan' poem) composed.

Unfortunately, the endeavor was a dying gasp, for in completing the task, human progress advanced to the rear, back towards monarchy.

"What a perfect little doll."

"How manly he is."

"The beginning of better times," and so on, as the ceremonies drew to an end.

At last, Isobel rose and gestured for silence. A great hush fell over the multitude. Just as the Pope upon achieving his popedom receives special dispensations from God, so Isobel, everyone was sure, had been transformed by her coronation into an omniscient presence as well. The regality of her bearing could not be denied and pulses pounded in anticipation of her first queenly words.

"No more screwing in public and no more private enterprise orgies, that's number one!"

The Actor-Robot, still sprung, still unhinged, still propped against a tree, sat listening to himself rust during Isobel's proclamation.

Buck Alice, still flat where he had fallen, smiled happily during Isobel's diatribe.

Titheria, still on her stretcher and lying quite still, threw rocks at dinosaurs during Isobel's oration.

Apart from the rest, still in the bush, Maytag hunched hiding, glicki-ing and crying during Isobel's recriminations.

On and on it went: item two, item three, item four, each numerical elevation a complete revolution of the clamp tightening around the throat of Now-Newer Hope Settlement.

In a tent nearby, oblivious to Isobel's ranting and to life and to death, sat Sam with Celeste. He played with her fingers, he toyed with her thumb, he held close her cold hand.

A short distance away at the edge of the crowd, Morris stood with Louella who nodded on cue. "They don't know, they don't understand," he murmured aloud. "My father's flock led not by the shepherd but by the most woebegone, gone astray, spindley-legged lamb of all. What am I to do, father? Am I to do nothing? Silence is pain far worse than nails. What am I to do? Surely, it is time I step forward and take the lead, to show them the way, but then, how—how to proceed? Give me a sign, father."

As if following Morris' lead, the entire community looked up to the heavens at precisely the same moment. Although everybody saw it at the same time, no one was sure they believed what they saw. The gleaming space-ship descending into the jungle held no more reality for them than an Alpine landscape on the screen of a steamy drive-in movie in Pittsburgh. That is, of course, until it landed and this naked chalk-white creature jumped out screaming, "Don't be afraid! I'm one of you!"

"Charge!" commanded Hank as everyone started racing in the opposite direction. Suddenly, another space-ship was landing in front of them and the mob reversed its field again.

"Stop!" implored Joshua, jumping into the center of the pack. "Honestly, I'm a human being, just like you."

Nobody seemed impressed.

"My name is Joshua Chaplin, I'm Rochelle Chaplin's

little boy, and I was an insurance salesman before the
invasion.''

They knew he was lying now; whoever heard of a
Jewish insurance salesman. Joshua tried again. ''Cookie
Lavagetto got the nineth inning double that broke up
Bill Bevans' no-hitter in the Dodgers-Yankees World
Series of 1947.''

Nothing.

''Jane Wyman was the deaf mute opposite Lew Ayres
in the movie *Johnny Belinda*.''

Still nothing.

''Hello, nephews, nieces too, mommys and daddys,
how are you? This is your Uncle Don, all set to. . . .''

''Kill the little bastards!'' Someone had yelled out the
password.

''That's it, that's it,'' Joshua shouted back, and the
crowd surged forward to shake the hand of the prodigal
son.

Unnoticed in the subsequent backslapping confusion,
Imhor stepped from his ship. He reached Joshua's right
side just as Morris, threading his way through the crowd
from the other direction, reached Joshua's left side. The
crowd fell back dramatically as they saw Imhor. The
three men were left quite alone in the center to stare at
each other.

''But you're dead,'' said Morris.

''Huh?'' said Joshua.

''We'll all be dead if you don't convince these people
to go along with my plan,'' said Imhor.

''Holy shit,'' said Joshua, ''now I remember. You're
the guy—what's his name—Morris, Morris Tate, the
guy in the war in the foxhole. I've got you to thank.
Without you I wouldn't be here. I was scared. What
fat-assed kid who nobody ever said 'sensitive lad' or
'bright boy' to, whose father died while he was twelve,

wouldn't be? But I kept remembering that once, once I really did do something great, that once I had saved a man's life, that once I was a hero, a *real* hero, and that I didn't need Friday afternoons after work to think about it. Well, when I remembered that, I knew for sure that I hadn't turned this color for nothing. No sir, I mean I am a God-blessed hero and I'm not a coward and everybody all down the line was wrong. I'm sure as hell not going back into life insurance. Maybe I'll become a soccer player for the Argentine team—or was it Brazil—after this. And to think, you're the guy. . . .''

"Quick, tell these people about my plan. . . .''

". . . . *my* plan.''

"I beg your pardon, *my* plan.''

"Yes, I'm the guy,'' said Morris, "and you're the honk. You were there, only you—not Louella, not the Doc, not the lampposts, only you. And now I will have the *sign*. You will tell me at last.''

"*My* plan.''

"You're definitely mistaken—*my* plan.''

"I remember now so clearly,'' said Joshua. "How could I have forgotten? Together in the foxhole and now you're here—*still alive*. To meet you at last and again, my God, if that isn't a sign. . . .''

"All these years of suffering,'' said Morris, "and now you're here, God's will come to tell me, that it was war—not my fault—that I suffered for mankind, not for myself. . . .''

"My plan, my plan, my plan!''
"*My* plan, *my* plan, *my* plan!!''
"That time in the foxhole,''
"That time in the foxhole,''
"When we turned and we fired''
"When we turned and we fired''

"And the enemy soldier fell dead at our feet."

"And the enemy soldier fell dead at our feet."

"That shot that was fired"

"That shot that was fired"

"it killed one poor man"

"it killed one poor man"

"but saved all the rest"

"but saved all the rest"

"Why else if not God's will that we meet at this time."

"Why else if not God's will that we meet at this time."

"Tell them about the plan!"

"I, His Son, have come to you with a message."

"You have come to me, His Son, with a message."

"Listen, everyone, the human race will not survive. They know where we are and they will come and destroy us, unless we bait a trap with ourselves. We must be prepared to stand before the aliens. This man here, this Milliginian, for his own reasons, will act with us. He will pull a switch that will destroy all of them."

"Only a few of you at most will die," Imhor helpfully interjected.

"Some of us will die for mankind?" Morris asked. "Then I am with you, of course."

"And those that survive will survive for mankind," added Joshua, "and will lead us from the wilderness into a better life."

"Who else? Who else?" Imhor called out.

"Charge," bellowed Hank, leading the way into the jungle.

"Wait," screamed Isobel even louder, "I demand that you halt."

There was such command in her posture, such authority in her voice that everybody actually did. She had suddenly grown ten feet tall. Was this the same little monster, the same little troll? No, no, she had changed, had grown, had learned—no wonder she was queen.

"CHARGE!" she screamed as roots shriveled and the hungry trees died on the spot. "CHARGE," she repeated to let everyone know who was boss. "CHARGE," she blasted a third time, disappearing into the swamp with Arnold and the rest of the settlement close on her heels. Until at last there was nobody left but those in the middle, the two in the tent, the one on the stretcher, the one on the ground, the one against the tree, and the one at the edge of the camp.

"We are one," said Louella to Morris. "I am you— you cannot go without me."

"What of the rest?" asked Morris. "They aren't able to decide for themselves."

"We need them," said Imhor, enveloped in pain. "I was hoping for forty, not four. We will need everyone or they won't all come out. Gather them up and quick. You don't have much time."

"Neither do I."

"Me neither."

Morris went to see Sam who told him Celeste was sleeping, but because she wasn't he put his arms around him and led him to the ship. Then they loaded in Titheria, gathered up all the parts of the Actor-Robot, lifted in Buck Alice and just as they were departing, in scampered Maytag with no place else to go.

The ship then took off.

"Me-you-fire-sky," thought Titheria.

"I'm gonna do big things, I'm gonna fight," thought Sam.

"Sputter-cough-chug-ping-sputter," thought the Actor-Robot.

"B-4-p-m-c-2-. . . . . s," thought Buck Alice.

"At last we're going to get even," thought all the Imhors.

"I am the Son of God and I am prepared to die," thought Morris.

"I am the Son of God and I am prepared to lead," thought Joshua.

"Now," said Isobel to Arnold at the site of Newest Hope Settlement deep in the swamp, "the first thing we gotta do is get us some babies."